## SHE WAS GETTING

"Burr?" Even though she'd said his name softly, it made him jump and ___ his hand on something. "You're tinkering with the combine? You still think you can make it run again?"

He yanked out his hand.

"Oh, no. You've cut yourself. Let me see." She reached to touch him.

"No. Don't."

"Don't what? Don't touch you?"

He focused on what he was doing. How was he supposed to answer a question like that?

*Don't make me want to be part of your life, Meredith. Because you'd never want to be part of mine. You're bringing something of me alive that it's best if I let die.*

Books by Deborah Bedford

*A Child's Promise*
*Chickadee*
*Timberline*
*Harvest Dance*

Published by HarperPaperbacks

# Harvest  Dance

DEBORAH BEDFORD

**HarperPaperbacks**
*A Division of HarperCollinsPublishers*

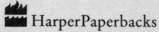

**HarperPaperbacks**
*A Division of* HarperCollins*Publishers*
10 East 53rd Street, New York, N.Y. 10022-5299

ISBN: 0-06-108512-X

Cover illustration by Jim Griffin

First printing: August 1997

Printed in the United States of America

❖ 10 9 8 7 6 5 4 3 2 1

This book is dedicated to my father, James Calvin Pigg, who understands so well the solemn magic of soil, seed, and sower.

And to Dorothy Beatrice Shell Bunting, William David Bunting, and Virginia Taylor Pigg, old-timers and upstanding citizens of Bryan/College Station, Brazos County, Texas. It is because of my own grandparents that I can write of love that transcends generations.

# Acknowledgements

I am grateful to those who shared their memories, their knowledge, and their farming homes with me and thus made this book possible:

Marvin and Sheila Schmidt, who let me drive the combine and help with the harvest; Gottlieb Fink, for his old-time Wyoming farming expertise; Nancy Effinger, director of the Teton County Library in Jackson Hole; Bill Kuntz, Case dealer and combine expert in Mount Pleasant, Iowa; and Annie Pike Greenwood, author of *We Sagebrush Folks*, who became a farm girl so long ago and was willing to eloquently tell her story.

To the precious friends in my life who have given me courage and laughter when I needed it most:

Pam Micca, Maria Lennon, and Catherine Smith; Tim Sandlin, who's always offered a shoulder and the use of his outhouse; Bobbi and Tom Wild and the rest of the Wild bunch—Jake, Matt, and Charlie, who have given long, sunlit days of tadpole catching and lots of Jedediah's sourdough pancakes.

Much love, to one and all.

I look into your eyes and see
reflections of lost melody,
a love gone by with fleeting song
when he who played the tune is gone.
When joy has come, its damask touch
like love is tattered just as much,
A harvest night, a fiddle's sound,
I dance, reborn on hallowed ground.

—DPB

# PART ONE

*Autumn, 1934*

Pastor Charles Burleigh watched the girl bend low as she walked, hiding—or so it seemed—in the protection of the gully where the fence around the cemetery had rusted down amid the brambles, where nothing much but thistles and sagebrush and wheat grass grew. He left the dooryard and followed, passing as the girl passed from shadow to light to shadow again, moonlight and darkness dappling her hair. The girl wore only a Hooverette housecoat three sizes large, as if she'd climbed out of bed upon a moment's notice and had run away.

"I'm the preacher here," he called out as she moved like a spirit from dark into light, and in that moment, that fatal, perfect moment, he wished for his wife, wished Delia'd stayed with him instead of traipsing off the way she always thought she must traipse off when the women of Melody Flats organized themselves. They'd done so tonight, with their pies and cookies and cakes, taking it upon themselves as the upstanding and the faithful in the valley to attend the refreshment table at the dance and make certain no overzealous farmer dumped liquor into the Shiloh punch. "I can help you."

"There's nobody who can help me. Not anymore." She spoke with something strange, presageful, in her voice, as if, despite the earthiness of her situation, she needed someone to bring her back to ground because she soared a little. She turned toward him. Charles Burleigh recognized the taut, enormous belly ill disguised in the Hooverette and the sad, delicate smile of the Wilkins girl who lived a mile up the road.

"Your baby is almost here."

She nodded. "It's coming tonight." Fear left a ragged edge on her voice. In the moonlight he could tell she'd been crying. "I've got pains."

He clasped one large, certain hand against her shoulder. The darkness around them tasted dusty. "The Father is with you. He always is, even when He doesn't seem to be. Sometimes, especially when He doesn't seem to be."

As he spoke she gripped her stomach, both hands pressed low against her belly. Her body tensed. Even though the night breeze was cool, perspiration melded dark curls to her face.

She closed her eyes, squeezing out a fresh allotment of tears, looking for all the world like a young, tragic Claudette Colbert. He caught at the girl's elbow, angry at himself for his human thoughts, his hopelessness. Worst time a girl could go into labor in Melody Flats was the night of a harvest dance. Particularly if that girl was a Wilkins. Particularly when that girl was somebody whom everyone said had gone wrong. He'd heard them talking about her in the foyer at church, offering up prayers for her on Wednesday nights, saying how they'd all seen the enormous belly and the exhaustion on the young girl's face, saying they knew she didn't have long to go.

"I'll go up to the parsonage and get the Pontiac. We'll drive down to the dance, get your father or some of the ladies to help us."

She shook her head. "Don't want anyone in my family helping me. It's a good thing, the baby coming this way. I'm glad Papa's away at the dance."

"He ought to be with you."

"Don't want this baby to be born into the arms of someone who already hates it. Babies know things. They come into the world a great deal wiser than we are."

"Then I'll drive you to the hospital in Riverton."

"Can't afford no hospital."

"Have you been seeing any doctor in particular?"

Again she shook her head. "Couldn't afford a doctor in particular, either."

When he'd been a boy, Charles Burleigh had thought this sort of thing rare. But since he'd come to pastor a church, he knew all too well that these ill-kept prejudices, the daughters who strayed, the parents who nursed haughty bitterness, were as common as highland weeds. "Surely someone in your household must be concerned about your health."

"Oh, Papa's concerned about my health all right. He's concerned I won't be able to help harvest when it's time to get the barley in." She gripped his arm restlessly as she spoke, the pains absorbing her attention. He recognized the throes of a building contraction. "I'd rather have the baby be born in the churchyard cemetery than back at home. The things he's said to me, I'm scared he'll get ahold of it and take it out to the creek and drown it the way he'd drown a cat."

"You'll come inside, won't you, child, when you can walk?"

Her upturned face dispelled his qualms. Her dark eyes glittered with trust and diffident pain. "I will." And later, when she could speak, the girl said again, "Best time for this to happen is tonight. It's the best time, while everybody's away at the dance."

He'd call Doc Forester once he got her inside, Charles decided, although he didn't know who would pay. He suspected, given these circumstances, that the deacons would approve some debit from the church benevolence fund. Wouldn't do for him not to find help for her. He wasn't the one who could assist her. He'd been seminary trained to counsel parishioners and disciple souls. He knew nothing about delivering babies.

When she could move, Charles walked her toward the house, supporting her elbow in silence. The parsonage sat on the sunset side of the church, a one-story post-and-beam whitewashed to brilliance by a fervent congregational work team, severely reminiscent of the farmhouses that had been springing up like buckwheat ever since immigrants had begun tilling the fawn-colored soil. The houses that stood empty now because of the drought, because the government had given assistance and moved so many people to better ground near Sheridan and Lingle.

He guided the Wilkins girl through the windless, dusty night, in through a side door that led to a room filled with study papers and framed degrees from Wheaton, the desk and chairs lit golden by filigreed lamps with discolored shades. His onionskin notes for next week's sermon lay in disarray on his desk, his black leather Bible fallen open to a page often touched, often read.

"You want to walk, or lie down?"

He felt inept, bizarrely unsure of his next move. The parsonage had several rooms in which he could make her comfortable, but none seemed antiseptic enough for birthing.

"Maybe both," she said. "Or if the pains get bad, I can crouch."

He took her to his bed and Delia's, the wrought-iron one they always left in a hasty fit of morning tasks. The Wilkins girl sat on the edge of the feather mattress, testing it, the Hooverette gathered demurely around her knees. "Guess this'll be fine," she said.

Charles rang up the doctor on the odd-looking newfangled phone, holding the earpiece to his head while he dialed the number. Seemed so funny not to have to crank that handle anymore and ask for Central. Riverside East-6334. On the other end, the telephone rang. And rang. And rang. "Crazy thing," he mumbled. "Even the doctor's out to the dance." He knew it without asking. But he asked anyway, breaking the connection with a flip of his thumb, then direct dialing "O." "You know a way to get hold of Doc Forester?" he asked Adele Merriman, who'd been the operator ever since they'd brought telephones into Melody Flats, when she came on the line.

"Not without driving out to the dance," she said. "I'd bet my last dollar you could go out there right now and find him in the crowd."

"But he can't be rung up?"

"You might try calling over at Moley's place. Could be somebody scrounging around in the kitchen who'd pick up and be willing to go in search of the doc." She stopped, waited, then: "So. You feeling poorly tonight, are you, Pastor? In need of the doctor yourself?"

He could hear her bated breath as she paused for him to explain. But this wasn't the sort of thing in which he wanted to involve people. He could think of nothing more formidable than to implicate Mrs. Merriman—who had a way and a means into over half the modern homes in Fremont County—in details of the Wilkins girl's labor and delivery. "Thank you, Adele. There isn't anything. Except if Forester calls in, will you have him get in touch? Tell him I'm in need of him."

"Sure will, Pastor. Sure will."

Charles rang off and dialed the number out at the Moley place. He waited for somebody, anybody, to answer. As it, too, rang over and over again, he began to despair. In his bedroom on the side where Delia slept, the girl crouched beside the mattress in the harsh electric light just brought in by the cooperative, her fists knotted around two sections of quilt, her face ashen with pain. She cried out once, only once, a sound both primitive and ethereal, a woman's measureless proclamation, and a woman's alone.

He hung up the telephone with a *whack* and spoke as if he knew what God must be thinking. "Surely you wouldn't intend me to do this by myself."

The clouds outside the parsonage threaded apart like rending, antique fabric. The clouds've given up again, he thought. There won't be rain tonight. But at that moment, as moonlight deluged the churchyard, he looked out the window and saw a familiar figure enter the church cemetery through the side gate. Fiona Trichak. Perhaps the only soul in this county besides himself who hadn't deemed it necessary to attend the dance. He watched as, with purpose, she picked her way exquisitely through the headstones. She halted, leaned low beside her husband's grave.

With a glance of vague reassurance at the Wilkins girl, Charles Burleigh tossed open the door and crossed the brittle September meadow. When he came to the iron fence, he vaulted it as effortlessly as a boy, coming upon his parishioner as she reached with one work-gloved hand to pull a Russian thistle from among the thatches of cured grass that had at last grown over Ray Trichak's final resting place.

He knelt beside her. The ground felt dry and hard beneath his knees. He knew that beneath the sparse grass, a crust had formed and ants had widened their hills. "Mrs. Trichak. Fiona." He reached toward her and touched her arm.

Fiona jumped. She'd been so entranced with her homage at Ray's graveside, she hadn't noticed anyone coming. She held up the thistle in her gloved palm, the prickly bract that necklaced a vibrant purple bloom, the nettlesome leaves, the deep hearty root clumped with dirt. "Seems a great injustice, doesn't it, Pastor Burleigh? That a man would struggle his life long to rid his barley fields of these thistles. He goes to his grave and, as sure as growing season comes again, even when there's scarcely been enough rain for barley to grow, this damned thing roots over the top of his head."

Pastor Burleigh took the thistle from her, flung it over the rusty fence as far as it would go. He said in a far-off voice that Fiona barely recognized as he watched the thistle fly, "There's a girl inside the parsonage I don't know what to do with. She's in labor with a baby."

"The Wilkins girl."

"Yes."

"That poor child."

"Yes. 'Poor child' is right. She doesn't want her father in on this. And, from the way things are happening, Doc Forester won't be in on it, either."

"You need help with a delivery, Pastor?" Even as she asked the question, Fiona'd all but forgotten her first purpose for coming. She gathered the gores of her organdy skirt around her the way a mother duck gathered ducklings and stood.

"I do."

"Where's Delia?"

"At the dance. The United Christian Women are policing the punch tonight." He spoke in hushed tones among the burials, as if talk of dancing might cause stirring amid the souls.

"That's where Michael's gone, too. Seems silly letting a six-year-old boy go to the dance with just friends, but I did it. I found it too difficult to go this year. Not without—" She broke off, thinking of Ray, missing him.

The clouds drew together again, dousing the light, like curtains gone closed at the end of a play. "How long has the girl been here?"

At first he didn't answer her. He gave his full attention to the sky. "Wilkins's crop was one of the worst this season, and none of the crops in this county were any good."

"No sense talking crops right now, Pastor Burleigh. A baby's being born."

He backhanded his forehead. "I'm not just talking crops. I'm talking about the entire scheme of things. Wilkins girl included."

"Let small problems be small. And big problems be big."

"She's been here long enough for me to call the doc and figure out he won't be coming."

"She'll be thinking you've deserted her, you've been out here so long."

"Didn't want to frighten you. Didn't want to

run straight out here and interrupt you grieving over Ray's grave."

As they walked and talked, they did not rush. They made their way side by side, drawing strength from each other for this task of birthwatch. "Fiddlesticks. This is a good thing for me, didn't you know? It's good to know there are living people still needing you worse than those that are dead." They breathed the smell of dry earth as they talked in darkness.

The girl had climbed onto the bed when they arrived. She'd thrown the quilt onto the floor. She rose on her knees, water and blood mixed to form a vague pink stain on the Hooverette.

"Let me see you, child," Fiona whispered. "I've come to help. How far along are you? Do you know?"

The girl shook her head almost violently. Sweat and dust and dried tears made vehement streaks down her face.

"Hand me a warm rag, would you, Charles?"

The girl shook her head again, moved an arm's length away.

But Fiona didn't change the timbre of her voice. "I'm going to explain as much as possible. So you'll understand what's happening. And you've got to help as much as you can."

Charles brought Fiona a tea towel from the kitchen. He handed it to her in one big, damp clump. "It's cold. I've gotten a fire going beneath the kettle to heat the next one up."

"It'll have to do for now."

Fiona Trichak unwadded the cloth and gently— oh so gently!—dabbed the cotton linen across the girl's cheeks. Streaks of dirt and dried salt disappeared. "What's your name, honey?" The Wilkins household boasted so many children that counting them and telling them apart was like identifying one in a group of downy nestlings. "Aren't you Kay Lee?"

The girl nodded.

"I thought it was you. You are the eldest, aren't you?"

"I am."

"I'll help you as much as I can. If you'll help me. I bet, with the pastor here, we can get through this together and it'll be fine."

"Okay."

"I'm going to have to have a look at you, child. Down between your legs where the baby's coming. That's the only way to tell how far along you are."

The girl stared at her in disbelief for a beat, then scooted sideways on the mattress. Charles knew that if Fiona hadn't been sitting so close at hand, Kay Lee Wilkins would've bolted off the bed and into a corner. He understood the panic that shone in the girl's eyes. For baffling reasons that had nothing to do with knowledge, Charles felt the girl's fear more keenly than he might've felt his own. "I've seen you at the market," she whispered, her voice quivering. "You're Fiona Trichak."

"I am."

It became obvious that Kay Lee Wilkins struggled for some common thread, something to establish a footing with this relative stranger. "Papa says you're gonna lose your farm without your husband. What with it being so dry and all."

Fiona smiled, and a rare, pure expression came across her face, a firm certainty that seemed to illuminate every cell in her body. "Folks've been saying that for months now. Hasn't happened yet, has it?"

"But you haven't turned out a barley crop. There won't be any grain to turn in when the government comes to collect on your loan. That's what Papa says."

"There's other crops besides what grows in the ground. I've got animals to sell." And Josh Harrison down at the bank had been trying to loan her money to put in sugar beets, although she hadn't made up her mind about that.

The girl's terror had, like fading vespers, begun to subside. "You come all this way to the church to help me?"

Fiona bit her bottom lip and lied. "I did."

The girl let out a rush of breath. "Thank you, Pastor Burleigh. Thank you for finding someone to help."

He'd never felt so humbled in all his life. "No," he said. "I didn't—" But his discounting words became lost in Fiona's next commands.

"You should be up and walking, Kay Lee. I'll walk with you, okay? That'll keep the baby coming faster." Fiona brushed the girl's hair back from her temple, soothing her the way soon she, herself, would learn to soothe her newborn. "Women have been doing this a long time, honey. It's how the good Lord works it."

"Yeah," the girl said at last. "My mama did it seven times. And with the last one, she died. It's how He works it all right. It's God's punishment. The curse. Papa says it gets you, no matter how hard you try. Sneaks up and takes everything away. Soul and body and strength."

Fiona glanced up sharply, met Charles's eyes. "I think your father's wrong about that, child. Dead wrong." She took Kay Lee's face in her hands. "There's a whole lot of people worrying about the Father's punishment when they ought to be doling out the Father's love. Now, Pastor, we need some privacy here, if you don't mind. You ought to be out of the room while I perform this first examination."

"Oh. Yes." It almost startled him to realize the grave necessity of Fiona's request. "Of course." But he was intrigued by the way Fiona Trichak looked at things, by the way she portrayed the situation as something magical and intriguing and fine. As a blessing instead of a curse. He didn't want to miss any part of her wisdom. So he remained in the doorway as long as he deemed suitable, still listening to Fiona.

"You wait and see," she said. "When somebody dies or is born, that always changes things. You're the same person, but you become a different person, too."

"I don't get it."

"It's the same way a dancer changes her steps to different tunes, to a new, unique pattern as the music shifts. Think about it, child. You will still have a parent. But you will also *be* a mother. It makes a difference in how you do things."

"Can't think of being a mother, Missus Trichak. Can't think of it in that way at all."

"You'll think of it all right. You'll see when you hold your baby that God doesn't overlook details. The way your breasts will spurt with milk. The baby's toes and hands, perhaps the way you expect them, perhaps not, but just the way He plans them to be. When Michael was born, that's the way it was for me. You'll look into its little face, one perfect life that wouldn't exist if you hadn't been used as a vessel. And you'll think, How can something like this form in the darkness inside of me, away from anyone's eyes?"

"I've thought about seeing a little face, the face of someone I know well, but someone I don't know at all."

Fiona laid a small, capable hand against the girl's neck and helped her adjust her head on the pillow. Charles knew it was time to depart. He paced around the house for five excruciating minutes. When he returned and knocked on the door, Fiona gave him a list of household supplies to find.

He went through his own house like a scavenger, pawing through the low drawers of the chiffonier to find the oilcloth Delia used whenever she served fried chicken to a crowd. He rummaged through the junk drawer in search of cotton twine and the kitchen shears. He retrieved the sewing basket with its miscellany of thread spools and its needles poked neatly into the sections of a tomato-shaped pincushion. He fetched a basket of rags Delia kept beside the washstand. He proudly handed Fiona the assortment, glad beyond measure to have someone with which to share this ordeal. He wouldn't've known to do any of this. Any of this.

"The scissors and needles need to be boiled," she said, handing those back. "You can put them in the water you've already got going."

He didn't move right away. The girl lay with her eyes closed, her skin as translucent as a moth wing, her face gone deathly pale. "She's hurting, isn't she?"

"The contractions are getting stronger. It won't be long now. She's progressing."

"Have the waters broken?"

"Not yet. But they will soon. As soon as we get this tablecloth in place, I may help that along a bit. The baby's head is almost ready to deliver. Feel." She reached for his hand. "Here. Do this."

Surprised, he stooped beside her. With her own petite hand, she guided his palm, showed him how to press with great care against Kay Lee's belly.

"There. Feel that?"

"What?"

"That."

"I don't feel anything."

"Yes, you do. Find all the shapes. Think what they could be." With noble precision she moved his fingers and showed him how to palpate the outline of the unborn rump and find the peaked, triangular shapes of two tiny, tiny feet.

"Amazing." He stared not at the girl's massive tummy, but at Fiona.

"That's the way you find out it isn't breech, that

the baby's head will present itself first." She beamed as if she'd told him she'd arranged for him to have a fireside chat with Franklin D. Roosevelt himself. "It's a good thing. This delivery should be okay. We're lucky. *She's* lucky."

"You're the good thing, Fiona. Sent by God himself to save this girl's life, and me. This has nothing to do with luck at all." For some reason, as he said the words, he couldn't quite catch his breath. Charles found himself astounded by her confidence at this, by everything she knew to do. He waited until she turned away from the swelling of the girl's abdomen and met her eyes, eyes the same powerful hue as a cloudless high-country sky.

In that moment, that one endearing moment, it seemed to Charles as if he looked into her eyes and saw a place he longed to travel, a place very different from the one he knew, a place far away, where he couldn't go.

Fiona released his hands with an uncharacteristic nervous motion, her fingers playing over the quilt the way they played over a string of piano keys. Her gaze skittered from his. She focused her attention on the frayed black shoestring of his left wing-tip oxford.

"Ten years running a family farm is plenty of time to learn things," she said shakily. "Ray taught me how to deliver calves. Something like this can't be much different."

As Delia had dressed for the dance, she'd opened the window. The wind had come up outside. Dust poured in over the sill like acrid smoke.

Charles jumped up and tugged down the sash, choking on the heavy smell of chaff from years gone by and the stench of dirt where automobile and wagon wheels had milled the high road beside the church.

He stood for a while at the window, peering out, fighting the need to swallow. He felt lost, as if he'd stumbled onto inappropriate ground, as if—in the midst of his own life—some part of himself had perilously taken flight. He knew well enough that the events in this past hour had estranged him from something. If he hadn't been hanging on to the sill, the suddenness, the electricity, of what he felt would've brought him again to his knees.

"Charles?"

He cleared his throat and turned back to Fiona. "You want me to get that tablecloth on the bed?"

She looked past the place he stood, somewhere in the vicinity of the mousetrap that waited, loaded with a dollop of cheese and ready to spring, in the corner. "I—if you would. Please."

"Do I put it under her? Like a sheet?"

"Over the mattress, to protect it. But under the sheet, so it won't feel awful."

"She'll have to stand up. I can't get to it otherwise."

"She needs to stand up."

"I can't. I'm too tired to stand," Kay Lee said. "I just want to rest, please."

"No, you mustn't rest just yet. Here. I'll help you." Fiona hoisted her up by the armpits. With Charles's help, the girl extended her feet to the floor and put her full weight on them. Fluid began to trickle down her legs, to splatter on him and on Fiona, too, warm and clear, a miraculous baptism of life. "There you go. Your water's broken by itself, and I didn't have to do anything. Everything's as it should be, child. There isn't anything mysterious or out of the ordinary about it."

"I've messed up the floor."

"The floor is nothing. That's why they've invented mops and pails."

While Fiona marched Kay Lee Wilkins in a wide circle around the room, Charles made preparations. He yanked the sheet away from the mattress, flung it over the wrought-iron bedstead. With only minor difficulty, he positioned the tablecloth across the foot of the mattress. When he retucked the cotton linens, he smoothed each wrinkle with an economic, precise motion. His shoulders didn't stiffen and his hands didn't start to feel fumbly until he straightened his back and met Fiona's awkward, grateful smile.

"What is it you need me to do now?" he asked, dusting off his hands on his trousers and feeling like a schoolboy.

"Those shears and things, remember?"

"Oh, yes."

Charles helped her readjust the girl on the bed, then dealt with the hygiene of the shears and the needles. He carried them to the kitchen and dropped them inside the kettle, watching them dance in the roiling water before he crowded another log and some sagebrush into the stove's firebox. The flames intensified. He set another water bowl on the hearth so they'd have some warm and not too hot.

He hadn't been gone long before he heard her call him. "Charles. Please come." It was the first time he noticed Fiona sounding anxious. "We're going to need you in here."

When he ran back he found her kneeling between the girl's legs, the yoke of her organdy dress splattered with blood. Kay Lee's face had gone rigid with the strain. She began to bear down, pushing the baby out of her womb, making a long, low sound like the lament of an ancient, swaying tree. She raised herself onto her elbows and spread her legs wider.

"Stoop beside her shoulders," Fiona ordered. "Let her lean on you."

He positioned himself behind the scruff of Kay Lee's neck, taking the full bore of her weight upon his chest. With his chin he spooned the crook of the girl's left shoulder blade. He wrapped both arms around Kay Lee in a fervent embrace. He felt the knobs of her spine pressed against him.

Wet ringlets of hair plastered her neck. She felt so slight in his arms and smelled so sweet, like a little child herself, someone much too young to be birthing a baby of her own. Charles mustered up all his strength for her, wishing there were something more he could do, that he could bear down for her and take up her struggle.

But he could not. He could only lean with solidity against her, rubbing her elbows with an occasional hand, touching the skin of her arms as humans are intended to touch others, saying *I am here for you. I care, child. I fight along beside you.*

She strained through another contraction, this one so fierce and compelling that she crossed her arms and dug her stubby, cracked fingernails into his wrists. Fiona stood and reached for them, prying Kay Lee's fingers loose. "No. Not that way." The girl left ten half-moon indentations upon him before Fiona convinced her to release her grasp. "This is what you do." She placed the girl's hands upon her own knees so that when she dug into something, she plied wide her own limbs, her elbows, her legs. "You're doing fine. Fine." Fiona stroked the girl's bare feet as this contraction subsided. "The opening gets smaller each time a pain ends. But it won't be long now. Not long at all."

"You don't get the—"

"Its little head is crowning, Kay Lee. It has lots of hair. Dark. Like yours."

Despite her trepidation, the girl's eyes went wide with wonder. "It does? Really?"

Fiona smiled, a smile contrary to the one before, one that bespoke great assurance and joy. She said, "Really."

"My baby has dark hair," the girl repeated. "Dark hair like me." But even as Kay Lee spoke, the amazement in her eyes began to wane. When the labor pains came, nothing mattered but the ridding of them as they crested. As if she'd become battered by free wind and soaring waves, Kay Lee's girth went taut and expectant. The contraction built. Charles tightened his grip around her shoulders. Perspiration shimmered on her face. Her jaw squared with effort. Kay Lee groaned. Her breath came in fast, sharp gasps, then, as she pushed full bore, she held it. Blood and birth fluid gushed onto the bedsheets.

Fiona gave her faith to the broad little body, the strewn legs before her. "You're doing it, child. You're making this look as easy as pie. Keep your legs relaxed. Your bottom, too. Push against it, sweetie. Just open it up and let the baby out."

Charles made no unnecessary movement; he committed himself only to the strength and to the fineness of women. His back ached something awful. Still, he held the girl upright. When the baby's head came through facedown, he could see pink ears as perfectly formed as a clamshell, the scribble of dark hair. "The head's out. The head's out," he told Kay Lee and Fiona as if they couldn't see. Fiona moved closer between the girl's thighs, cradled the tiny skull within her two hands. Tears rolled down her cheeks.

The minuscule face pivoted toward Charles, its eyes and mouth covered with mucus and blood, still closed. Shoulders and torso burst forth with marvelous speed. Legs, enveloped for months within the young girl's womb, slipped easily into the world, straightened, made ready to kick. For all the world this baby reminded Charles of some ancient, wizened old being. In the years that would pass, long after he'd aged into an old, dispassionate man, Pastor Charles Burleigh would remember and place great stock in the moment he looked upon this baby's wee, profound face for the first time. Along the course of his lifetime he would think, if not for that child, that night, my life would not have been the same.

The blue gray umbilical cord attached to the child at its belly, the thing yet pulsing with nourishment from its source, a mother's body. Fiona lifted the baby to examine it, and all seemed to be in order. Charles grinned at the physical aspects. "Looks like a boy to me." The baby opened its mouth and began its bleating cry.

Charles went immediately to the other room, brought back a warm blanket from the hearth, and wrapped it around the girl's shoulders. He made a second trip for the warm bowl of water, the needles, the shears. "Let me lay him here." Fiona snapped open the Hooverette and laid him atop the girl's bare breasts. "This is where he wants to be. He knows already who he belongs to. See."

The girl began to shake her head as the tiny boy rooted for her nipples. "No. I can't—"

"Sure you can. Don't be afraid to touch him. That's all he wants now is to be held close by you."

But Kay Lee Wilkins pushed him away. "I don't want to hold him close. I don't want him to even know me."

"What do you mean?" Caught unawares, Fiona suspended the babe in the air between them, her face gone as colorless as dust in the midnight road.

"I can't bring him home. Don't you see? Papa won't let me come there with him. He said he'd lock me out if I tried to come back, bringing a baby. He needs me in the fields."

"No father could be that—" She'd been about to say "cruel," but Charles put his hand upon her arm and stopped her. She switched the conversation with firm artistry. "We won't talk about it just yet. You'll be having another contraction any minute. I'll press hard on your stomach and help you deliver the afterbirth. I want you to be prepared."

"It hurts when you push on my stomach that hard. I wish you wouldn't."

"We have no other choice, Kay Lee." And her own words echoed in her head as the contraction did come and she pressed and the placenta wrenched through, looking like a gigantic slab of liver. *No other choice. No other choice.* She didn't know much about obstetrics. She did know enough to examine the afterbirth and note that it came out as a whole, uniform, and ordinary. "You could try with him again."

The girl waved her wrists in the air as she talked, wrists as slim as flame. "No sense trying. I've tried to get my way before."

"But never this."

"No," the girl agreed. "Never this."

"I'll need the rags, Charles. After you fetch those, could you get the twine and scissors?"

"They're right here. All ready."

Where Fiona's hands had once seemed assured, now Charles noticed that they trembled. She dipped a corner of fresh cotton linen into the warm water and dabbed mucus from the baby's nose. The infant wriggled and bellowed, its fists clenched, its eyes squinted shut against this indignity.

The opaque gray cord that stretched from the girl's groin to the baby's tummy began to turn white and to wither. It shriveled even as they watched it. Fiona said, "Here's what we'll do with the string you've brought." She reached for the ball of twine, her face still bleak, and unwound a length. She snipped off two sections. She tied them around the umbilical cord in two places, tugging the knots so they'd stay tight.

"You want to do the honors?" She handed the sterilized scissors to Charles.

He rocked backward on his heels. He'd never considered cutting membrane and flesh. The thought made him dizzy, almost frightened. Yet the thing had to be done. And something about the idea of severing an organ that had served well its purpose and could be ceremonially, victoriously broken brought forth a perfect portrayal of the living Christ in his mind. He took the shears from Fiona and cut the cord.

The baby wailed gloriously, as if the infant, too, heralded its final release from mother's womb. "Let's get him wrapped up," Fiona said.

"Here. Let me." Charles took the baby and swaddled it inside one of Delia's nicest towels, one that had been toasting beside the stove in the kitchen. He held the boy snugly yet with nonchalance, as if— because of this night—the infant might always belong to him. When he spoke, he said the words to cheer Fiona more than anything else. "Hey, little guy. Welcome to Wyoming. Welcome to the Dust Bowl."

The bleakness wavered and Fiona laughed as he'd hoped. "Now, don't start him out in such an optimistic way, Charley." When she realized she'd used his familiar name, her cheeks tinged with faint color. "Telling about the state of agriculture in Melody Flats before he's even five minutes old."

"Well, somebody's got to tell him not to grow up to be a farmer."

Fiona helped Kay Lee straighten her legs. She cleaned the girl off with fresh warm linen and covered her with the quilt. The girl still bled a bit, but not an inordinate amount. Fiona tucked the coverlet tight around her legs, making sure she'd stay warm. "He'll be getting home from the dance soon, won't he? If I'm there, he'll have no idea I've been away. My sisters and brothers won't tell him. I've got chores to do. Papa didn't get the cow milked before he took off."

"You can't do the milking tonight."

"If I don't take care of Jersey, her udders'll get constricted. We lose that cow, it'll be all my fault."

The situation might have been laughable if it hadn't been completely dire. "Your father might've stayed home from the dance himself and taken care of it. Or he could've given the chore to someone else."

"But I'm the oldest."

"Dear child."

"Would you take him?" She leaned her head against the pillow and looked into the distance with a peculiar, drifting manner, as if the wall and the baby that had been inside her and the church-yard outside had never mattered. "He wouldn't be much trouble, would he? I've saved three flour sacks to make diapers and a little slip."

"Kay Lee . . ."

"I'll bring them over so you can stitch them up. Ought to be able to bring them over one day when nobody's watching."

Charles placed his own nose close to the infant's. The baby's eyes were navy and clear, breathtaking, like deep pools of quiet water. He said, "You can't pretend this hasn't happened."

"I'm not pretending. I'm doing the only thing I can do. I try to keep him on my own, we'll both of us starve."

Charles gave Fiona one quick, penetrating glance, and she took the words up for him. "But you ran away from the house. You came to have your baby here. You can . . ." But she didn't know what else to say. She couldn't urge the girl to leave her own family. And to Charles, the significance of Kay Lee's words, of her searching for a place where the baby would be born—not into hatred, but into something safe—began to take on new, unexpected meaning. The infant rooted and wriggled inside his arms.

Kay Lee touched Fiona's arm. "Please." She raised her eyes in a last ditch effort, a final plea. "Raise him like he was your boy."

Fiona choked back a tremendous lump in her throat, one that had begun to form the moment she'd handed the infant to Kay Lee Wilkins and the girl had pushed it away. "You'd trust me to do that?"

Charles held the little fellow upright so the girl could have a better look at him. "I'll go with you to your house, Kay Lee. I'll have the baby in my arms and let your father get introduced to him. We'll take over some of those preserved fruits from the church basement. We'll take custard and some of Delia's prize-winning butter. You won't have to do any sewing, either. The Women's Literary Society is good at putting together layettes. This child is so precious. If you brought him home, I don't see how your family could turn either of—"

"You're used to kindness in people, Pastor." Kay Lee cut him short with a sad, sharp laugh. When she turned away suddenly, he knew it was to hide the tears in her eyes. "You're used to parishioners making much of you. You're used to details being weighted your way whenever you've got an opinion."

He hadn't ever thought of things in exactly that way. But, yes. Yes! Certainly his opinions carried significance in Melody Flats.

"You haven't run up against my papa in church, and you won't. He's got need of me teaching my brothers and sisters how to plow and plant and harvest in the field, not in the house taking care of babies. He's made it clear."

Fiona Trichak and Charles Burleigh looked hard at each other. In their hearts, each fostered the same thought. It seemed such an odd question, such a strange moment. "Have you wanted another child, Fiona? A second son?"

She lowered her eyes, could not meet his gaze. For no one could know, no one, how alone she'd felt, how often she and Ray had talked about it, how disappointed they'd been when she hadn't borne more children. "My husband and I, we'd always planned to have a big family. . . ." She trailed off. When she started up again, she spoke deliberately. "I'm sorry, Pastor Burleigh. This isn't something I've discussed with anyone but Ray."

He touched her chin with his finger and lifted her eyes to meet his. "Fiona. We've delivered a baby together. You've been calling me Charley for this past hour. I ask you something so important, and now I'm Pastor Burleigh again?"

"Yes."

"Please. I'd like always to be a Charley to someone."

"Aren't you?"

"Some Sundays, I stand up there preaching and I realize the words I'm saying aren't from the Lord at all. They're words from me. Words I've picked out because they're what everybody wants to hear."

"You think we expect everything you say to be the inspired word of God?"

"Folks think it's easier for me because I am a pastor. Folks think it's easier for me to look around and have hope. And, for a while, it was. Guess I figured that because of my calling I had some sort of special market on hope. But I've offered up prayers for seven different families who've lost their farms since then."

"I know all those families," she said.

"The last one was Gilbert Beasley and his wife, Hedda. He came into the parsonage twisting his hat, and I wanted to say, 'Go away. Ask anybody else for prayers but me. If I pray for you, it's a sure sign things won't go your way.'"

"Charley . . ." Fiona felt something burgeon

within her heart, a concern for him that took wing and lofted like a bird, a sense that she'd been brought here to him for worth and goodness and purpose.

"It's not that I don't understand God, Fiona. It's just that I don't understand what God is *doing.*"

She looked at him with a calm, level gaze. "You often can't know where the good is going to come from. You mustn't judge for yourself, standing where you stand."

"I've told myself that. I've told myself I'm not big enough to comprehend people's struggles, to understand God's plan. But there's a part inside me that keeps me wanting to *try.*"

"You need only to understand your own struggle, Charley." Then she gave a little laugh, because he'd finally made her see it. A soft pleasure came over her expression. "Except that your own struggle is always tied to everybody else's, isn't it?"

"Yes. It's easy to let it be like that." He lifted the child upright again, like a Shoshone child on a stiff cradle board. "So tell me about this boy, Fiona. Would you take him, the way he's being offered?"

She touched one tentative finger to the knob of this tiny, perfect nose. "Ray always talked about it, how he wanted scads of boys to pass along the farm to. He had in mind growing old and teaching a horde of young men how to plow and harrow and cultivate. I always thought maybe it was good that we only had the one, that Ray's plans for a tussling pile of sons never came into fruition. For what if, after all the sons had come, there'd been nothing left to pass along to them?"

"I'm not asking about the farm. I'm not asking about Ray. I'm asking about you. Do you want this boy, Fiona? If you'd like him, I believe he's being given to you. In the presence of God, with me as an eyewitness."

Fiona took the baby from him finally, clutching the bundle close to her chest. She sat beside Kay Lee. "Oh, child. You don't know what you're offering. Please. Take him in your arms and then say it, if you still want him to be mine."

Kay Lee waved them both off. "Get away. Don't bring him close." She threw back the quilt on the bed and hopped to the floor before Fiona could stop her. Blood gushed down her legs and splattered onto the floor. Blood forged a line down the side of the mattress. It gathered in a massive pool where the girl had lain in the bed, splaying out fiercely with the weave of the cloth. It puddled where it found nowhere else to go.

"Child. Lie down. You're still bleeding." Fiona shoved the baby at Charles and grabbed Kay Lee as the girl started to topple. Fiona'd never seen so much blood. She felt faint. "Charley. Help me."

He found a place for the baby among his shirts in a bureau drawer. The girl said, "It will stop soon, won't it? Maybe you're right. Maybe I've tried to go home too soon." As she talked, her words slurred. "My brother can milk the cow tomorrow morning."

"Yes. We'll have your brother do the milking. You've tried to get up too soon." And it terrified Fiona when, this time, the girl didn't reply. In a matter of moments Kay Lee'd sunk into a stupor.

"We've got to stop the bleeding. She won't last if it goes on much longer."

"Maybe cold compresses would do. Maybe ice, like to a nosebleed. Dear Father God." Words he'd uttered in scripted prayer, he now repeated in earnest desperation. "I'll call Doc Forester again. Maybe Adele was able to get him out of the dance. Maybe he's on his way."

"There isn't time, even if he's already coming."

Charles thought of something. "Shepherd's purse. I'll bet there's shepherd's purse still growing."

"What's that?"

"The weed beside the woodpile. I've seen Delia point it out for bleeding. We could make a poultice."

"Or a tea." She touched the girl's face.

He slammed out the door and fell to his knees in the yard. Sure enough, the shepherd's purse still grew in the protection of the parsonage, but barely; most of it had gone dry and brittle from the cold. He ripped it from the earth in fistfuls, stalks, roots, and all. He filled the crooks of both arms with it, careful not to shatter the tiny, heart-shaped leaves.

"Don't know if this'll do any good. But at least we've tried."

When he dropped them on the drainboard inside, Fiona had yanked open the metal ice trays from the Servel and had folded ice inside a towel. "I don't even know where to apply this, Charley."

"Maybe against the outside of her stomach. Or between her legs." He reached above to get a crock and spoon to bruise the herbs. "It's going to be the same with this. I won't know where to put it."

"I'll put ice on her stomach. The poultice would go into her, if we could get it there."

"Dear sweet heaven."

"And the tea. She should drink the tea."

Fiona ran to the bedroom and pressed ice against the girl's stomach again and again. Each time she put pressure on Kay Lee's belly, blood spurted in every direction. "Hurry."

He brought in his poultice. "Here. Fiona, I—"

"I'll apply it. You just get the tea going. We'll have to get some down her, although I don't know how."

Fiona applied the wet shepherd's purse with a gentle hand. Blood mixed with the mush of leaves and ran in rivulets between her fingers. Charles brewed the tea and rang up the doctor again. "Come on," he said to no one. "Come on. Answer." He tapped his foot on the floor.

Adele Merriman came on the line. "Doc Forester," he bellowed without preamble. "We've got to have Doc Forester out at the parsonage."

"He's never been found, Pastor Burleigh. I'll try again for you, though."

The tea steeped in a cup, steam rising from the warm water. He set it on the lampstand by the bed and knelt again beside the girl. He lifted her, and what he felt chilled him to the bone. Before when he'd supported her, she'd felt warm and alive and struggling. Now her body felt like the ice Fiona applied, cold and listless, dead weight. He shook her. She opened her eyes halfway, her face gone the frightening blue shade of shadow on snow. "Kay Lee. You've got to drink this."

From somewhere far away, she seemed to hear him. She pursed her dried lips and waited for him to raise the teacup, thin and dainty as an eggshell.

"It's warm. Watch out."

She nodded, took in some tea. Then more. The sheer effort exhausted her. She fell back and dozed.

"You've got to take a little more, Kay Lee. Just a little more."

But the girl didn't respond. Her body had gone limp. Her head lolled sideways. Fiona had begun to cry again, the tears glistening unregarded upon her cheeks. He caught her eye. She shook her head. "No matter what we do, it isn't stopping. I've never seen so much blood in all my life."

From the bureau drawer where he'd laid the baby came a rustling, no heavier than the rustling of a mouse as it skitters across floorboards. Tea sloshed out of the cup and burned his hand. Despite the burn, a numbing cold settled over him. He willed the girl to move, to open her eyes, to breathe. Fiona laid aside the poultice, shoved damp hair from her eyes with the back of her hand.

"Can you get any more down her?"

"I could try to force it. But it'll run down her chin. I don't want her burned."

"She's past the point of feeling anything."

From the bureau drawer, the tiny baby boy began to cry. Charles had never felt more incapable in his life. He'd done everything he'd known to do, and everything hadn't been enough. He drew a grating, pain-ridden breath.

Fiona stood and took one step toward him. "Charley . . ." *This isn't your fault,* she wanted to say. *Don't think it's happened because you're the one who's tried to help.*

Charles set the cup on the nightstand. He placed his hand on Kay Lee Wilkins's chest just below her left breast. Nothing. No heartbeat at all. "Kay Lee," he sobbed with rage. "Kay Lee. Kay Lee. Come on."

Fiona grabbed the coverlet with her own fists as if she were the one laboring, as if she were the one in great pain. He tried another place on her chest, moving his palm to the left. For a fraction of a second he felt something like the flutter of a butterfly there, some faint, imperceptible movement. He felt it again. Again. And again. "There," he whispered. "There. Her heart's beating."

"She won't make it to the hospital."

"I know that."

They stood and looked at each other, both of them awash with blood and birth fluid and immeasurable sadness. How alone they felt, as if the few steps between the foot of the bed and the head of it evoked a stretch of desolation that neither could vanquish or overpower.

Later, when they'd each lie awake thinking of it, neither of them would remember who had moved first. They'd each been buffeted by something so primordial, they did the only thing possible to do. They needed to hold on to each other. And so they did.

"Fiona . . ." Charles whispered her name just as he took her into his arms, just as he discovered that their bodies fit together as if they'd been hewn to fit together, hewn by the God he'd struggled lately to understand. The broad angles of his chest aligned with the gentle expanse of her shoulders. The cradle of her hipbones swathed the firm plane of his abdomen.

How good it felt after watching Kay Lee's life wane away to stand tall and firm and solid for the other, to match even their very breaths, to inhale as the other sighed, to exhale while the other's lungs filled. Their hearts clattered like hammer irons against each other, fierce and strong and violent. As they hung on to each other, they hung on to life.

The door to the parsonage flung open.

In ran Doc Forester, out of sorts and bellowing all the way. "Once I found out, got here as quick as I could. Knew you wouldn't mind if I let myself in. Is it you who's sick, Pastor, or is it someone else? From what Adele Merriman told me on the phone—"

He stopped in midsentence. In silence, breathtaking silence, the doctor stared at Fiona Trichak and Pastor Charles Burleigh as they stood close, so close. Seconds, a minute, ticked by on the clock in the hallway. A bee buzzed and butted against the screen door, trying for escape.

Presently Fiona decided it would be best to begin with some sort of explanation. "The Wilkins girl has had a baby, Doc Forester. She came here for help and we've ended up delivering a nice boy.

But she started bleeding. We've been desperate. We didn't know what to do, how to get it to stop."

"So I see," Doc Forester said, his measured glare taking in the placement of Charley's hand upon the small of her back, the position of her hand upon his shoulder. "So I see." He shook his head. When he spoke again, he spoke as Fiona had spoken, as much to bridge a silence as anything else, until the pastor of the flock in Melody Flats could trust to use his voice. The doctor eyed the poultice set aside on Delia's dressing table. He began to dig for something inside his huge telescope bag. "You've used shepherd's purse, have you? Smart idea. Who knew to come up with that?"

Charles said, "I did."

"A good choice."

"She's still alive. Is there something more that can be done for her?"

Doc Forester turned his back against the clandestine activity he'd walked in on and examined Kay Lee Wilkins with thorough professionalism. "She's lost a large amount of blood. You've dealt very well with it." He examined the afterbirth Fiona had kept and found nothing wrong there. "She's a bleeder, that's all. Some people are prone to hemorrhaging. There's no rhyme or reason for it. But look. She'll live. She's stopped bleeding."

"She has?"

"The poultice did its job. I trust you gave her shepherd's purse internally as well."

"Y-yes. Ch-Charl—I mean, Pastor Burleigh was able to get her to drink some."

The doctor examined the baby next and pronounced him surprisingly well. "The infant hasn't suffered any ill effects out of all this. But we've got to get Kay Lee to the hospital in Riverton. I think it best if I drove her there myself."

Charles said, "We'll help you get her out to the car."

"Old Man Wilkins was still down at the dance when I left," Forester said. "You can drive the baby down to him after I leave with Kay Lee."

Fiona stood quietly beside them both.

"I don't want to do that," Charles Burleigh said. Then he proceeded to tell Doc Forester the entire story, how the girl had come to them because she'd feared for the life of the infant, how she'd begged Fiona to keep the boy safe and to raise him as her own.

"Is that so?" the doctor proclaimed, examining the silver moons of his big fingernails as if he examined fine jewelry. "Well, Mrs. Trichak. Looks like you've got yourself a new young one, then. And poor Old Man Wilkins is a lucky fellow, too. You two've just saved him the life of his eldest daughter, the best barley hand he's ever had."

# PART TWO

*Autumn, 1997*

**1**

Come September after the barley had been cut and threshed, after the oats and sugar beets had been stored away, after the hay had been cured and lifted into bread-loaf heaps to await the winter, everybody in Melody Flats, Wyoming, congregated for the harvest dance.

Nobody could remember exactly when the dancing started. Some folks said the tradition'd begun just after the new century turned, when mountain parties lasted until morning, when women numbered so few that ranchers tied their arms with bandannas and stepped in to take the place of a lady. Others thought the hoedown began during a drought year, when rain withheld its favor like a stubborn matron, then—just as bullheadedly—bestowed itself furiously upon the dirt, making everyone affable enough to clean up, fork out genuine money to hire musicians, and sweep out the Moley family's cowshed.

But dance every year they did, even now, for whatever reasons, fiddle music spilling from the rickety makeshift stage, its melody both a token of the season and timeless. To its strains the folks in Almer Moley's barn paired up with people they'd known a lifetime. They paced heartily through jigs and square dances and "The Salty Dog Rag" exactly as they'd gone through them the past sixty years or so, twirling and stomping beneath the rafters, setting cobwebs to billowing in the eaves.

This night, when the stranger came to town, the music had ebbed and everyone saw him standing at the door, a young man waiting in silence as if afraid, his hand resting warily against the weather-bleached barn door.

"Who's that?" someone asked.

"Darned if I know," someone answered.

Outside, an opulent moon hung poised above the mountain, its light bathing the sage and the newly shorn turn rows in silver purity. Seemed, as the dancers watched, that something more than breeze pushed the fellow in from behind.

"Never seen that guy before."

"He looks familiar."

"Everybody looks familiar around these parts. Only problem is, there's nobody here he looks familiar *with*."

He took one step toward the dance floor. Sam Grigg stayed his bow, his fiddling arm poked out like a wing on some mad Plymouth Rock hen. Joe Hester lowered his banjo clear to his hip. Taylor

Kew, with his fingers still poised over his mandolin strings, said, "Is somebody going to start playing, or are we going to stand here all night squared up and staring at some fellow we don't know?"

Hard to say what age the man might be. He had the look of youth about him, his body limber and sure. Only his eyes made him appear older; they shone hard and wary, like a range coyote's eyes.

He swallowed once, waited with his feet planted apart, as if he stood firm against a high-plains wind. "Been on the road awhile. My Jeep's broken down." Even though he stood two ax handles wide, he didn't walk into the midst of the dancers. From where she stood beside the punch bowl and Lorna Johnson's homemade M&M's cookies, Meredith Trichak sensed his fear. "Thought I might find work around to get me by."

"What sort of work you looking for, boy?"

"Harvest work."

Laughter circled the room.

"I've got a strong back and a good mind. Know you've got grain to bring in."

"Oh, you know that, do you?"

"I have experience driving an Allis-Chalmers combine in Kansas—"

Everybody looked at everybody else to see who might get brave enough to tell him. Finally Taylor Kew did just that. "Think you got your dates mixed up a bit. We're finished with harvest work. We're doing our damnedest to *play*."

"This here's the high country. We have to get grain in the silos before the snow flies."

"You want work, you'd best get back to Kansas."

"Or Texas. In Texas they've got a crop of winter wheat to cut when everything else peters out."

"Maybe something else, then. Some other job." He sounded desperate. "Been driving in second gear for the past three hours. Jeep won't make it up the highway to the Conoco station, much less to Texas."

From beside the punch bowl, Fiona Trichak laid a hand upon her granddaughter, the aged joints like burled wood against Meredith's small, impracticable fingers. Fiona whispered, "There's something about him. But I can't figure what it is—"

"You recognize him from somewhere?"

"Don't know as I *recognize* him, exactly. But an odd notion I get. Like I've—" But the old woman stopped, shook her head. In one shaky, deliberate motion she tucked a piece of white hair behind her ear. "Don't know where such a feeling could've come from." She let her hand fall away from Meredith's. She stepped around the table, her pale blue eyes never wavering from the stranger, her expression a baffling mixture of weariness and joy. "Almer," she said aloud, although Almer Moley wasn't anywhere near her. "Maybe I'm wrong. Maybe my eyesight's bad. But I'll bet Almer can see it, too. Where's Almer?"

Despite discouragement from the townsfolk, this fellow made no indication of leaving. Seemed to them all that whatever endurance he might have had had gone out of him. Joe's wife, Mavis Hester, said, "There's work to be had in Melody Flats all right. If you're good at milking holsteins, you can always earn your keep on a cold morning."

"I can milk a cow, I guess."

"Come around to the house tomorrow. We'll discuss it."

"Tomorrow?" he asked, as if he didn't often think that far. "Not tonight?"

"No. Not tonight. Because we're dancing."

He tipped his head to Mavis. "Thank you." At this he began to back away, pulling his odd leather coat tightly around him. A dog materialized at his feet. The dog, so near to the color of night, could be seen only by a small white crest on its bosom. And as if the animal understood all too well the meaning of its master's retreat, she began to slink forward into the light, nosing her way dangerously toward the rows of pies.

The dog stalked the length of the plywood table. She rose on hindquarters and peered at the food. With no further ado, the animal buried her nose inside the crust of a rhubarb pie and began attacking it, gulping down great bites and heaving portions of the other baked desserts onto the floor.

"Get that dog out of here!" somebody hollered.

"Damn thing's eating the food."

"Mildred spent an hour making that pie. Best crop of rhubarb I've grown by the front stoop in years."

The stranger bolted forward. "Cy. No."

Meredith grabbed the dog by the scruff of the neck and forced it to the ground. Only then did she realize how bony the dog was and how it shook with hunger.

"She's worse than a wild—"

But she never finished. The fellow came toward her, his eyes and cheeks bright with distress.

"My dog's hungry, is all, mighty hungry."

"Ought not bring a dog in with people if you can't control what it'll do." She backed away from him. And when she did, he began to totter, his eyes unseeing. She tried to grab him and soften his fall as he went over, to no avail. He probably weighed half again what she weighed. He went over flat on his face. Meredith heard his nose crack, saw blood begin to spread across the barn floor.

"Good heavens," Mavis Hester said.

"He's fainted dead away." Meredith knelt beside him, not wanting to touch him. "And probably broken his nose to boot."

"Why would a grown man come into a party and do such a thing?" Mildred Carney asked.

"He didn't know it would be a party. He's starving," Meredith said, "the same as his dog."

"He's homeless, that's what he is. We don't need that kind around Melody Flats."

"The faster he leaves, the better."

Fiona lingered beside the table, gently pressing her fingers upon its surface as if she, too, needed something to help her stand. "Best get that man up off the floor." Sam Grigg made a wide circle with his arm in an effort to escape the crowd. "Wake him up with water."

"There isn't any water out here in the barn. There's only red Hi-C punch."

"And whiskey. There's got to be whiskey. Ten bucks says Almer's got a bottle of Crown Royal hidden up there in the hay somewhere."

"Take him outside. That'll bring him about," Sam suggested. Tonight was a crisp autumn evening, cold enough to make the children glad to come in from playing "capture the flag" in the corrals.

"Does somebody have a bandanna?" Meredith asked. "I need something to stop this bleeding."

"Hi-C. Douse him in the face with Hi-C."

Meredith accepted one of the several bandannas proffered and labored to roll him onto his side. She pressed the cloth against his nose, felt the cotton linen go warm and damp beneath her fingers. "Once he comes around, ought to order him off," Ralph Carney said. "Mavis never should've suggested he come around to her place."

The fellow began to moan, pitching his head from side to side. He streaked blood over everything. "My," Meredith said, trying not to be squeamish. "He's worse than a toddler who won't have his face washed."

"He's a tramp, that's what he is. Wouldn't take much for his toes to come sticking clear out of his shoes."

"Can't order someone off," Taylor Kew said, "just because you don't know his history. Try as you might, Ralph, you don't own these fields and mountain places."

"He doesn't belong. Strangers never belong." Ralph raised his fists and rolled his bovine eyes as if he fully expected the matter to come to blows.

"He's got as much right here as anybody else," Joe Hester said. "You can't blame a man for traveling in at threshing time. Everything's full of promise when the grain's coming in."

"But it ain't threshing time anymore. Threshing time is *over.*"

"It ended yesterday. You've got to be more flexible than that, Ralph."

"I've got everybody's good at heart. Didn't you see him looking in at the door? His eyes were as wild as a coyote's."

"Some folks'd say that'd be a fine indication of how we affect people." Fiona knelt beside her granddaughter at last. "I can't find Almer, Meredith. All I want is to find Almer."

"I'm here, Fiona. I've been here all along. Right behind you."

"Would you take a look at him?"

"I've been looking at him ever since he walked in through the door."

"Don't know as I trust him. Especially because he seems familiar. Doesn't make sense, does it, Almer? That someone so young could look like—" She stopped, never finished her sentence. The stranger opened his eyes.

He opened his fingers.

Inside his work-leathered hand lay a small, crude object. A wooden whistle. Through no fault of his own, it rolled from his palm and out onto the floor. Fiona picked it up, stared at it.

"Hey." He grabbed for the whistle.

Fiona jerked it out of his reach. She raised it to her bifocals and studied it. "D.W.T." She read the irregular, childlike initials carved in the cracked aspen wood. She said them aloud once, twice, as if she found them astonishing. "D.W.T."

"What is that old thing?" Meredith asked.

Fiona stood without answering. For one long moment she adjusted her shawl back and forth across her spine, not satisfied until it lay perfectly draped across both shoulders. "Where did you get this?" she asked, waggling it at him as he sat up and blotted his nose with his jacket sleeve.

"None of your business." He reached out, made once again as if to take it from her. "It's mine."

She handed it back to him reluctantly, watched while he examined its odd, jutting angles again, rolling it against his skin with deliberation. Fiona stood up, then reached down to offer him a hand. "Where are you spending the night?" she asked.

He shook his head. "Don't rightly know." Apparently he felt too groggy to cover for himself just now. "Probably in somebody's barn, like I've been doing the past month. Where's my dog?" He glanced around the room.

"Meredith." When Fiona spoke, her voice moved in riffles the way water moved beneath light wind. "Wouldn't do to turn a man out after a fine dance like this. Let's go to the house and see about fixing up a bedroom."

"Grandma. You can't mean that. You don't know who he is. He could be a . . . a thief. Or worse. A murderer."

"Maybe. Or perhaps we're all wrong. Perhaps it doesn't matter who he is. I've decided to give this boy a roof over his head tonight."

"Grandma. Think about this. Take a few minutes before you decide. Why don't you come and dance?"

"I'm an old woman," Fiona told her. "Damn near too old to dance."

"Maybe damn near. But not too old. Sam Grigg, tune up the fiddle and get the music going again, would you? If I can get her doing the schottische or 'Oh, Johnny, Oh,' maybe she'll think better of all this."

"I'm not dancing."

"He's afraid of us. And people aren't afraid unless they have reasons. Feed him, if you think you must. But don't invite him home to stay. I live there, too. I should have something to say about this, at least."

"No." Fiona headed for the parked cars in the pasture without turning back. "We'll drive him to the house. You can help me air out the guest bedroom."

# 2

Fiona Trichak's lifelong home stood atop a swell that overlooked acres and acres of unused, overgrown grainfields. In the pale starlight, the rises and wanes of the land made soft, dun-colored curves against the black pearlescent sky. The high-pitched roof jutted upward at sharp angles, a vast contrast to the rolling spread that had once been cut and plowed and coaxed from the sagebrush land. Along the sunset side of the house ran a low, long porch with white posts, gingerbread scrolls, and a porch swing—dangling from chains—that wavered slightly sideways in the breeze.

They'd driven all the way from Almer Moley's packed in the cab of Fiona's thirty-year-old Dodge pickup like a trio of sardines, Fiona peering out low over the steering wheel, Meredith straddling the gearshift in the middle, the stranger pressed up against the passenger-side door with the handles and the ancient steel ashtray imbedded in his rib cage.

"Grandma, you should've let me drive the truck. It's one reason I'm here, so I can do these things for you."

"You can drive tomorrow, Meredith. I'm in the mood tonight to be in charge. I won't be treated like an invalid, you know. I'm not a convalescent."

The truck pitched and yawed over the road's rocks and washouts. Behind them in the bed of the truck, the dog who had feasted on rhubarb pie ran back and forth, back and forth, checking the right side of the road, then the left, leaping over the fellow's dilapidated guitar case as if playing some witless child's game.

"Can't you make your dog calm down?" Meredith asked, scooting closer to Fiona in an attempt to get some breathing room. She arched her eyebrows at him. "He's making me dizzy, going back and forth like that."

Fiona downshifted as they made the corner. Meredith did her best to get her legs out of the way. But the turn threw her right back to where she'd been, next to him. He hung on to the door handle for dear life. "He is a she," the man said without looking at her. He kept his face pressed to the window, his dilapidated Stetson pulled low over his nose, which still showed traces of blood and was beginning to swell. Fiona parked in front of the barn and turned off the lights.

"Meredith. I'm going to need help upstairs

directly. I've got to get the feather comforter down from the top shelf in the cedar cabinet, and you know I can't reach that high. Oh, it's nice having a tall granddaughter who can stand on her tiptoes and reach for things."

Meredith shot one last, suspicious look at the stranger as she climbed from the cab on Fiona's side and went toward the house. She wouldn't concede; she knew her grandmother. Fiona Trichak could be a levelheaded, sensible woman. "Let him stay out in the barn, why don't you? There's that old cookstove out there, those bunks where the farmhands used to sleep. That'd be enough kindness, Grandma, just to give him a roof over his head."

"You been out to look at those mattresses lately, young lady? They've served as fine homes for generations of field mice. There's nests in them the size of a guinea hen."

"I'm right to be worried, and you know it. He's a complete stranger. He'll have the run of the house if you set him up in the guest room."

"Wouldn't serve for any human to sleep out in that barn. Not until me and you and a dozen others've given it a hard scrub."

He lagged behind them and Meredith lowered her voice. "Don't forget about Aunt Kakin's antique brooches you keep stashed in your dressing table. He could help himself and be clear into Idaho before you knew he was gone. He's going over to the Hesters' in the morning to milk cows. If Mavis is softhearted enough to give him a job, let her and Joe give him a clean place to stay."

"See here." The two women went inside and

Fiona lowered herself into a kitchen chair with the heavy weariness of someone privy to wisdom others didn't understand. "He's not going anywhere in the morning. That boy is sick with hunger. He's in no shape to get up at the crack of dawn and go over to Mavis's and milk cows."

"He told everybody at the harvest dance he was in need of a job. You heard him."

"Some folks think they need one thing when they're direly in need of something else. Offering him that job wasn't an act of kindness on Mavis's part. Mavis is sick of pushing holsteins into tie stalls and scouring the floor in the milking parlor, and I don't blame her. Fifty years is a damned long time to pull teats."

With each objection her grandmother overcame, Meredith's need to banish this stranger become more acute and certain. He posed a peril she sensed but couldn't comprehend, the menace all the more threatening for its vagueness. "This is a fine state of affairs, isn't it?" She put out her hand and took her grandmother's in a judicious squeeze. "You intend him to lay around and recuperate, doing nothing when he's got the chance at an honorable job. Mother and Dad will never put up with it."

Fiona turned the tables. "I remember the summer you spent here when you were ten. Your mother and dad would've never put up with you skinny dipping in the cattle trough down the road, either. But I sure didn't ring up first thing and tattle."

"You don't intend for me to tell them, do you?"

"That boy will stay until he's strong."

"I've gotten myself approved for extended curriculum so I can stay here and keep a watch over you. I am responsible for you. If something happens with him here, I'll be held accountable."

"Like they held me accountable when you were ten and I let you dip in Moley's cattle trough. Oh, goodness, he hasn't even come inside, has he? Still sitting outside on the porch with that reprehensible dog of his." Fiona hoisted herself out of the chair, lifting herself with some effort by the wooden arms. "Excuse me. I'm going to find him. You get that leftover flank steak and put it in the microwave. There's potatoes cooked, too, those little red ones done up with parsley and butter."

Meredith opened the old Servel refrigerator and poked in her head. They had other leftovers, the remains of a Tater Tots casserole, three pigs in a blanket still frozen from Sam's Club. Fiona had instructed her to serve him their best.

"Grandma?" she asked with false nonchalance while she pulled out bowls from the shelves. "What was that old whistle you picked up off the floor at the dance? You acted so strange about it."

"There's biscuits in there. And pinto beans. Don't forget the pinto beans. Pile him high a whole plate of everything, would you? Then put the bowls on the table, too. Don't want him to be too proud to ask for seconds."

"You haven't—" But Meredith stopped. With her grandmother, to feed creatures was a natural expression of respect—her sparse array of chickens, the mule she kept, an occasional deer that wandered over from the woods past Hester's place, and this one particular, hungry stranger. There could be no stopping Fiona; she'd already made good on her word and gone to the porch.

Meredith heard them coming in, the screen door grating on its rusty hinges. They entered the kitchen together, Fiona with her chin lifted at a decorous angle, the stranger with those piercing, wary eyes and his sweat-stained hat held in two immense, grimy hands. For a long time not one of them—not the stranger, not Fiona Trichak, not Meredith—said anything. The stranger shifted his weight from one broken-soled cowboy boot to the other. Meredith planted her hands on her hips, flipped her head to one side so her dark hair fell behind one shoulder in obvious defiance.

The microwave rang out, broke the silence. *Beep. Beep. Beep.*

Meredith busied herself opening and shutting things. The silverware drawer, where she grabbed a knife and fork before she slid it shut with vigor, taking perverse pleasure as utensils clattered against each other. The wooden cabinet, where she seized a tumbler and pelted ice cubes into it one by one. The microwave door which she *throing*ed open and shoved closed with a satisfying metallic slam.

"Your plate's ready." She set it down hard before him. She set it down so hard, one of the potatoes rolled off.

He didn't move to sit in the chair. "It's nice enough of you to feed me," he said. "I'll just take that plate and eat outside. Cy's waiting on the stoop."

"Nonsense." Fiona gave the table a good *thwack*. "You sit right here and eat your supper. You've been hanging out with nobody but that dog for too long. You'll eat in here tonight." The old woman located herself in the chair again. After she'd gotten comfortable, she looked up at her granddaughter with a curious gleam of authority in her lively, deep-set eyes. "I also expect you'll sleep in here tonight. No matter what seems prudent or practical, I'm not putting you out to the barn like some new cow."

He took one deep breath, and Meredith had the sudden, unnerving sense that he was caught in something he couldn't hold himself back from, that he'd happened upon a circumstance that repelled him as much as it offered opportunity. He stood rigid as a windmill, hanging on to his hat for dear life.

"Go ahead." Meredith waggled a tea towel at him. "Don't have to wait for me to say anything. It's obvious I'm not in charge around here, isn't it?"

He laid his battered Stetson brim side up on the table. He sat down, pushed up his sleeves, and rolled his backside sideways in the chair as if it, too, made him uncomfortable. He situated himself, raised his eyes to Meredith, and nodded. "Looks real good." He reached across the table, picked up the potato with his fingers, and replaced it.

She found a bib apron on a nail behind the kitchen door, turned from him to put it over her head and tie it on. She heard him begin slowly, the way his mother must've taught him to be mannerly when he'd been a boy, sawing at the flank steak one bite at a time, then laying the knife across the rim of the plate. She heard him begin to eat fast, to devour steak and biscuit, too hungry to slow down or even take a breath. Meredith spun and watched him with fascination, noticing how his hat had left a crease around his head, how his hair tufted in curls behind his ears, how his thick, slovenly hands quaked as he jabbed a potato and raised it toward his mouth with the knife.

His plate was about half-empty when he caught her eye and stopped, his knife in midair. "I was wondering something about my dog. I m-mean"— it obviously embarrassed him to bring it up—"Cy's out there, and she hasn't had anything."

"What do you mean, 'she hasn't had anything'? She ate a whole pie at the harvest dance."

"Don't think that pie counts for much. Rhubarb might not be so good for a dog's constitution. You know, it being stringy and all. I was thinking, maybe some meat—"

"You'd better stop thinking meat. You've gotten the last piece of steak yourself."

"That's why I'm asking now. If it's okay with you, I'd like to go out there on the porch and give Cy what's left of it."

"As hungry as you are, you'd stop and give the rest to your dog?"

"She's a mighty fine dog. She's stuck by me, walked halfway across New Mexico and Colorado with sore paws and me with sore feet. A person would've given up on me long before now. In fact, some have."

"You haven't got a lick of sense," Meredith said.

And she might have said much more if Fiona had not put up a hand to stop her. "We've always had enough food to feed a hungry mouth when it wanders onto this place. There's that Tater Tot casserole, isn't there? Warm that up and heap it into a bowl for the dog. Then we'll see what we can do about putting this fellow's bed together upstairs."

For the second time in twenty minutes, Meredith plopped a plateful of food in front of one more hungry mouth she didn't think it necessary to feed. Hard to decide who gobbled down dinner faster, the stranger or his dog. She surveyed the pair once more, long and hard, before she followed Fiona upstairs.

"There's the comforter." Fiona pointed high over her head to a shelf she couldn't reach without a chair. "You know the sheets'll come down when you yank it. They're on top."

Ever since she'd been a little girl, Meredith had loved it best when she came to visit and her grandmother pulled down her hand-tied feather comforter from the top shelf of the cedar cabinet. In those days Fiona had kept a stool close by, and she had balanced upon it precariously, pulling a corner here, a fold there, whatever she could reach, until the whole thing toppled down upon both their heads. The linens came down tonight as always, engulfing them fully in the redolence of cedar, keen and penetrating, and setting forth remembrances of a hundred different nights when grandmother and granddaughter—one of them grown and one of them small, now one of them old and one of them grown—had prepared a bed.

With her small, wavering arms, Fiona wafted the sheet over the four-poster bed. *Flap snap.* Like a sail, it hung high in the air before it settled onto Meredith's side for her to tuck.

"Wish I'd put out five dollars and gotten those fancy sheets at the church rummage sale last summer," Fiona said. "They were Martex, pima cotton. These have worn so thin, they might bust through if he rolls wrong."

"These sheets are fine, Grandma. Clean and soft." *And good enough for a stranger whom nobody knows.*

Next came the fancy feather comforter. *Flop.* Fiona situated it square on the mattress, smoothing wrinkles with her aged fingers.

"Please, Grandma." Meredith tried again, one last ditch effort to make her grandmother see reason. "He could do something awful to us. Steal something, or . . . or hurt us."

Fiona plumped the pillows, deliberately arranging them at angles to her liking, the meager frown on her lips the only indication that she did not take Meredith's admonitions lightly. "You are my granddaughter," she said, "someone I've helped care for since you were a little child. Do you think I would put you intentionally in harm's way, Meredith?"

"Given tonight, I don't know what you'd do. I've never seen you take such an ill-founded interest in someone. You've taken him in and haven't even asked his name."

Fiona took her granddaughter's arm and began gently quoting Scripture. "'For I was hungry and you gave me something to eat,'" she cited. "'I was thirsty and you gave me something to drink, I was a stranger and you invited me in.'"

*That was all fine, don't you think, for the olden days?* Meredith wanted to remind her. But Fiona's expression made her hold the words in check. She'd never before seen such melancholy hope, such girl-like fascination, on an elderly woman's face.

"Wouldn't've invited him home if I hadn't got reason to believe that fellow may not be what he seems. I believe there's more to him than what he lets everybody see." She said it intently, confidingly, while she arranged a clean towel on the dowel in the bathroom. "Things haven't changed so much as you might think." As if she knew Meredith's contemplations exactly.

"I'm afraid, Grandma. I'm afraid because you don't feel wary of him."

"I do feel wary. I've said already that I don't trust him. But some things, a woman doesn't have a choice about." Fiona jiggled the handle on the commode. "Never did get around to calling someone over to fix these rattling pipes. Every time this thing flushes, sounds like a Union Pacific's coming through."

"If you'd put him in the bunkhouse, you wouldn't have to worry about the pipes. That old outhouse behind the barn doesn't make nearly so much noise."

"Got to remember to warn him about that

racket when he flushes, else it'll scare him clear out of his wits."

"Funny thing, you worrying about *him* being scared by the commode pipes, when I won't get any rest at all tonight."

"That can't be helped, Meredith." And for the first time, Fiona sounded stern.

The dog came upstairs first, extending its skinny flanks as it ascended, the clicking of its claws peculiar and out of place on Fiona's polished hardwood floor. When Meredith peered down, the stranger waited at the bottom of the steps, peering up, his battered hat perched precariously upon his head, his battered guitar case hanging beside one leg.

"You got enough to eat finally, did you both?"

He addressed Fiona. "Yes, ma'am. We did. And it was a mighty good meal. Mighty good."

"No need to wait down there. Got your bed all done up for you here."

He leveled his eyes on Meredith. "I'd be just as comfortable sleeping on a haystack in the barn. Wouldn't want to make anybody feel put out."

Meredith didn't say a word. She held her breath, hopeful again. But Fiona asked, "How many haystacks've you slept on this past week, boy?"

He looked back and counted. He screwed up his chin, bit the inside of his mouth while he figured. "Four, I guess, ma'am. I've slept in four barns in the last four nights."

"And where'd you sleep the night before that?"

He calculated mentally. "Guess it was in somebody's alfalfa field. Somewhere outside of Walsenburg, Colorado."

Fiona gave the wall a good *whack*. "There's a four-poster up here with clean sheets and a feather mattress. No matter what my granddaughter thinks is appropriate, I'll be darned if I'll let a guest sleep where animals chomp cud over his ears."

Her words seemed enough for the stranger. He cast one frugal glance at Meredith, then lumbered up the stairs with the instrument case banging against his knee, walking as if he'd become eternally weary. "There's a clean towel in the bathroom so you can shower. Warm water's on the left, cold is on the right. I warn you, the toilet sounds like a foghorn when you flush it."

"Heard all that."

"Maybe I'll be the one to be out on a haystack in the barn," Meredith announced. "Maybe I'll be out there in the morning, because it's the only place I feel safe." But she wouldn't carry through with her threat, and they knew it; she wouldn't leave her grandmother inside alone with him, not as long as the prospect of thievery or something vile remained.

Meredith tried to sleep that night in the room she'd slept in as a child, with the autumn wind reeling past the windows, bringing the heavy scent of ripe grain stored away. She lay in bed and watched the light thread from beneath her grandmother's doorway, listening to Fiona move about in her room. By half-past midnight the moon began to sink behind the sweep of the grassland.

The gambrel-roofed barn, the twisted fence-posts, the poplars that rose like giant exclamation points beside the house, took on odd lengthy shadows in the yard. At last, in the wee hours of morning, she rose, donned her bathrobe, and prowled the length of the hall. She passed the open door of the guest room and peeked in to see them both, the man with his head slipped sideways, still buttressed against pillows, the dog who'd merrily assaulted the pies curled on the threadbare rug, her head and ear propped atop one muddy, worn boot that he'd tossed aside.

The dog raised her chin as Meredith passed. Meredith raised her chin, too. She lingered. She surveyed the stranger's sleeping countenance, his eyelids closed against a face that appeared, without the probing canine eyes, gaunt and vulnerable with exhaustion. His nose was still swelling to a massive size. It had peeled and was still peeling, sunburned beyond remedy.

Despite the early hour, the sky had already begun to fade to gray, giving things the look of being very near and very soft, like flannel. She noticed he'd tucked all those curls behind his ears as if he didn't want anyone to see them.

She'd come upon him at that time before sunrise when all movement stopped. As she'd lain awake she'd heard night breezes stirring the poplars. Now the treetops kept still, the gentle hiss of breeze and leaves had subsided like a breath held.

When she didn't pass, the dog rose and growled. The stranger opened his eyes. He stared a good three seconds before it seemed he recognized where he lay. He sat bolt upright. The comforter tumbled to his navel.

She realigned her bathrobe upon her shoulders, clenched it tighter around her middle with one fist.

"What're you doing here?" He grabbed at the covers, adjusting them in great folds around his middle, as if he felt the need to protect himself.

"Nothing," she lied.

"You guarding me all night, is that it? Trying to make sure I don't run off with the family jewels or your grandmother's hairpiece?"

"My grandma is being unreasonably kind to you. Don't poke fun at her. As if she wears a hairpiece and you would steal it."

"But that's it, isn't it? You think I'm here to take advantage, to try something."

"Wouldn't you think the same thing?" She smiled. She regarded it as an accomplishment that she'd made him uncomfortable.

He took his hat off the nightstand and placed it on his head. The dog remained at attention. "Might as well be standing in the hall with your shotgun over me."

"Yes. Might as well be." Their eyes met, two young things, one's eyes skeptical, the other's exhausted. "You ought to have stayed at the Hesters'. You ought to have stayed where there was a man around the house. Because of you, my grandmother isn't sleeping."

"Seems like you're the one not sleeping."

"The light's been on in her room all night."

He reached toward the nightstand, and for the

first time she noticed he'd laid other belongings there. He picked up the odd little whistle that he'd brought and fingered it. "You're afraid of me, aren't you?"

"I'm afraid of anything that comes to disrupt Grandma's life."

"Burr Colton, born to disrupt." He put the whistle to his lips and blew. Out came a thin reed of sound.

"That's your name, isn't it? Burr Colton. Grandma never even asked your name."

The dog set down with a heavy sigh. He said, "So, now you know it."

"Burr fits well. Like a burr under a saddle."

"Like the one you've had ever since I got here. Look. No matter what you think, I'm not here to cause anybody trouble."

"Your nose looks awful."

"Thank you. That's because I fell flat on it."

She took a step toward him. "It's swollen to three times its normal size."

He scooted back on the bed to get away from her. "Don't touch my nose."

"It could be broken."

"It's been broken before. Always heals up without any help from anybody."

"It is dangerous to let it heal by itself, though. The septum could—"

She reached for his face, and his dog growled for the second time.

"Cy doesn't want you to touch me."

"Make your dog be quiet," she demanded. "I'm going to examine your nose."

As if he'd never had any choice in the matter,

she sat on the four-poster bed beside him, looking as tiny and harmless as a hummingbird. She tilted his hat back out of the way. With one finger from each hand, she applied pressure along each side of the bone.

He winced, and she had the strange sensation that he drew away from her touch as much as he drew away from pain. "Damn, that hurts."

"Hold still, would you? I can't tell anything with you jumping around like a jackrabbit."

He steeled himself and said nothing.

"I've seen second-graders who handled this better than you." She went at him mercifully with only one finger this time, probing along each bony ridge that made up his misshapen olfactory.

"You've done enough. You ought not be up here with me."

"I'm not finished yet. Hold still." At last she sat back and seemed satisfied. "It isn't broken. You've mashed your septum. But you haven't done damage to the posterior nares."

Before he had a chance to ask her just what the hell was a posterior nares, she'd gone to the medicine cabinet for ointment. "This'll take some of the swelling out," she told him. She plopped back down with a brown glass bottle and a wad of cotton balls in her lap.

She tilted the bottle upside-down and let salve soak into the cotton. When she began to dot ointment along his nostrils, the fumes rose and stung his nasal passages clear up behind his eyeballs. His eyes started to water. His body was as tense as a stretched wire when she touched him.

"I don't care what my grandmother says about you staying around to recuperate, Burr Colton." She dabbed salve along the ridge of his septum with a firm, confident hand. "You've got to move on."

"I'm aiming to."

"I'm glad you see that." And she kept after him until she made him commit. "You won't still be here by the end of tomorrow, will you? You've gotten a meal out of my grandmother, and she's given you a roof over your head for the night. But I don't want you to think there's any work around this place."

"You could've fooled me. You two've been doing nothing but working since we got back."

"That's *house*work. My grandmother hasn't been running a producing farm for over three decades." She lowered herself to his level and gave him a stare not much different from that of a hawk pinpointing prey. "She's been letting me spend summers with her since I was ten years old. I've stretched out two semesters of UCLA med school so I can return the favor. I'm not letting anybody horn in or disrupt her life. There's too much at stake."

He still held that funny, crude whistle he'd brought, as if he needed something of his own to hang on to while she went at him. He fingered the tiny, hand-carved thing, ran one rough finger along the edge of it before he spoke in a low but somewhat unnatural voice. The rims of his ears had turned red.

"Sure, you want me out. Don't worry. I'll be gone from here by tomorrow."

"Good." She sat back, satisfied. "You won't be sorry. There isn't much to do here. But you'll find there are jobs everywhere else in Wyoming, in every town from Gillette clear on down to Rock Springs."

"I told you I'd be gone from here, this farm, this place." As he talked, he pointed directly at the pine-planked floor below him. "I never said anything about leaving Melody Flats."

Meredith didn't like that idea. She wanted him out of the valley, considering the odd way her grandmother seemed to have taken to him. "You can get yourself a good job down at that trona mine in Rock Springs."

"Not going to Rock Springs. I'll go as far as Mavis Hester's and that's it. Never intended to come to one place and stay. But there's something I gotta look for—" He bit off his words as sharp as he'd bite off a piece of tough jerky.

She grabbed the closest of the four posters. "There's nothing to find here—"

And that was as far as she got before she stopped. They both heard the sound at the same time. "What's that?"

At first the soft noise from down the hall meant nothing to Meredith; she didn't recognize it, heard it only as a faint, low wisp of sound. But its volume grew until there could be no mistaking it, for either of them.

"Shh-h-hhh. Listen."

"I'm listening."

Meredith looked hard at Burr Colton. "You've caused this."

"I have?" He flopped his hat upside-down on the nightstand. "You saying it's my fault?"

"She's crying," Meredith said. "All my life, and I've never heard my grandma do any such a thing."

"I hear it all right."

"Sh-hh-hhh."

When Meredith left the stranger behind, his dog lifted its head to watch her go. She tiptoed up the hall to her grandmother's door, waited with her hand on the knob, uncertain whether she should enter.

She heard Fiona inside, alone, weeping like a young thing lost.

# 3

As the sun rose over the Trichak farm on Sunday, it set the small order of chickens to cackling and scratching the dirt in their dilapidated houses. The rooster crowed huffily from where he'd been dozing on the pole fence. From all around came the morning sounds of autumn, leaves scuffling as they blew across the gravel drive, the Canada geese honking, their cries like distant woodwinds as they ascended and flew circles around the sunburned, stubbled fields.

Fiona puttered around the kitchen, making little blustery noises, taking out a pan from the cabinet, rattling the packet that contained the coffee, setting the juice pitcher on the counter with a firm ring. Oh, why wouldn't someone wake up! Didn't they know that everything was just beginning?

Presently she heard the shower running upstairs and felt rewarded. She waited for the young stranger to descend the stairs, and when he did, she saw that he'd dressed for the day. He was probably cleaner than he'd been for weeks. He'd wet-combed his hair until it lay flat as a rug against his head. The dog followed close at his heels.

"Well, good morning," she announced cheerily. "Good to have somebody up. Good to have company."

He walked to the screen door and let the dog out first thing. "You always get up this early? Always start fixing breakfast at the crack of dawn?"

"Not always. Only when I know I have hungry mouths to feed. Used to do it all the time when we had hands over helping in the fields." Fiona ground the coffee and siphoned water into the coffee maker. In no time at all, the coffee machine began gurgling and shooting steam. "Did you sleep good?"

He didn't know exactly what to tell her, what with having his nose doctored and being given ultimatums and hearing her cry in the night. He worded it carefully. "Can't tell you how long it's been since I've slept in a bed."

Fiona pulled a roll of sage sausage out of the refrigerator and twisted open the end of the package. "Now that doesn't tell me a thing." She put the meat on a cutting board and began to slice the sausage into even, perfect patties. She dropped them in the pan and turned up the fire beneath it. "I've heard stories about people who can't sleep in beds because they've gotten so used to sleeping in haymows or on floors. Thought you might be one of those."

"When I was asleep, I slept fine," he said.

This time when she opened the refrigerator, she took out a full box of eggs. "Good. I had hoped you would." She began to break them against the side of a Pyrex bowl and drop them in, one by one. She didn't stop until the box was completely empty.

"I reckon I made a spectacle out of myself, falling over on the floor the way I did last night."

"I'll admit I've seen prettier sights all right."

"Guess I shouldn't have let Cy eat that lady's pie. Everybody got real mad."

"Don't see as you had much choice with that one."

The sausage began to bubble around the edges, singing in the pan and filling the kitchen with the fragrance of sage and meat. He stood in the middle of the kitchen and didn't move. "You shouldn't've brought me into your house, lady," he said. "Why did you, in the first place? You don't know me. It was a dangerous thing to do."

Fiona ran the fork in fierce circuits around the bowl, scrambling the eggs without looking at him. "I know Meredith will want something to eat, too. When she finally wakes up. Thought you'd probably be the first one down this morning. She's used to college hours, you see. Late nights studying and late out of bed in the morning."

"Aren't you gonna answer my question?"

"No." She opened the oven and took out a plate of velvet-browned hotcakes. "No, I don't think I can. Just a feeling I've got, is all. A feeling." She placed that plate piled high with hotcakes on the table beside him. She brought over a tub of butter and syrup, too.

"A feeling of what?"

She stopped what she was doing at the counter and eyed him good, up and down. "Like you're all pride on the outside and lost on the inside." And then she shrugged. "A feeling that there's more to you than meets the eye."

He gave up and sat down hard. "Wrong on both counts." And then, as if he thought he needed to add more, "That's no good reason, anyway."

Fiona dusted the flour off her hands. "You in Melody Flats for some purpose I should know about?"

He leaned forward in the chair, balanced his elbows on his knees, and found something interesting on the floor. "Don't suppose so."

"Don't suppose you've got a purpose? Or don't suppose I should know about it."

"Maybe both."

She laid down the spatula and faced him squarely, pressing the knot of her apron and the aged joints of her hands against the edge of the kitchen counter. She watched his eyes, and something in his demeanor told her that his answer to this question was grave, that he took it with far too much seriousness to reply. Something more wrenched in her heart, something that gratified and enraptured her. She felt safe from everything, was where she wanted to be, where she ought to be. She thought, *A plant that's been washed out feels this way when a farmer puts it gently back into its own earth.*

"Never mind my silly questions, then. I really don't need to know." She began to bring the rest of the food to the table. She brought the plate of eggs. She carried over the dish of sausages. She set a basket of biscuits, a jar of jam, and a bowl of apple butter before him. She brought the juice pitcher and poured him a mug of coffee. "Cream?"

He shook his head.

"Sugar?"

"No, thank you, ma'am."

She poured herself her own mug and carried it with her to the chair. Before she sat down, she extended her hand to him and he took it, as she'd known he would. "My name is Fiona Trichak."

"Missus or Miss?"

"Mrs. Trichak. I am a widow."

"Missus Trichak." He smoothed down hair the color of river sand. It had started to dry and burst into curls behind his ears. "Pleasure to meet you, Missus Trichak."

"And my granddaughter's name is Meredith."

He helped himself to a pile of frothy yellow eggs. Fiona settled herself opposite him to watch him scarf his breakfast, never minding that her scrutiny might make him uncomfortable. She fingered her mug, perfectly in control of the conversation. "And what should I call you?"

He took a bite and swallowed. "Burr."

"Burr." She had reason to believe his name might mean something. "Is that short for anything else?"

"No. Ain't short for anything. Just 'Burr.'"

"You got a last name?"

"Colton. Name's Burr Colton."

"Of the Teton County Coltons?"

"No, ma'am. Not of them. I grew up in Belle Fourche, South Dakota, a long way from Teton County."

A long pause, long enough to make him look uncomfortable. "Heard you say something about Kansas and Texas last night."

"I've been there."

"You been traveling a lot of places?"

He stopped with his fork in midair, syrup dripping. "Don't know as I'd call it traveling. I've been working. Working in a lot of places."

"What kind of work?"

"Everything. I mean, anything to get by. Mostly just coming in to somewhere and meeting folks like I did last night. Seeing who needs somebody to do odd jobs around."

"Like Mavis Hester and her cows?"

He nodded.

"You know how to milk cows?"

She could tell by his expression, he wished she'd stop asking questions. "I've milked a few."

Fiona kept silent for once, just looking at him with her head cocked to one side as though she didn't believe him, her gray hair gathered twisted into a wispy bun at the back of her neck.

He acquiesced under the scrutiny. "I milked

cows once down in Colorado. But I didn't last long at it. Herding cows is more my thing. I herded cows once on the Rafter S over in South Dakota."

"Know anything about running machines?"

"Know my way around one. Did some rough-necking on an oil rig down off the Gulf Coast for a few months. Learned about a lot of machines there. After I lost that job, I drove a truck for that supercollider project the government started up and then gave up on down near Waxahachie, Texas."

"Truck driving's an honest profession. I imagine that's a fine way to see the country."

"It was a fine way to see Waxahachie, anyway. Until—" He cut himself short, as if he'd started to say more but figured he didn't want to.

"Until what?"

"When you work for the government, they run a background check on you and all."

"And?"

"And I got a background. Fired me the minute the report came over the fax machine. Wouldn't've lasted much longer even if I *had* checked out with the government, though. Boring as hell, driving a truck."

Fiona Trichak began to realize that every story this young man told ended with something dismal.

"Worked as a maintenance man for a family motel down in New Mexico. You know, one of those motels that has electrical tape to fix the holes in the carpet and a bottle opener on the wall in every bathroom. Got fired there, too."

Fiona didn't ask. She figured he'd tell her if he wanted; the reason didn't matter, anyway.

"Lady from California, she complained to the housekeepers that I took money out of her suitcase."

"Were you the only one with keys?"

"No. Housekeepers had keys."

She'd asked him difficult questions all breakfast long. But perhaps the most difficult one she had to ask was this next one. She kept fingering her mug, looking down at light reflecting in circles on dark liquid.

"During all that wandering and working and getting fired, didn't you ever want to go home?"

He slumped in his chair. He made a long inspection of the crumbs that'd been trapped by his knife in the butter. He rolled his weight from one buttock to another, as if he were in an uncomfortable seat.

"Why would you ask me about home?"

"A feeling I get."

He jabbed his fork into his sausage all of a sudden, as if he'd speared some vicious animal. "Missus Trichak, your granddaughter's been right from the start. A woman like you, you ought to've never let me in here."

He'd thought she'd take that as her cue, that after his string of stories she'd open the front door and point him out where he could go. But she didn't.

"You ever done any farming?"

"No. Lots of other things. But no farming." Burr knew how she was getting him to tell her the truth. This lady was plying him with food. He wasn't too stupid to figure that out. Just couldn't figure why she'd think any of this was important. "I lied about working in Kansas and driving that Allis-Chalmers combine. Just read about that in a magazine coming here."

"You've never been to Kansas?"

"Oh, I've been *through* Kansas plenty of times, getting to other places. But I ain't never worked in Kansas fields. I was desperate last night, is all. And I learn fast. I'm good with my hands. Good enough to fool anybody."

After all this, she had one certain subject she wouldn't let him back off from. "When's the last time you visited home?"

He met her gaze head on. "Nobody wants me around back there. I come around, my mother does her best to hide me."

"No mother could feel that way about a son."

"That's where you're wrong, lady. Sons like me, we don't fit into family portraits too well." He poked one entire biscuit in his mouth. He wanted to be done answering questions. He wanted to be done thinking about this.

"How long's it been since you been home?"

Took a good while for that biscuit to go down. He swallowed and held up his hands. "We're coming from there now. Me and Cy stayed eight hours for a funeral, then took off again."

As calmly as if they'd never had this conversation at all, Fiona announced, "I'll get aloe lotion for your nose soon as breakfast is over. Or maybe I've got something else to take out the swelling and help the peel."

He pressed his nose gingerly with two fingers, just to make sure that, yes, despite its injury and subsequent doctoring, it was still there. "Don't need lotion or anything," he said. "I've already had plenty."

Meredith's voice came from the top of the stairwell. "Your nose doesn't look better this morning."

Neither of them had heard her above them. She came down carefully in her slippers, with her bathrobe cinched tight as a saddle around her middle. She'd pulled her hair back with a velvet band, and when she sat at the opposite end of the table from him and propped her elbows on the table, he saw tiny gold loops like diminutive cymbals dangling from her ears.

He said, "Seems it'd be hard for you to see my nose from all the way up there."

She said, "It's still huge. Anyone can see it from a long way off." Then, "You're up early, Grandma." She clasped her hands together, peering sideways so as not to look at him anymore. One of those little dangling earrings hung right at the tip of her thumb. "What's going on?"

"Made a big breakfast early. Figured our guest, Mr. Burr Colton, would be hungry this morning. Then I thought we'd go up early to church."

Burr Colton sat bolt upright in his chair.

He cleared his throat as if he had something unpleasant to say. And, indeed, he did. "Church? You never said anything about me going to church."

Fiona stacked three empty plates, carried them

to the sink, and turned on the water. "It'd be a good thing, is all. Folks are sure to be talking this morning. It'd give them a chance to look at you and figure out you aren't going to bite."

"You'll get me in a lot of places. You'll get me riding a horse behind the butt end of cows. You'll see me out on a platform in the middle of the ocean bringing up oil. You'll see me patching up toilets with my head in the bowl. But you won't catch me inside any church. No, ma'am. You can ask anybody who's ever known me. That's the last place I'd want to be."

From where he sat, he saw Meredith look pleased. So, he'd given the right answer. She leveled her eyes on his with a "Remember what you heard last night and what you've agreed to do" stare.

"Got to get my Jeep picked up and over to the garage this morning, anyway," he said, taking up Meredith's visual prompt. "Thing's still parked out on Highway Twenty-six if the sheriff hasn't impounded it."

Fiona said, "Sheriff hasn't impounded it. He was too busy doing the do-si-do with Martha Crumbs last night. You've got time. You've got time to stick around and recuperate."

"This breakfast was enough to recuperate an army." He stood up and pushed in his chair. "I'd best get on over to the Hesters' and see about that job she's offered me."

# 4

I nside the Dinwoody Municipal Library of
Melody Flats, Wyoming, the rows and rows of
old volumes stood like hushed guardians, their
spines perfectly aligned along the shelves. The
ancient card catalog, which formed an inviolate
fortress smack dab in front of the librarian's cubi-
cle, afforded Meredith a constant view of the double maple doors and the knowledge that she could
duck in one direction or the other to avoid company. Every time she recognized someone who
walked up to the central desk, she scooted this
way or that and hid.

Only the study carrels were new, a recent
library addition proudly funded by a Harlequin
romance book sale and a committee that sold
baked goods in front of the Elks Club on Saturday
mornings. Meredith sat in the carrel she liked

best, piled a third medical book on top of the
other two she'd been reading, and flopped it open
to the page marked "Senility—Alzheimer Type
(SDAT)."

When she came to the library, she always
brought her own books from UCLA. A library like
Dinwoody Municipal would never have the re-
sources she needed. But she'd discovered that this
place provided neutral territory, a place away from
the farm where she could regroup and focus on the
life and the friends and the studies she'd left behind
at university.

Meredith began reading at the top of the
page. "A form of brain disease that leads to con-
fusion, restlessness, problems with perception
or excit-ability. The disease often starts in later
middle life with slight defects in memory and
behavior. The exact cause is not known, but
real breakdown in the cells of the brain does
occur. There is no treatment, but good nutri-
tion may slow progress."

Not anything she hadn't known before.

She scrutinized the same paragraph twice
before she gave up on this volume, too, and
buried her face in her hands. She closed the three
medical books with a loud *thwack,* one upon the
other, then scrubbed her eye sockets with her
palms. She finished up by running her fingers all
the way through her hair.

Thank heavens that homeless man would be
out of her grandmother's house by this afternoon.
He'd be at Mavis Hester's to milk the cows. It
couldn't be helped that he wouldn't go any farther

than that. So she'd managed to get Mr. Burr Colton out of the guest bedroom, but not out of Fremont County.

Of course, Fiona had admitted to being wary of the stranger. But what troubled Meredith most was the curious way her grandmother had taken to Burr Colton, her haunting tears, her eccentric, rash decisions when she'd taken this stranger into her home for the night.

No matter how ageless her grandmother seemed to be, the years had begun to tell on Fiona Trichak . . . yes, that was true. And Meredith doubted her grandmother suffered from anything as degenerative or clinically recognizable as Alzheimer's disease. She didn't understand why she'd let reason disappear completely in a situation like this.

Meredith took a scrunchee from her backpack and wrapped her hair into a tail at the base of her neck. The librarian, a friend of Fiona's, turned from the magazine rack where she'd been tamping together the latest issues of *Sports Illustrated, Popular Mechanics,* and *People.* "Are you at those medical books again?" she asked in a discreet whisper.

"Yes," Meredith whispered back, her expression a study in nonchalance. "At it again."

"I've never seen anything like it, a student as faithful as you. But I guess you'd have to be, wouldn't you, with being accepted to med school and then leaving to come out here the way you did?"

Again, the obliging smile. "I'm trying. The Department of Educational Development and Research accepted me for a new program. This is my 'decom-pressed' med school time."

"Doesn't look decompressed to me. Out here on Sunday morning, when everybody in town's sleeping late after the dance last night. Quite a dance, wasn't it?"

"Not everybody slept in. My grandmother was up at dawn, despite all the excitement."

"Or maybe because of it. I heard you had a visi-tor out at the farm last night."

"We did. But he's been well taken care of. And he'll already be gone when we get home at lunchtime."

She checked her watch and gathered her notes and pens. She poked them both into the side pouch of the backpack where she kept them. She disentangled the three medical volumes she'd been researching, careful not to reveal the exact pages she'd been reading. She closed them delib-erately and loaded them one by one into her pack.

*Oh, how I wish I were only studying.*

She slung her backpack onto one shoulder and made her way outdoors into sunlight. Along the sidewalk came a troop of middle-sized boys shout-ing and taking turns running out to catch a foot-ball. She stepped off the curb and crossed Main Street.

Down the way, Sam Grigg whistled and swept the stoop of his pub, which would open for busi-ness and the Denver Broncos versus Kansas City Chiefs football game at noon. Farther along, the broad windows of Big Horn Farmer's Cooperative glimmered with cars' passing reflections. At the farthest point of Main Street, the siding of the huge Simplot warehouse presented a sheeny tower of corrugated metal.

She had just enough time to make the phone call she wanted before meeting Fiona as arranged. She crossed the immense parking lot to the new Kmart, put her backpack on the shelf of the phone cubby in the line of pay phones, and charged the call to her calling card.

The entire time the phone clicked and whirred toward a connection, she didn't stop thinking of her grandmother. Despite her years alone, Fiona had commanded her destiny in a wise and effective manner. Her reasoning was just off; that was certain. Some chemical imbalance in a beloved brain growing old.

The phone began to ring on the other end, its tinny bell almost giving Meredith a shock. She'd been so worried about Fiona, she'd scarcely planned what to say to her parents. And she felt somewhat guilty because Fiona had reminded her of the episode of the cattle trough swim when she'd been ten.

"Hello."

Meredith plugged up her other ear so she could hear. "Hello. It's me."

"Oh, good to hear from you. Michael, pick up the phone in the other room. It's Meredith."

They were both on the line. "How are you doing out there? How's your grandmother?"

It was too quick to tell them. "Fine." *Only she took in a stranger last night when no one knows him or why he's here or where he's come from.* "Grandma's just fine."

Barbara, knowing her the way she'd always known her, picked up on the hesitancy she heard in her daughter's voice. "And you? Are you fine, too?"

"Yes. I'm fine, too."

There proceeded a long pause while they tried to figure out what she wasn't saying and she tried to figure out how to say it. A pause in which they heard background noise and knew she wasn't at home.

"Where are you calling from?" Michael asked. "I hear other people in the background."

"I'm at Kmart. I'm supposed to meet Grandma here at noon when she gets out of church."

"You didn't go to church with her this morning?"

"I wasn't in the mood."

A trio of teens sauntered past, rumpling their paper sacks and reading off a list of songs from the Blues Traveler CD they'd purchased. "You aren't calling from the house." Barbara's voice oozed concern. "Honey, what's wrong?"

Michael cleared his throat. "If that place is getting to you, I want you to come home."

Barbara added, "We've been talking about it some this week. Your medical studies have placed such a demand on you. You're drained, and now you're giving more of yourself for this. It isn't a financial burden for us to hire someone to take care of your grandmother. We've expected to have to do it for a while. We don't want you to lose the standing that you've worked for. We can even hire her a nurse if we can't convince her to leave the farm."

"Grandma doesn't need a nurse. She just doesn't need to be alone."

"Then why are you calling from a Kmart, Meredith?"

She hesitated, groping for the right words. "Guess I'm worried about her, is all."

Michael asked, "Why? What's made you worry?"

Here it came. She couldn't put this off any longer.

"I don't think she's thinking straight."

"About what?"

"Has your grandmother had a breakdown?"

"A man walked into the harvest dance last night. A total stranger. She invited him to come home with us and spend the night."

"Good God."

"Honey, are you okay? Sweetie, did he do you any harm?"

"He didn't do any harm. And the situation's taken care of. I've talked to him and gotten him to leave. But it was a rough night. I don't think I slept at all. And Grandma seemed agitated."

"Agitated?"

"I heard her crying last night. In the middle of the night. For no reason."

Here, Barbara and Michael began a conversation in their house—from separate lines—while Meredith listened to them long distance. "She needs to go to the doctor again, Mike. She needs a thorough physical examination."

"I don't see the point. Mom's already had a physical examination. What's the doctor going to tell her that she doesn't already know? She's on medication for her heart. He isn't going to give her a clean bill of health."

"But her head. It sounds like her mind is going as well. She goes too far, and she could be detrimental to herself and to others. To *Meredith*, for heaven's sake."

Meredith broke in, for the first time feeling the need to defend her grandmother to them. "She made an odd decision, is all. One I don't understand. But that isn't a reason to think she'd be harmful to anyone else."

Her words reminded both her parents that she waited on the line. Barbara said, "I think she's being selfish, agreeing to let you stay there."

"I'm giving her time, Mom. Please. Just a little more time before she has to move into town. She isn't being selfish. It's just that this is the only thing she's ever known."

Michael asked, "Is that man gone now? Has he left the house?"

"Yes, he's left by now. Someone's promised to give him a job milking cows."

"If you get back and he's still at the house, I want you to call the sheriff's office, do you hear me?" And he might have been talking to a young girl instead of a grown, mature woman. "If he is still there when you get back, I want you to call the sheriff's office and have him forcibly removed."

Behind the customer service counter, the cashier dropped an entire register tray of coins and receipts. The plastic tray clattered. Quarters, nickels, and pennies rolled past her shoes.

"I have to go," Meredith said. "Church is out. I see Grandma walking over from across the street."


Meredith followed her grandmother as Fiona went about her Kmart shopping in an uncustomarily brusque fashion. Fiona didn't search the aisles for anybody she knew as she passed them. She didn't stop in three different places at three different times, as was habitual, to complain that this Kmart should never have been built because it had put Rickman's Drug Store out of business and made Jake Kramer, who had farmed the land beneath it, a rich, despondent man. She didn't pause when they announced a blue-light special advertising English ivies at $.50 a pot when only yesterday they had sold for $3.97.

Odd that she bypassed the yarn and knitting section and detoured instead to check prices on a twin mattress that stood enshrouded in cellophane.

"Something on your mind, Grandma?" Meredith asked as they passed three towering pyramids of laundry detergent.

Fiona shook her head. "Nothing important."

"You thinking about that stranger, wondering if he's left the house?"

"That, and more. I was thinking about how people talk in this town. How they put their noses in other people's business. You should see the pile of notes I got passed down the pew to me during the church service."

"They're worried about you, is all."

"Well, I don't want to be worried about. Lived in this town seventy years and nobody's worried about me before. Fine time for everybody to start thinking my life is their business at this late date."

Odd that when they hurried down the rows of plastic-packaged Santas with movable heads and wreaths with tiny battery-operated candles, she didn't go into her regular diatribe about Christmas decorations already being out in September.

Odd that when Nancy Ann the pharmacist said, "Your hair looks so pretty today, Mrs. Trichak. All piled up on your head that way, makes you look like a young woman," Fiona thanked her but didn't pat her head and turn around so Nancy could see how the back of it fell in wisps around her neck. Fiona just said, "I need a refill on my Digifortis, Nancy Ann. Another month's worth, if you please."

She laid out exact change for her medicine and one package of Doublemint chewing gum without making her usual small talk with the cashier. They walked to the truck, which was still in the church parking lot, and Meredith opened Fiona's door. Meredith took the driver's seat before they both peeled wrappers from pieces of gum.

"Well, what are we going to do this afternoon?" Fiona pitched the piece of foil into the litter bag and folded the gum into her mouth. "You already finished with your studying, or do you need more time?"

Meredith braked at the red light at the intersection, then peered high over the steering wheel and turned the Dodge into traffic. Meredith held the stick of gum in front of her lips. She kept glancing at the right-of-way as fenceposts skirted past at regular intervals. "As finished as I'll ever be, for one day." As they drove farther and farther into the country, the truck began to lurch into the washes and sway over rocks. They neared the Trichak acreage, and while it was still a good mile off, Meredith could see an unfamiliar vehicle parked in front of the house. "Who's parked at the place?"

"No telling." Fiona shaded her eyes and leaned forward. "Looks like somebody's old mud-splattered Jeep. Oh, see. License plates from South Dakota. Why, he must've gotten it started easier than he thought." Odd, that she sounded pleased about it. "That rig belongs to Burr Colton. Must've gotten it started up and driven it over here. Kept hoping he hadn't left yet. Wanted to catch up with him about something before he started over to Hester's."

"You mean, that's Mr. Colton still at the house?"

"Doesn't look like he's *still* there, Meredith." She clutched her leather church purse in her lap. "Looks like he left and came back."

Meredith pressed harder on the gas pedal and got to going faster. The truck teetered back and forth as she barreled in across the front cattle guard, sprayed gravel and dirt when she spun in, and parked beside the Jeep. She climbed resentfully out of the passenger side after what she considered a bad morning, a bad night, a bad conversation with her parents, a bad ride in the old Dodge home from town. She made sure Fiona alighted safely from the truck's running board, then she didn't wait any longer. She stomped on ahead and slammed in through the door.

"Hey. What are you doing in here?"

He didn't answer.

"Mr. Colton!"

She couldn't see him anywhere. He must be upstairs. She went up, taking the steps two at a time. "Hallooo." She gentled her voice a bit, like a hunter trying to coax its prey. "You up here, Mr. Colton?" Again, she heard nothing. She began to feel afraid. Perhaps he'd set up some sort of fortress. Perhaps he'd decided to hold them hostage or to accost them. He tried anything out of the ordinary, and she *would* call the sheriff.

"Mr. Burr Colton?" This time she measured her voice as though she were aching to get her hands on a wayward little boy. "Mr. Colton, why won't you answer me?"

As she neared the top of the stairs, she began to hear odd sounds from above her, a tap on porcelain that made it ring out like a bell, a jiggling of a handle, the rush of water pouring, the sound of something heavy dragging and scraping across the floor. When she entered the room where he'd slept, she found the bed made as best a man could make it, wrinkles running hither and yon to prove he hadn't swiped the sheet hand over hand the way a woman would. He'd just tugged everything to the top and called it good.

She'd lost track of how many tones she'd used in her voice in the past five minutes. She spoke quietly, not warmly, and as if she meant it. "We made a bargain that you wouldn't be here."

"Hm-m-mmm?"

She followed the sound and peered inside the bathroom door. He'd built himself a fortress indeed! He'd lain tools and a length of old pipe and a plumber's snake across the length of the bathroom. One of his scuffed workboots lay sideways beside the door.

The second boot was tucked up higher, attached to the bent, angular leg of the man who'd promised Meredith he'd be long gone by now. Both boots were connected to socks woven with seed pods and spear grass, shoved up beneath dusty jeans, inches too short for the lanky limbs that were clad in them. Burr Colton lay like a contortionist on the linoleum of Fiona's guest bathroom, where he'd proudly dismantled the very thing that gave the room its function. The white glistening toilet sat in the middle of the room, disconnected and empty and looking horribly out of place. He had his arms up to his elbows down the middle of a hole in the floor, the sweat-stained armpits of his blue cambric shirt a testimony to his labor.

"What have you done? What are you still doing in my grandmother's bathroom, with this"—she gave a sweeping gesture toward the commode— "taken apart?"

"I'll bet you can figure that out for yourself," he said, and she realized that behind all that hodge-podge of tools and the mud and the porcelain fixture, he had on his hat and he'd tipped it at her.

He maneuvered himself out of that hole and sat up far enough on one elbow to give Meredith and her grandmother, who stood behind her now, a heartening wink. "Missus Trichak, I promise I'll have this back together in short order. Hope you don't mind. Had to cut off the water to drain the pipes."

Meredith crossed her arms beneath her breasts. "You've cut off the water? To the house?"

"Got to thinking of a way I could pay back for that supper and that warm bed and then all that breakfast." With the wrench in his hand, he twisted two pipes and gritted his teeth. "Got to thinking I could drain these pipes. Got a sewer snake I used at that motel. Thought I'd drain these pipes and run the snake through and blow the air out of the lines. Then the next guests that stay over won't have to worry about the sound."

Fiona sat on the fixture, right in the middle of the bathroom where he'd been working. "I was right about this, wasn't I? You flush the thing and it sounds like a freight train's coming through. I knew those pipes'd make an awful noise and keep you awake all night."

"No, ma'am." He kept his eyes on the pipes and said cryptically, "If anything kept me up last night, sure wasn't these pipes." He gestured with his wrench. "Careful sitting on that thing. It's a little wobbly without the screws in the floor."

"I am getting deathly tired of everybody I know telling me to be careful." Fiona took a second stick of gum from her church purse, offered the pack around but had no takers, and read-justed herself on the seat. It wobbled, but she paid it no mind.

"Learned this at that New Mexico motel. Was there for two months. Took toilets apart the whole time."

Fiona bent over and stared with some concern inside the pipe that went down through the wall. "So. This will go back together again?"

"Yep. All it'll take is a tightening here and a tightening there. And you'll have it."

For the first time he realized he ought to have gotten permission before he started disassembling the house. "It's that I could . . . I mean, I thought—"

Damn, but it was hard to explain what he'd been thinking. He hadn't had any reason to be grateful to anybody in so long. He wasn't the sort of fellow people did favors for.

"It's just, I could've hid out in somebody's field last night, been as cold as the dickens sleeping out there. Aw, hell. I could get this toilet reattached in the next fifteen minutes if somebody needs to use it."

Meredith asked, "You been over to Mavis and Joe Hester's yet to see about starting your job?"

"I've talked to them all right. Starting over there first thing in the morning."

"You drove over?" Fiona asked innocently. "Seems quick, how you got your vehicle fixed right away on Sunday morning. Didn't know the garage was even open on the weekends."

He had the grace to look sheepish. "Actually, it wasn't."

"Then how did you get your Jeep up and running, without a garage?"

"Well, you see, guess that's something else I wasn't a hundred percent straightforward on last night."

"What? What weren't you straightforward about?"

"Said I'd broken down and there was no way I'd ever make it down as far as Texas. But that was a lie." He picked up the wrench again, used his fingernail to peel off a fleck of rust. "Wasn't anything ever wrong with that Jeep out there. Was out of gas, that was all."

Meredith laid a hand against her grandmother's shoulder and didn't like herself much for the vindication she felt at his words. Good, she thought. Grandma, please see this fellow for who he is. He's been telling stories ever since he walked in the door of that dance.

"Was about a half mile down the highway from where y'all were having that dance when it gave a little cough, and right then I knew we weren't going to make it all the way in. Should've filled up in Thermopolis, but I didn't have money—"

"But you got it filled up and running this morning?" Fiona asked.

"I did."

From downstairs, the telephone rang. A good time, perfect. When Fiona went to answer the call, Meredith was relieved. She wanted her grandmother not to trust this man. But with the condition of her heart, she'd already been in on too many accusations. "You didn't have any money to fill up last night? But you found a way to do it this morning?" She had to wonder if he'd searched through her grandmother's belongings. Where else, when he'd had nothing before? Fiona kept an amount of spare change in the junk drawer downstairs by the stove. "Did Mavis Hester advance you on your salary?"

"No."

He poked both his arms into the hole up to his elbows and applied the wrench. He pushed it as tight as it would go, then he pushed it even tighter. "Hesters didn't advance me nothing."

"Where'd you get the money?"

"You got no right asking."

He untangled his body from the plumbing and sat up on his haunches. If this had been any other place, in any other little town, in any other God-forsaken state besides Wyoming, he would've let her think what she wanted.

Burr could see it written plainly in her green, skeptical eyes. She would never trust him.

Before, when folks had stared at him with skeptical eyes like that, it'd been simpler on everybody for him to concede and back away. He didn't have that choice this time. His eyes—calm, mocking, sarcastic—locked on hers in the bathroom mirror. "Didn't take money from anybody, if that's what you're thinking."

"Don't know how you did it, then. Must be magic."

"You don't think it's magic. You think it's stealing."

Her tone was cold and final. "Could be stealing. Could be. How else have you traveled all over the countryside without ever holding down a job?"

"A man learns how to get by without much." Burr Colton's countenance had gone hard as granite, a sculpted stoic face, stone cold. He stood from his hams and went after the porcelain fixture, maneuvering it one inch forward on one side, one inch forward on the other, as if it were taking toddler steps. The sound made them both cringe as it scraped across the floor. He bowed one knee forward, lifted Fiona's guest-room toilet, and fitted its various appendages down through the hole.

"Would you hand me that putty over there on the floor by you? Got to putty up these joints so your grandmother doesn't have a flood."

She picked up the little putty can and held on so he couldn't take it. "You tell me how you got money to fill up your Jeep."

He took a breath and found something interesting on the wall beside her shoulder. "Never got any money for anything. I traded the guy at the gas station. A fair trade. A fill-up for my guitar."

Her fingers went limp. The can of putty sat unheeded in her palm. "You did what?"

"Traded my guitar at the gas station."

"Why did you go do a thing like that?"

"Wasn't any big deal. Guy at the gas station, he said he didn't have need of a guitar. He's taking it to the pawn shop next door on Monday. I can buy it back if I save up the money working at Mavis and Joe Hester's place. And I will. I've had that old thing since I was thirteen. I'll buy it back."

"You gave up a perfectly good guitar for a twenty-dollar tank of gas?"

"I didn't say it was a good guitar. It's pretty banged up after all the places it's been."

Meredith studied him with quiet intentness. "I've never heard of anybody doing something like that."

"You never been in a pawn shop before?"

"No."

"You'd better hand me that can of putty if you expect me to finish this up and get on over to the Hesters' this afternoon. I get these pipes finished, Fiona'll be up flushing and hearing the difference in no time."

She gave it over and studied him more.

"Look. I had to get the Jeep off the highway or they'd've towed it away. Have to stay in Melody Flats. And nobody around here was going to trust me enough to advance money. You sure wouldn't've."

Meredith watched while he daubed bits of mud-colored putty around fittings on the copper pipes. She stood with her back against the door-jamb and watched while he matched up the holes at the base of the commode with the holes in the floor. He lined everything up, corresponded bolts with nuts. His lips got thin, the muscles got stringy over his jaw, when he forced the nuts tight. He puttied over them, too, and put those white plastic caps over the bolts in the floor. He wiped his putty-covered fingers on his jeans and left little mud-colored streaks on his thighs.

"Got to go turn the water on."

She barely moved her shoulder out of the way so he could get past. Downstairs, she could still hear Fiona talking on the telephone. A few seconds later she heard the water start to run, a gentle hiss of spray that kept up until the tank had filled. He tromped back up the steps and stood beside her. "Well, what do you think? She's all done." He walked over and pushed down the handle, and the swish of water came. The pipes didn't vibrate or hoot. "Think that'll be enough of a 'thank you' after she took me in for the night?"

He took off his hat, picked up the various tools, and lined them inside his Stetson. He had a set when he'd finished gathering them, a handsaw and a set of wrenches, a hammer and a box of assorted nails, a pair of pliers and some rattail files.

"Are those your tools?" she asked.

"They are." He fingered the wrench for a second. "They've gotten me a million miles, too. Had to decide which to let go of, my tools or my guitar. Had to figure I'd get more mileage out of these. And see, they've already come in handy."

He carried his hat and the tools balanced in his two putty-covered hands. He held them as if they were the only thing in the world that belonged to him. "Best get on the road. You tell your grandmother I'm much obliged for her hospitality."

"I will. I'll tell her that."

Meredith moved out of the way so he could go.

# 5

Fiona held the telephone away from her ear and grimaced at it. She could hear Mavis Hester's words clearly even though she held the receiver a good half foot from her head. She also heard Burr Colton tromping down the stairs a second time, a sense of finality in his heavy foot-falls.

She put the mouthpiece back where it belonged. "Mavis, I need to hang up. I hear him coming down again. He's leaving just this minute. . . .

"Yes, I think you should tell Joe that he's gotten in the way of your Cow Belle's meeting. Just tell him it's all planned, that you've got to have the house on Monday night and he can't invite the staff from the farm bureau to watch football. Mavis, I have to go—

"Joe could take them to the pub. Sam Grigg

always keeps his place open for the Denver games. . . . No, but he always sells food. I've seen it on the sign. Tacos or chicken wings every Monday night . . .

"Tell him that you're making Christmas ornaments out of rosehips and barbed wire and that you're going to need to spread out in the living room."

"Mavis . . . I have to *go*. . . . Mavis . . ."

Burr Colton had climbed in his Jeep and shut the door. She heard the engine start up, and for a moment, the windshield wipers ran.

"Mavis . . ."

Fiona took a deep breath and hung up. She stared at the telephone hanging on the wall for a moment, feeling only slightly contrite. If this made Mavis feel unfriendly for a while, she'd explain that they'd gotten cut off. She'd explain that someone was digging a hole somewhere and had cut the cord and the number couldn't be redialed. After thinking about that, she lifted the receiver off the hook and laid it on the counter. She gathered her gingham apron in her hands and hurried outside.

She found him out of his Jeep again, wiping his windshield with a tattered cloth. He said, "Drove through a fly hatch when I came along the river. Could hardly see out the window. Thought when I got settled, they'd let me wash off the whole thing with a hose."

"I'll get you a better rag than that. One that's clean, at least."

"This is okay. It'll get me where I'm going." He

pitched it over onto the front seat. "I'm glad you're off the phone, though. Wanted to thank you, but I didn't feel right to interrupt." He stuck out a hand. "Missus Trichak, I'm much obliged for the supper and the breakfast and the good night's sleep in a bed."

She gathered the folds of her apron and held her two hands together there, not reaching for his. "Don't want you to go over to the Hesters' this afternoon. Want you to think about staying here and working on this place for me."

Burr stared at the woman. After he did that, he glanced above at the upstairs window as if he could see Meredith and all her accusations there. "I'm set to start tomorrow morning over at the Hesters'. Don't know why you'd want me to stay with you instead."

"I've just talked to Mavis on the phone." *And hung up on her, too*, though she didn't say a word about that. "She wouldn't mind if you didn't come, although she's looked forward to an extra set of hands in the milking parlor."

"Don't know what she'd do if I didn't show up."

Fiona had, in truth, convinced Mavis that she'd be better off hiring someone who knew his way around a dairy cow, perhaps a Future Farmers of America student from Fremont High School. A high school student wouldn't cost as much and wouldn't take room and board. Fiona had, in truth, told a little white lie. She'd said to Mavis, "We were talking about cows this morning, the stranger and me. He was telling me he knew about the butt end of them, but not much more.

He asked what side of a cow he had to sit on in order to get the milk out." And Mavis had said, "Oh, merciful heavens!" and that had been victory.

"Mavis is prepared for that now. She wouldn't mind at all if you stayed here and worked for me on this farm."

"What farm? What sort of work is there to do around here? These fields haven't been worked in a long time."

Fiona glanced around at the weeds and the sagging porch, the neglected chicken coop and the holes in the barn roof and the general disarray. "You're right. Fields aren't the only thing that haven't been worked. None of it has been. It's time to put a barley crop back onto this ground. And I'd like you to be the one to do it for me."

He couldn't believe she'd want to employ him after the string of failures he'd listed. And the largest failure, his biggest shame, he hadn't bothered to mention at all. "Already told you I didn't know anything about farming."

"That doesn't matter. I'd be willing to teach you. And what I don't know, you could ask questions around the co-op and learn for yourself."

It seemed almost like an omen that this lady had proposed for him to stay. As if, because she'd first taken him in, she'd become a part of the inexplicable riddle that had guided him to Melody Flats. Whichever job he took, he wouldn't be here long enough for it to make any difference, anyway. His eyes grazed the upstairs glass again. "I don't know."

"Don't you go worrying about Meredith. She's

got a strong view of things all right. But this is my house and my farm, and I have the final say. She wouldn't have too much to complain about anyway if I set you up in the barn the way she wanted in the first place. Barn needs a good mucking out. And there's holes in the roof, but you could start working there. You think you could figure out how to roof a barn?"

"Never roofed a barn before. But I'm good at learning. I'm good with my hands."

"I'll buy a new mattress for the bed in the bunkhouse. Looked at them at Kmart when we went in after church. It stays plenty warm out there. We've had that wood stove out there since Ray built the place."

"You kept me around here, Missus Trichak, I'm afraid you'd be coming up with busywork all winter long."

"I don't think so." Fiona rubbed the back of one hand with the other, pushed the fingers of her left hand between the fingers of her right. "You come walking with me, boy. Come look inside the barn and tell me what you think. There's things you ought to know about this place. There's things you ought to know about me."

Without turning from her, he opened the door to the Jeep and called his dog. "Okay. I'm willing to listen." He resituated his Stetson on his head and fell into step beside her. Cy fell into step, too.

For a long time, the walking seemed enough. Although it was heavy autumn, the sun flared down on them through a summery bleached sky. Clouds wafted overhead in high puffs too airy to cast shadows. Missus Trichak's hair reminded him of airy clouds, too, gray and wisped around her head, the bulk of it coiled higher on her neck than yesterday, the same intricate shape as a glazed cinnamon twist.

"That field's twenty acres," she told him as she pointed to first one side of the driveway and then the other. "That one's twenty-five more. The bigger field down by the granary." She pointed straight ahead. "That one's thirty-five. Eighty acres in all."

"That's a fair amount of land," he said.

"Yes. A fair amount."

Fiona untied her apron, arranged it, carried it wadded in her hand. She seemed tiny walking beside him with her shoulders stooped. Her gait was that of a younger woman, her arms swinging in wide arcs, her steps purposeful and sure. When they came to the barn, he waited while she unlocked the massive double doors. He helped her walk them open wide.

The old hinges creaked. Webs tore asunder. It took a good while for Burr's eyes to adjust to the darkness inside the barn. Along one wall stood a gallon oil can crusted with dirt and oil, a roll of baling wire, and a rat-gnawed mule collar. Several stalls along the far section were still heaped with musty hay. Behind a hastily constructed partition stood two swaybacked cots and a nickel-trimmed stove, the trappings of home sweet home to farmhands. An abandoned boot sat crumpled beside one cot as if its owner had, just hours ago, stepped out of it.

"It isn't much," she said.

"No," he said. "It isn't."

"It'll be warm all winter. A little cleaning out, this place'll be comfortable."

"Where was Mavis gonna let me sleep?"

"You judging jobs by the sleeping arrangements? Same setup as this. Only her bunkhouse is over the milking parlor. You'd've heard cows lowing and moving about in their stalls all night."

"Sounds like a Christmas card."

"When we spoke, Mavis was frank about salary. She told me how much she'd agreed to pay you. I'll give you the monthly wages she offered plus a hundred more."

He took off his hat, tossed it onto the mouse-eaten cot, and looked around him. This place certainly wasn't as fancy as the four-poster bed he'd been given last night. But then, it'd been a long time since he'd been choosy.

Burr stared straight up at the rickety haymow and the plank ladder with missing planks and the holes above in the rafters where he could see daylight. The stark bones of the barn. "I'll have to buy new sheet metal if you want a new roof up there." His voice echoed in the rafters and made something fly. Probably bats. Or, with luck, barn swallows.

"Got a charge account over at the co-op. Or I can give you cash for the Sunrise Lumber. You can purchase all the tin you think you'll need from Taylor Kew. Got an account at the implement dealership, too. I've had credit all over this town for the past fifty years. Just haven't needed to use it until now."

He poked his hands in his pockets and jiggled things. "I don't know."

Fiona came upon an old disk plow that lay propped and rusted in the corner. Absently she turned one bumpy blade, ran her finger beside the rotating circumference. "Me and Ray, we home-steaded this land in the early thirties, back when the agreement between the Shoshones and the U.S. gov-ernment said more farmers could come if the U.S. built an irrigation project. Only problem is, you don't get anything for free. Don't now. Didn't then."

"Must've been rough getting started."

"It was rough all right. Sometimes I think Ray worked himself to death, what with pitching all those rocks that came up with the winter freezes. What with burning off all the sagebrush and fight-ing off jackrabbits and trying to break through a thousand years of roots and stone and animal dens. They say it was pneumonia that killed him. I think it was starting up this farm."

"He died a long time ago, didn't he?"

She nodded, stood from the plow, began to pace. "There comes a time where you have to decide whether or not to give up on something. Comes a time when you have to decide whether to let some-thing go because it beat you, or whether to hang on to it for dear life for just that same reason. Me, I decided to hang on."

"You're different from me," Burr said.

"Maybe I am." She turned and faced him. "Maybe I'm not."

"What do you mean by that?"

For a moment, Burr thought she looked sad.

"It's something more than love that makes a man do what he has to do. It's a passion. Ray said once, passion traps a man as often as poverty does. It kind of places you at a disadvantage in life. You can never be free to make any other choices."

"If you would've done something different with your life," he asked, "what would you have done?"

Fiona gave a sharp, mirthless response, more like a cough than a laugh. "That's just it. There isn't anything else I would have done. If it had been up to Michael and Barbara, I would be living in a prestigious retirement community in Southern California, conveniently close to their hourly scheduled activities. But then, perhaps I've been selfish. If I'd agreed to their decisions, I would have seen family more. I might have gone to Meredith's ballet recitals and tennis matches and cheered her on as she grew up. I might have joined their lives instead of keeping my own."

"For better or worse," he said, "you've made your decision." And Burr thought, Perhaps we are alike. She's made it very much the same way I've made mine.

"Well, it's time to do something different now. Michael and Barbara have long been after me. Now they're after me to sell the land, with some good reason. I'm going to have to let this place go eventually, and move in closer to people who can take care of me." Then she popped it on him the exact way she'd popped it on Michael and Meredith and Barbara when she'd called to say what was going on. "My heart's going out, you know. It's stopping. Winding down like an old clock."

He plopped on the cot beside his hat. The aluminum springs made one loud, raspy twang.

"Oh, don't look at me that way. It isn't going out just yet. I'm not going to die on you today. But I've had tests done. A body can tell when there's changes coming on. A body can tell, just like the earth can tell, when a different season begins to move in." Fiona glanced out the door, toward the house and Meredith. "That's why she's here, you see. I used to take care of her, get her out of the city and into the fresh country air for summers. Now she's decided she has to take care of me."

Burr could scarcely see Missus Trichak in the darkness of the barn. "How long? How long will she be here so you can stay?"

"She's gotten an extended curriculum approved from the School of Medicine at UCLA. She's out, doing light studying and on-line work with faculty, for a year. So I have until early next fall. This same time."

"A year."

"Yes. One more of each of the seasons. And I intend to enjoy them all."

"Well." He slapped his open palm on top of a fist. "That's something."

"I'd like to grow one more barley crop, Burr. I'd like to see this land put through its paces once more before I have to leave it. You've wandered in this weekend like a last chance. I don't want to waste a single moment."

He fingered the brim of his hat. He felt sorry, mighty sorry. And then he said, "What you said about being passionate about things. Guess I'm the opposite of that. Never been passionate about anything, except maybe leaving one place and heading for another."

"Would you do it for me?" she asked. "Would you stay?"

"Do folks around town—" He stopped, unsure how to ask.

"Know how sick I am?" she finished for him. "No, they don't. Just that doctor who comes over to the clinic from Riverton every Tuesday. And Nancy Ann at the pharmacy over at Kmart. She's the one that sells me my heart medicine, so she ought to know."

He walked to the massive door, clutched the huge jamb, got splinters in his fingers. Outside, the afternoon had gone soft, tingly, and mellow, warm with an edge of chill to it, like breathing gold.

"Don't want to fool you," she said. "It'd be hard work. Real hard work. That much hasn't changed in sixty years."

"I don't know anything about farming," he said, "but I learn fast. I'm good at learning. Good enough to fool anybody."

"You don't need to fool anybody. Not here."

"You mind me asking why you stopped? Why's it been so long since anybody's kept things up?"

"Don't mind you asking. Sometimes I ask myself. Then I answer, 'It's people who make a place.' I lost people, and I lost my passion for a while, too. That was a mistake. Shouldn't've let this place go to disrepair."

He gazed up at the rafters again, quiet a long time. She had a good argument, a good way of convincing him to stick around. "If you want me to," he said finally, "I'll stay."

And so their agreement was wrought, with the doors flung open and late afternoon sunlight streaming into the barn, shining through whirling motes of chaff and dust.

Burr Colton put out a hard, lean hand. "It's a deal, Missus Trichak."

Fiona rose from the disk plow and took his hand inside her own. "Thank you, Burr."

They shook to seal the bargain.


Meredith puttered around the house attending to the late afternoon chores. She straightened the Sunday *Melody Flats Gazette* that Fiona had left in disarray, set out a dish of milk on the back stoop for the cats, carried in an armload of wood—the night's supply of split pine—and heaped it into a tumble beside the hearth.

She stood at the mantel for a moment, absently dusting the dark pine with her hand, rearranging the photographs and frames so they stood parallel to one another. How long ago it seemed when she'd first stood at the mantel and seen them, how long ago that first trip when she'd flown in for the summer.

She'd been ten the first time she flew to Wyoming, her first plane trip alone, to a landscape she'd seen as outlandish and remote. The first night she'd ever visited her grandmother's farm, she'd walked around in her pajamas before bedtime, touching these frames on the mantel, as if the motion of touching itself might make everything of Fiona's seem not quite so foreign.

"Who's this?" She pointed to one picture after another. "What's that? And this?"

If Fiona minded this microscopic examination of her mantel and her life, she didn't let on. "That's your grandpa Ray on his old horse, Hi-Gal. . . . That's me the year I bagged a bobcat up on top of Togwotee Pass. . . . That's a whole group of folks the week the government came in and built the reservoir."

"What's this one?"

"That's the combine."

"What's a combine do?"

"It harvests grain. Separates the barley from the chaff."

Meredith stared at it a good while. "Seems funny to have a picture of farm machinery in a frame. It's lined up here like a member of the family."

"I reckon that combine is a member of the family. You ever want to take a good look at it, it's parked in the field out behind the granary. Bought it myself not long after your grandpa Ray died."

"Does it still run?"

"No. It hasn't run for years."

"Who's in the picture driving the tractor? Is that my dad?"

"Yes. That's your dad all right. Michael loved taking off on that thing."

Meredith held on to the mantelpiece with both

hands and tried to make out the sepia details. "He's driving it all by himself? How old is he?"

"Oh, let me count." Fiona ticked the years backward on her fingers. "In that picture, I'd say he was just about your age. I'd say he was ten when I took that."

"He never told me he used to drive a combine."

"You'll have to ask him about it. Although I imagine he has other things on his mind now."

"He works all the time."

"Does he?"

Meredith peered hard and long at her father's face. "Does it still run, or is it broken down like the combine?"

"Does what still run? Your father? Or the tractor?"

Meredith started to giggle. "The tractor, silly."

"No. Just used that to harrow the fields in the spring and drive the combine when harvesttime came. They came together from the dealer. See, it says 'Case' right on the front grille. A matched set, they were. Supposed to run together like horses."

"I wish they would still go. I wish I could drive them around the place like my dad drove them."

"Should've put them away or gotten them in out of the weather. Meredith, wasn't long after that picture was taken, I had a year when I just gave up on the farm. Had a year when I just parked the whole contraption out by the silo and forgot about it. Left both parts to rust and die together."

Even now, Meredith remembered the details of that first precious visit she'd had here, how Fiona tuned in the country-music radio station every evening, and to the voices of Hank Williams, Jr. and Crystal Gayle, they played games like two hands down and Shanghai rummy. Every night they'd put together a rousing game, and sometimes they'd invite the neighbors, old people with hearing aids in their ears named the Moleys, and go into the wee hours of morning, fighting for a run of seven and a set of three, or three sets of three, or three runs of five. If somebody tried to discard something that could be played on the table, everyone would scream all at once, "Shanghai! Shanghai!" Meredith wiped dust off the old photograph of her father and remembered asking, "Why hasn't he let me spend summers with you before?"

"He and Barbara have their own lists of things they think are important, I guess. Priorities. My old place isn't much of a priority to your father anymore. Used to be."

"It's a priority to me. I don't understand why my father doesn't come here often. I would have liked to come to the farm when I was a baby, and then when I was growing, but still very small."

"He's let you come now."

"Only because I begged him."

And here Fiona, in younger days, had taken her hand. "I begged him, too."

"He's your son, Grandma. You ought not to have had to plead with him to let us come visit. It ought to have always been something understood."

"Meredith, don't blame him so much. There's things between Michael and me. Your father was angry at me about something when he was young. With plenty good reason, I suppose. Sometimes boys run away from lives that don't suit them. They start a whole different existence to cover hurts that have gone before. Until folks grow old, they can't always see that the thing they've covered up is still where it always was, buried underneath, like a seed that's got roots but not foliage."

That night Meredith lay in her bed and stared up at the ceiling, grief filling her in a way that she could neither understand nor measure. Past midnight, she went to Fiona's room and climbed beneath the quilts with her grandmother. She put her feet on Fiona's feet. She wrapped her arms around Fiona's arm.

"What is it, child?" her grandmother asked. "What's wrong?"

"When I leave tomorrow," Meredith said, "you'll be here all alone."

Fiona sat back against the pillows and gathered Meredith inside the crook of her arm. "I've been here alone a long time. I've gotten to like it."

"Most people don't."

"I'm set in my ways, Meredith. I like my own company. And I like not having to please anybody but myself." She offered up a quiet laugh, like the warbling of an evening bird. "Everyone thinks I keep myself too far away. But I like far away. Far away keeps things simple."

"When you get old and you need someone to take care of you, I'm going to come here. I'm not going to let you be far away. I'm going to stay with you here so you won't be all alone."

"Oh, child." Fiona had backed away, had chaliced Meredith's cheeks in her hands the exact way she'd taken them at the airport when she'd needed so desperately to recognize and acknowledge the features of her own granddaughter's face. "Little girls ought not make commitments like that when they're ten." Then she threw back the coverlet where they lay and took Meredith's hand. "Come with me. I want to show you something."

Hand in hand, they walked barefoot into the yard, the summer grass like cool lace beneath their toes. Their nightgowns billowed against their bare calves. "Look up." Fiona squeezed her granddaughter's fingers.

Together they gazed into the darkness above them. And as they bravely searched the night, the darkness became not darkness at all, but a swirl of gentle, living light.

"It's beautiful." Meredith squeezed her grandmother's hand back.

"I want you to understand, child. I could never be alone, as long as I had this."

Over their heads the night sky hung like a canopy, breathless and clear, its stars so thick and endless, they might have been seeds strewn by some lavish sower's hand. The full moon shone like a friend, a verdant cameo that seemed to throb and call to them, *Come. Remain. Be filled.*

"This is the light of the land"—Fiona spoke to all that was above them—"and nothing to be afraid of. This is the sort of light that reveals things about people, not the sort that makes it easy for them to hide away. Often, I think that's what scares people most about darkness."

Even now Meredith remembered how Fiona had said it, even after all these years. She remembered how they stood in silence, watching the sky, watching the stars, listening to the moon and occasionally a car that passed like a firefly along the road to town.

She knelt and built the fire with careful precision, crinkling up a page of last Wednesday's newspaper and positioning it loosely beneath three stacked logs. She set a match to it and watched, gratified, while the paper began to turn black and curl and the dry pine ignited with little pops.

Sunday nights caring for her grandmother were good nights, easy nights, with sandwiches in front of the fire and *3rd Rock from the Sun* on television. She checked the banana pudding she'd put in the oven to brown, sat luxuriously in the midst of sofa pillows she'd just straightened, kicked off her sneakers, and propped her feet on the coffee table.

The sun was just descending behind the Wind Rivers, tincturing the sky with pastels behind the mountains. Meredith shook open the remainder of the local newspaper and scanned each page, reading only the articles that interested her with their headlines.

She read about a civil trial in which a man had sued his neighbor because a horse had knocked a hole in a front gate. She read down the list of public record sheriff's calls, a list that always made her

smile: one Mrs. Elizabeth Irons reported that someone had pulled up and stolen ten tulip bulbs she'd
planted; a tourist en route to Yellowstone, one Mr.
Edgar Neuhaus, reported that his cellular phone
had been stolen, but later the phone had been
found in the possession of his wife, who'd been
making a clandestined long-distance phone call;
Pete Johnson reported that two cows had gotten
out of the pasture and were missing; two small
boys, names not released because they were juve-
niles, had been caught shoplifting bubblegum and
baseball cards from the Conoco gas station, but
charges would not be filed because the boys had
agreed to sweep the floor of the garage for a month.

"I can always tell when you're reading the sheriff's reports," Fiona announced as she stepped
lightly down the stairs, "because you're always
smiling."

Meredith leaned her head against the headrest
and lifted her throat toward the ceiling. "They're
so funny. And you end up knowing half the people, anyway."

"Something smells delicious."

"It's banana pudding." She flopped the paper to
the side. "I ought to take it out. By now, it's probably done."

"I'll get it. You stay put."

"How are you feeling, Grandma? You getting
tired?"

"How can I be tired? I just got up from a rest."

"You know what I mean. It's been a taxing
weekend for you. I have to make sure that you
haven't gotten worn out."

Fiona ignored her granddaughter. She donned two hot mitts and took the meringue-topped dessert from the oven. She set it on the sideboard to cool. "It's good you've made that," she said, flopping the mitts back into the drawer. "We'll be needing—" She stopped.

"What? What do we need?"

"Nothing. It's nothing. Not for now, anyway." Fiona went to the window, held back the curtain, and peeked outside. "It's going to be a pretty sunset."

Fiona'd buried herself in newspaper articles again and crossed her ankles. "Hm-m-mmm. It is."

"Prettiest one I've seen in a month."

"Hm-m-mmm. I forgot to tell you. Mavis called a little while ago. Said the two of you got cut off."

"We did. Somebody must've been digging a hole somewhere and cut the line."

"Phone lines are generally above the ground out here, not down in them."

"Bird must've landed on a line, then. Big enough bird to take the whole thing out. Maybe a trumpeter swan."

"I found the phone off the hook, Grandma. I hung it up about an hour ago."

"Hm-m-mmm. Mavis expected me to do the planning for her Cow Belle's meeting, and I had other important things on my mind."

The house became quiet again. The fire in the stove crackled and hissed as the flames began to reach up over the logs and take earnest hold. Meredith heard the sound of the birds, of starlings chittering as they roosted in the trees and swallows swooping for flies en route to their mud nests in the eaves of the barn.

From outside came another sound, a startling sound, an odd scraping of hard steel and chains and the rolling together of rock.

Meredith's head lifted. She sat poised for a moment, waiting, for the harsh clatter to come again.

It did.

"What's that?"

Fiona lifted her head, too. "What?"

"That sound outside."

"What sound?" Which seemed ridiculous, because you couldn't miss it.

"That one. Listen."

Again the grating came, harsh and liquid, metal dragging, chains jangling, and stones toppling out of the way.

"Where's your old twenty-two, Grandma? Someone's doing something odd in your driveway."

Fiona narrowed her eyes. "These aren't the days of the Hatfields and the McCoys, where you automatically pop someone with a rifle who's encroaching on your property. Besides"—and here her face became a study of confidence and controlled dignity—"no reason to worry about that sound, anyway. That's just Burr out there, working on the road."

Meredith laid down the paper in one big sheet. She stared at the woman on the sofa beside her, Fiona's feeble fingers folded innocently in the middle of her lap. "Why is he out there at this time of night working on the road? Why isn't he over where he's supposed to be, at the Hesters' place?"

"There's still enough daylight to be working."

"I'm not talking daylight, Grandma, and you know it."

"He's gotten the idea he needs to smooth down the road."

"That road hasn't been smooth for twenty years."

"Well, he's smoothing it now. He's been filling potholes with a shovel. Now he's dragging that big piece of sheet iron behind the truck, evening out the holes and drawing rocks out of the way. A road grader would do the same thing. I expect the worst of the racket will be over shortly."

A sneaking, awful suspicion began to creep into Meredith's mind. "Don't tell me he's still working off his breakfast."

"No. He isn't."

"Grandma." Meredith clasped her grandmother's two hands inside one of her own, trying a different tack, being as gentle as she could be. "You have to let that man get on to his next job."

"He does wonderful work, Meredith. Why, after my rest upstairs, I went into the guest bathroom and flushed the toilet three times. The pipes didn't blow like a truck horn anymore. They didn't even whimper. He's good with his hands, good at fixing things."

The metal clanging out in the driveway kept grating and jangling, first getting loud and coming close, then moving farther away. "You'll have to go talk to him out there. You'll have to get him to stop doing these favors for you. If he's still feeling obligated, you'll have to let Mr. Colton know that he's done enough to pay back your meals and an overnight's lodging."

"He isn't doing favors, Meredith. He's gone to work for me. He's working off the first part of this month's salary. I've hired him."

Meredith found she had nothing to say. The odd thought came, *She's always known I'd be here for her. Why would she think she needs anyone else?*

"You look like a trout, Meredith. Close your mouth or you might get hooked in the lip. There's no sense taking exception. I may be an old woman, but it's my farm and I know what I'm doing."

"You've hired him."

"I have."

"Oh, Grandma. He isn't staying in the guest room. We've been through this already."

"Of course he isn't staying in the guest room. You've already raised such a fuss about that, and I trust your opinion. He'll make a place for himself in the old farmhand's quarters in the barn."

"You said yourself that those mattresses were mouse infested."

"That's where he's been this afternoon. I sent him back to Kmart to buy that nice mattress for the bunkhouse. That was an acceptable one. The one on aisle H that was wrapped in cellophane."

"You gave him money to buy a mattress? When Mavis had already set things up and given him a job?"

"I talked Mavis out of doing such a damn fool

thing as hiring some stranger she doesn't know to milk her cows."

"It's the very same thing you're doing."

"She doesn't have to know that. Besides, with Mavis, it doesn't matter so much."

"What matters so much? What matters that you're willing to throw caution to the winds when it comes to this stranger?"

"I'm growing a crop this year, I've decided. A barley crop, the way Ray and I used to have it. And now I'll have the two of you to help me."

"A crop? I don't know anything about growing a crop."

"It's something I've wanted you to learn since you were a little girl. A long time ago, you *wanted* to learn it."

"I've given up a year's worth of medical school to stay here with you, Grandma. So you could have one last year before you give up your household and move to a retirement center, where you can get around-the-clock medical care. I am here for that, Grandma, not to work in the fields and grow a barley crop."

"You're here to make banana puddings and read the sheriff's report and scold me for being an old, addlepated woman."

"I don't even know what addlepated means."

"You've been in medical school, haven't you? You ought to know everything after that." Fiona readjusted herself on the sofa and used the remote to power up the television. Meredith noticed she'd turned the volume three notches higher than usual so there could be no talking.

In total frustration, Meredith stared at the newspaper that lay open on her lap. She wanted to tear the paper in frustration, enjoying the crisp, satisfying rips. But she didn't. For that was a childish thing to do, and she wasn't a child. She felt at odds with everything, thinking there would be someone else her grandmother had hired to stay with them on the farm. After some time, her eyes fell onto the sheriff's report and she remembered promising her father she'd report Burr Colton to the authorities. She'd promised her father she'd have the man forcibly removed.

But that had been before her grandmother had offered him a job.

She practiced the conversation in her head. "There's a stranger been offered a job at my grandmother's house. He's up to no good. . . . Well, yes, Officer. I've asked him to leave, but he isn't listening to me. He's listening to my grandmother. . . .

"Well, no, Officer. I don't own the property. My grandmother does. She's hired him because she wants to have a farm again. . . .

"Perhaps she should have a farm again, and perhaps she shouldn't. She's an old woman who's dreaming of younger days. Her heart's going out, the doctor at the clinic told us that, but what if her mind's going out, too?"

She sounded like her parents. She didn't want to sound like her parents.

Meredith stared at the newsprint strewn along the cushions and wrote the headline in her mind as she went along. "Meredith Trichak, granddaughter of Fiona Trichak, reports that her grandmother has hired a stranger because she's touched in the head."

If she called the sheriff's department with a story such as that, everyone in Melody Flats would think Fiona was failing. The very thing she'd given up school and moved here to avoid.

From the depths of her came the confusing, unsettling thought: I don't understand why you needed to hire someone for the place, Grandma. You haven't for years and years. And you already had me.

Unless she'd be willing to bear witness to the authorities that Fiona Trichak was suffering from some degenerative, old-age malfunction, and have those very words printed in the newspaper next Wednesday for everyone to read, there was no way for her to rid herself and her grandmother of Burr Colton.

A man so destitute and unestablished, he'd traded off his guitar for a tank of gas!

Meredith supposed he'd been offered room and board, too. She supposed he'd be eating in this very kitchen tonight. Well, she'd cook and clean and keep things on an even keel around this place. But she would not attach herself in any way to the presence of a man who'd take advantage of an aging, heartsick, dreamy old woman. He'd figure out soon enough she didn't give a prairie dog's hill that he'd decided to stay.

She walked to the kitchen, found a serving spoon as big as a shovel, and dug out a massive helping of banana pudding. She slopped it into a bowl and began to devour it systematically, not tasting the rich bananas or the warm custard or the billowy meringue.

*You've trapped us, Burr Colton. Trapped us plain and simple.*

# 6

T aylor Kew's lumberyard, Sunrise Lumber, stood
catty-corner to Main Street and across the train
tracks from the city park. Its crumbly brick
facade faced the sunset side of town, its chain-linked
coverts and weatherproof storage shelves faced, as
the name suggested, in the opposite direction.

Old-timers said the store had been strategically
placed here by a keen merchant who'd understood
the reward of unloading boards straight from the
freight cars of a westbound train.

Union Pacific no longer ran this route; the
company had opted for the track that skirted
Interstate 80 through Rock Springs and Evanston.
And Taylor Kew had his orders delivered nowa-
days by Utah/Wyoming Freight Line, a trucking
company that brought its eighteen-wheelers into
this part of the country once every two weeks.

Taylor ruled the shelves of his establishment with a firm, organized hand, in much the same manner a good librarian ruled a library. He kept his timber and boards assorted by size and type, flooring separate from paneling, paneling separate from planks, planks separate from plywood. In one particular section he kept a selection of hardwoods, labeled with black grease pencil and divided into bins, oak, maple, sweet gum, tupelo, cottonwood, and beech. When customers entered the store, they always found him sitting in the same location, seated at his rolltop desk, the top of which was perhaps the most disorganized site of the entire store, its surface impossible to find through the muddle of yellow receipts, pink order forms marked "to be delivered," and an assortment of catalogs, factory blueprints, and price lists.

Burr Colton entered through the front glass door, his nostrils besieged by the mixture of fresh popcorn and pungent timber. He strolled up the aisle where Kew kept his most pressing seasonal stock—for September that meant bird feeders and displays of suet, plastic sleds, rigid bags of rock salt to melt ice off steps and roads, and flat, square snow shovels.

Evangeline Kew dusted the counter beside the cash register. "You need help with something?" She went after the Formica in small, circular strokes.

"Just looking, is all. Thanks."

While Burr traipsed down the hardware aisle, Evangeline stood her ground behind the counter.

She caught her husband's glance, notifying him with an uplift of her chin that he ought to keep an eye on the fellow who'd entered the store. Taylor thrust his pencil behind his ear and swiveled in his chair.

Burr walked back to the counter and tapped the glass on the red-and-white popcorn machine. "There a charge for this?"

Evangeline surveyed his face with an amount of caution. She pointed to the striped cartons stacked upside-down, suspiciously close to a list of September mark-down items. "Nope. No charge. Just something we do so people'll browse a while. Help yourself."

"Much obliged." He used the aluminum dipper hanging on a chain and scooped himself a boxful. He wandered around the store with the striped carton in one hand, eating a kernel at a time, absently reading the labels on finishing nails and box nails, sixpenny and fourpenny nails, flathead and roundhead screws.

Taylor appeared behind him. "Don't usually have too many customers before ten o'clock. Everybody's still down drinking coffee at the Sarvisberry Inn and talking about the weather. You have a project you want to get a jump on?"

"I do."

"Say"—and here Taylor stuck out his hand—"you that fellow who showed up at the dance Saturday night?" He saw his wife mouthing from behind the fellow's shoulder, "That's him. Don't ask. Just watch that he doesn't steal something."

Burr stuck his hand out, too, and introduced himself. "Name's Burr Colton."

"You got shopping to do? What can I fix you up with? Nails or something?"

"I'll be needing nails. And other assorted items. Just have to make the decision what."

"What project you working on?"

"Roofing a barn. Got to get the thing winterized. Roof's got gashes in it as big around as windmill blades." In truth, even with a fire snapping in the stove, he'd gotten mighty cold in the bunkhouse. And he suspected he'd heard bats fluttering in the rafters.

"What barn?"

"Missus Trichak's barn. Gonna fix it up for her. Doing work around the place for her this winter. And putting in a new barley crop for the spring."

Taylor heard Evangeline drop an entire tray of huckleberry candies on the floor. She made a little *humph* when she bent to gather them up.

Taylor's eyebrows arched at his wife. No matter the dubious character of the shopper, he wasn't one to risk losing out on a sale. He asked Burr, "You got measurements?"

"For the barn? Sure do."

"So Fiona's hired you, has she? That comes as a surprise."

"Yes. Other folks are telling me the same thing."

The entire time they discussed the dimensions of the barn, Evangeline Kew kept herself hefted halfway over the cash register, her ample bosom countering her ample build on the other end like an unbalanced teeter-totter. Although Taylor sent her several disapproving glances, she remained hoisted, anxious to hear and to repeat for posterity this wayfarer's every word.

"Walked out the proportions of the barn this morning before breakfast." Burr extracted a wrinkled paper from his jeans and gave it over. "Got 'em written right here."

"Let's have a look." Taylor extracted his pencil from behind his ear and did some figuring. "You want to reroof the whole thing?"

"I do."

"You gonna do structural work, too?"

"There's two beams that need replacing. I want good lumber. Something that'll last."

"No sense getting something too durable for Fiona's barn. I saw it last year when we went out to put a town council campaign sign on her combine. That structure won't be standing much longer."

"Want my labor for Missus Trichak to amount to something, Mr. Kew. Guess if the rest of that barn falls down tomorrow, I'd be proud to see these beams and that roof still holding."

Burr squared his shoulders and leveled his jaw. His entire countenance said, *Fiona Trichak's given me a chance to work at something that'll matter. Never had a chance at anything like that before.*

"You ought to be able to do with good pine lumber. You driving a truck?"

"Yep. I'm driving Missus Trichak's."

"If you'll pull it around to the loading gate back here, I'll have my stock boy bring out your tin."

Burr nodded. "That'd be fine."

"Come on back to my desk. We'll write up the order. It'll be cash?"

Taylor led him to the rolltop desk and thumbed through several different cubicles to find the correct receipt book. As he thumbed he said offhandedly, "You growing a barley crop out there next spring, you'd best get to plowing earth now."

That came as a surprise. "Now? Thought I had all winter to figure things out about farming. You saying I need to plow now?"

Kew stopped listing figures on the receipt and nibbled on the end of the pencil. He frowned. "You don't know much about farming, do you?"

"I don't."

"You'd best get yourself over to Big Horn Co-op this morning and ask advice," Taylor suggested. "Either that or over to the Sarvisberry Inn and drink coffee with those farmers. There'd be plenty of folks to give you advice there, too. Only problem is, you've got to decide who to believe and who not to."

"I'll do that. Thank you. I'll get right on over there today."

Taylor handed Burr's order to the stock boy and made a point of walking him to Fiona's old Dodge. Burr climbed inside the cab, but Taylor kept a grip on the door handle. "Fiona Trichak's been an upstanding member of this community since I was born. Those of us from around here, we keep a close eye on her, you know." As he said it, Burr couldn't decide if he was being upbraided or offered assistance. "You do the right thing by her, boy. And if you need help or advice from a lumber man, you holler."

• • •

By the time Burr loaded the tin and headed up Main Street to Big Horn Co-op, he'd bet a dime to a doughnut that someone at Sunrise Lumber had telephoned everybody in town. He parked diagonally in front of the farmer's co-op and shoved his way in the front door. The bell overhead gave a merry tinkle.

Funny, how a whole congregation of fellows seemed to be waiting in the co-op for him, all straddle-legged on bags of feed and seed, all carrying mugs half-full of coffee, mugs that said on the side, "Start Things Moving at Sarvisberry Inn."

He'd say there were about a dozen of them, spread out and somber, eyeing him as though they didn't quite know what to make of him. They held their noses low, their eyes level, like wolves sneaking forward, wondering if they'd found prey. "Howdy," somebody said. He looked around, but in all the crowd, he couldn't see who. "Come on in and join the group."

"You need help?"

"Heard you looking to farm out at the old Trichak place."

"You putting in sugar beets or barley?"

"What's your acreage out there?"

He'd been hoping to have time to peruse the bags of seed, the lists of fertilizers and insecticides, to get his bearings about him before anyone figured out how little he knew. But it was too late. Somebody'd warned them ahead of time.

"Evangeline Kew called over here, said you were on your way."

"She called over at the Sarvisberry, too."

"Waitress let us bring our mugs with us. But we've got to return them before the noon rush."

"It'll be good to see grain waving out on Fiona's place again. It's high time. High time."

Burr took their willingness to congregate and look him over as encouragement. Didn't matter if they offered advice out of curiosity or helpfulness, he appreciated the aid. "Kew says I need to get a plow in the ground now. I don't know a thing about it."

"Some people plow before winter. Some people don't."

"Only people don't are the sugar beet growers. They don't get their beets out much before the ground freezes. They'd do it if they had time."

"Can't plow this week. That'd be wrong. Got to wait for the wax of the moon."

"That's crazy, Darby. Ought to always plow ground when the moon is new."

"Ought to plant corn when the moon is filling. It'll ear out a good two joints higher than corn planted when the moon is waning."

"He's not planting corn, Darby. He's planting barley. And he's not planting yet, he's plowing."

"Evangeline said he needed advice. I'm giving her all the advice I know."

The proprietor came forward with a business card in his hand. "Never mind all these folks. They're just hankering to poke their noses into other people's business."

"I don't have much of a plan. Fiona just hired me on yesterday afternoon."

"Fiona doesn't have implements out there, does she?"

"She's got an old combine and tractor."

"I'm not talking about that old rig. I've seen it out sitting by the highway. That thing'll never run. I'm talking real implements. You'll need to go out and make a good set of turn rows, turn, say, eight to sixteen inches of dirt under before winter sets in. Breaks up the old roots, breaks up any crust and clods, gets it ready to absorb the rain and snow. Talk to this fellow over at the implement dealership." He waggled the card at him again. "He'll give you a fair deal, get you set up to rent something that'll do the job."

Burr took the card. "Any idea how long it'll take to get the thing done?"

"How many acres you working out there?"

"Eighty."

The fellow cinched his arms beneath his armpits. "Takes about an hour an acre to do almost anything. To plow. To seed. To fertilize. It could be quicker to combine. I'd say two or three acres an hour for that."

"That long to plow," Burr commented.

"Yep. So it'll take you eighty hours to plow the whole thing. Figure eight-hour days, that's ten days."

"Figure twelve-hour days."

"Then you'll get it done in a week, if you're willing to work that hard. It'd do that ground good to get the old roots clear under and the new soil up breathing before freezing weather comes. And I've got other advice," he said, grinning.

"Probably the most important thing anybody'll ever tell you."

"What's that?" Burr asked.

"Don't listen to too much advice."

And as Burr headed out the door he could still hear them behind him, talking about doctoring animals when the zodiac signs were right and planting potatoes in the dark of the moon.

Meredith knew that the sun had been up for a long time.

She'd opened one eye when the glow had first crested the broad horizon and had peach tinged the Wind River Mountains. She'd opened that same eye when she smelled coffee brewing, when she heard English muffins erupting from the toaster, and when she heard someone driving out across the front cattle guard.

So Burr Colton was already up and at it. She burrowed her head beneath a pillow and pretended to be a ground squirrel, tucked in for a winter's hibernation.

She'd been up until midnight on the Internet, on-line with UCLA MedNet, updating her files with the faculty and composing a proposal for an independent-learning report. Last night she'd been convinced that the paper was a good idea, a research study entitled "Biomathematics in the Micro-anatomy System" that would earn three credits toward her doctorate. This morning she wasn't completely certain of its merit. She felt far away from home and cornered this morning, not sure of anything.

She'd check her e-mail later in the day. She'd sent a message to her faculty adviser. He'd answer her quickly and let her know his opinion on the project.

From outside Meredith heard the unmistakable sound of someone overzealously bending and pitching metal. She opened the same eye and checked the digital clock beside her. Ten-thirty. She raised her head just an inkling off the pillow, moaned, and had the grace to feel somewhat guilty. Outside her second-story window, climbed halfway up on the roof of the barn, was Burr Colton.

Meredith closed her blinds. The entire time she dressed she could hear him, the interloper, pounding at the wood, removing nails, tearing the roof off with the dissonant arpeggio of bending tin. She dressed, went downstairs, took what was left of the morning's coffee, and toasted an English muffin. The entire time Meredith ate, tin came flying down in disjointed, corrugated wings and bounced on the grass outside the window. She heard Fiona, happy as a setting hen, humming in her sewing room.

She checked the wood box on the back porch and found it to be almost empty. They'd burned everything she'd brought into the house last night. Meredith suspected Burr had burned some in the barn stove last night as well. As if he thought he were the only one who could get any work done around here. She needed to split more firewood before sunset, and this would be the perfect time.

And even if this wasn't the perfect time, she elected to do it now anyway.

On the old cottonwood stump, right behind the barn, where Burr Colton would be certain to see.

If she didn't get decapitated by flying roof first.

Meredith yanked on her work gloves and picked up the splitting maul and wedge Fiona kept in the mud room. She opened the door and ducked just as a square piece of metal skittered past, catching a waft of air and spinning away into the clothesline.

"Hey," she hollered up at him. She shielded her eyes and could see that he'd chosen to work shirtless, that he'd worked up a heavy sweat despite the cool autumn day. "Be careful where you're dropping that stuff."

"Can't be careful," he hollered back. "Can't see a thing up here. I told Missus Trichak it would be best not to be in the yard."

"I have to be in the yard, Mr. Colton. I have work to do out here," she hollered back.

He yanked out a nail and shrugged his shoulders. "Suit yourself."

Meredith balanced the maul over one shoulder and trod out to the cottonwood splitting stump. It had stood in this corner by the barn for as long as she remembered, an old knot in one side where a thick branch had once grown, nicks and cuts taken out of its broad surface by the ax, the hundred or so growth rings still countable. She picked up one log from the woodpile and stood it on end upon the stump. She raised the maul over her left shoulder and let it fall.

The log cracked. Meredith shoved the iron wedge inside the crack. She spread her legs for leverage, lifted the maul over her shoulder, drove the wedge deeper into the crack. On the third hit, the log split in half.

Now she began the same process with the half, standing it on end, lifting the maul, and letting it fly, making a crack. Three minutes later, she had a nice pile of five split logs. Proudly she pitched them aside and began again.

On the roof, Burr Colton pried nails and staples with new precision, setting the hammer under the rusted nail heads and rocking each out with a single squeaking motion. One row, out. Second row, gone. Pitch a length of metal and watch it spin down on the side of the house; hear it *bong* onto the ground. Next. The landscape around him had no permanence to it, a temporary place where he would serve his time the same as the others and then move on.

On the stump, Meredith had gotten her wedge stuck into a knot. It wouldn't go deeper. She removed the wedge and went deeper into the crack with the maul. The maul got stuck. She hefted the maul and the log came, too. She banged the whole thing, maul and wood together, onto the stump. One side splintered off and was good for nothing but kindling, a spindly, uneven piece.

Atop the barn rafters, Burr dislodged the last sheet of roof tin. He lost his concentration momentarily as he peered into the eaves below. The beam he'd chosen to bestride had rotted almost through.

In his haste to move off the eave, he lost control of the metal. It fell against his hand and flopped asunder, cutting a nasty line across the width of his palm. He muttered an expletive it was good no one else heard. He'd hide this wound whenever he went into the house. After the nose doctoring he'd suffered with Meredith, he didn't want to give her another chance to find something to fix. He wiped blood on his jeans while he tried to figure out how to replace those two beams.

They managed to keep out of each other's way for almost two hours. The sounds of their labor rang out in the dooryard. He hammered new tin into place over the beams that had stayed sturdy. He hammered like a piston. *Whap whap whap*.

She continued to split with the wedge and maul. With each log that rent and splintered into halves, she found divine enjoyment. *Plank plank plank*.

They might have been able to ignore each other if not for the presence of those sounds, each reminding the other of who worked above or below.

A few minutes before noon, when Fiona still hadn't called them for lunch, Meredith swung the maul over her shoulder and left it stuck in the middle of the stump.

Oh, but it felt good to stand straight and stretch out her ribs.

She clasped gloved hands at the small of her back and arched her backbone. She wiped her brow with the back of her work glove and listened.

Burr's hammering had stopped, too.

She shaded her eyes and squinted into the sun. She saw him astride the peak of the roof.

He sat with his spine perfectly straight, his hammer in a hand at his side, and stared into the sky as if he'd never been so close to it before. And maybe, she decided, he hadn't been.

The sun and the sweat and the breeze had done their work on his uncovered head. All those curls he tried to slick down and hide and poke behind his ears had escaped and protruded like watch springs all around his head.

Seemed a long time that he watched the sky before he realized the sound of her wood splitting had ceased. He ran his palm the length of his thigh and glanced toward the ground.

And stared her down as though he'd come upon a bobcat in the brush.

She stared up at him the same way.

For several seconds they eyed each other, squared off like opposing infantrymen, angry and distrustful. Finally Burr spoke.

"I suppose you think I convinced her to offer me this job."

She set her hands on her hips, and even from where he sat, he could see she had wood chips covering her shirt. "Seems funny, doesn't it, Mr. Colton? Until you came around, my grandmother hadn't offered anyone a farming job."

He donned his shirt, buttoned it, and tucked it in all the way around. He mopped his brow with his sleeve, peered straight into the sun. "My guess is, must be about noon."

"No sense avoiding the issue, Mr. Colton. I want to have it out with you."

"I'm sure you do." She'd done nothing but have it out with him ever since her grandmother had invited him home from the dance. But he had no intention of sitting on top of a roof and shouting down the terms under which Fiona Trichak had offered him employment. He swung his leg over the summit of the roof the same way he'd swing his leg off a saddle. He worked his way down, spiderlike, to the brink of the ladder. He didn't say another word until he'd turned and started climbing down. And when he did, he punctuated every word with a step onto the next rung. "I know her medical condition. She told me the details when she offered the job."

That set Meredith back. He could hear it in her voice. "She told you about it?"

He'd reached the bottom rung and jumped to the ground. Cy trotted out of the barn and sat at his feet. Burr pitched his hammer into the pile of tools he'd left in the grass. "Everything."

"You know why I've come to stay with her, then."

"She told me that, too."

"My parents have wanted her to sell this place for a long time. If she would agree to move into town, she'd have professional care and she'd be close in case something happened. There's not much medical care here. Except on Tuesdays, when the clinic's open."

"You think she should sell the place, too?"

"Eventually. Just hate to see the time come, is all."

"It came as a blow when she told me. There's no telling she's in bad health, seeing her like she is."

"In that case, you should've understood that it wasn't a good idea to accept. From the moment you walked into that dance you've had some mysterious *draw* on her that no one in town can figure out."

Her words wrenched in his gut. "Folks are saying that?"

"You heard her crying the other night when she thought nobody'd hear. You ought to know, she isn't acting her normal self."

He couldn't get past her previous words. "Folks're saying I shouldn't be here?"

"Yes. I—I mean, *some* folks are saying it."

"You mean, you."

She bent down and started piling up an armload of split wood to take to the back porch. "There's others." She carefully avoided his face. "How long's she agreed to pay you for?"

He didn't see as how that'd be any of her business. "Figure I'll be around here about as long as you will."

"You're taking advantage of an old woman who is incapable of making sound decisions any longer. You are using your wiles—"

"Believe me, lady," he said, "I didn't have to use 'wiles' of any sort. She came to me and convinced me it will mean something to her to have a crop growing on this place again."

"She's convinced you of nothing. I think you've convinced her. Why else would she do such a thing after all these years?"

"I don't know anything about farming, Miss Trichak, but your grandmother thinks I am capable of learning. I cannot say, as you are doing, 'Mrs. Trichak. You are too old to have a dream.'" He pointed a finger directly at her, anger burgeoning. She had a right to her opinion. She did not have a right to take away the hint of dignity her grandmother had offered him. "I believe, if you'd stop being so set on diagnosing her with problems, you could stop to see that she is wise."

"I never said she isn't wise. My grandmother is a wise woman."

"You can't always look on the outside and see what folks need on the inside."

"I've known my grandmother my entire life. You say you know better than me what she needs *inside?*"

"From how she talks, I'd say your family is too busy to know what's inside her."

"Too busy? I'm here, aren't I?"

"There's other types of busyness."

She poked at a wood chip with the toe of her shoe. "Why do you call her wise, Burr Colton? Because she has seen fit to hire you?"

"Maybe." Despite his anger, he let a rare trace of vulnerability show. "Maybe I wanted her to see something nobody else would."

"So you *have* coerced her."

"No. I won't be held responsible for that."

"I hold you responsible for all of it."

"I think you ought to do something differently," he said. "I think you out to stop keeping your nose in your medical books and *be* with her.

There's times people need more than physical presence from a person. They need to be focused on, because maybe it's their last chance to know and to be known deeply by someone. Maybe that's why she convinced me to stay. That's something I learned from my grandfather. . . ." And then he stopped, clamped his mouth tight like a trap that had sprung shut.

"Why did you stop? What did you learn from your grandfather?"

"I wish I'd known him better, is all."

"Was he wise?"

"Yes. I think he was. Only it took me a long time to figure that out."

The screen door creaked on its hinges. Fiona, calling them to lunch. "Burr. Meredith. The two of you wash up." They filed inside, past her, like wayward children. Fiona pointed a finger at Meredith. "And don't you think you'll take chicken pot pie into your bedroom to eat it. There's too much excitement around here for you to miss a gathering."

They'd scarcely had time to sit down and hear Fiona say a short grace before she unfolded her napkin and began questioning Burr about the barn.

"So you've picked up the tin?"

"Already started putting it on. It's going to take a while, though. I'll keep at it today until sundown. May need help mounting those two beams."

"It'll be good as new when you're finished, won't it?"

"Yep. Good as new."

"Are you going to paint the roof, Burr? I've

always thought it would be lovely to have a barn with a painted roof."

"What color would you like it?"

"I've always liked red. Or blue. Or green. Especially green. I've always been partial to green, but Ray wouldn't have that. Said a green-roofed barn came too close to matching a John Deere tractor. Oh! We'll have to decide, won't we? We'll have to take votes between us."

Meredith couldn't resist a hint of sarcasm. All this excitement between them and she felt left out. "We could letter the roof, too. Something that could be read from miles away. 'Trichak Farm.'"

But they ignored her comments like she wasn't even there. Burr said, "Don't know if I'll get the barn finished all the way as soon as I'd hoped, Missus Trichak." He stopped, waited for her to ask why.

"Why?"

"Got another big job to start tomorrow. Something I hadn't planned on."

And Meredith thought, How could he have planned on *anything*? Grandma didn't hire him until yesterday.

Fiona leaned forward with her elbows on the table, her fingers entwined beneath her chin. "What is it?"

"Got plenty of advice from farmers this morning. Plenty of folks were willing to tell me what to do with this land."

"I knew they'd tell you."

"You said you had an account down at the implement dealership?" He pulled out the card he'd gotten, stood it on its side, and tapped it on the edge of the table like a fidgety little boy. "I'd like to call over there this afternoon and hire us a tractor and plow. Seems from all the advice I've gotten, I need to spend the next week or so plowing up these fields."

Meredith frowned. "That's crazy. You certainly don't need to plow now."

Fiona said, "You *do* need to plow now. But don't rent equipment from the dealer. Hightail it over to Almer Moley's in the morning. Almer's always awake at sunup. We've let those Moleys borrow our rig plenty of times. Almer's a good friend. Time we called in the favor."

"Grandma." Meredith touched her arm, just to remind her. "Those Moleys who borrowed your rig. Are they still *alive?*"

"No. But Almer remembers it. Almer knows everything. Get over there first thing tomorrow, Burr. I'd forgotten about fall plowing. Got to get those old roots turned under before the snow falls."

# 7

That night the stars broke as usual, shining over the Trichak farm with that glittery silveriness that early stars have in high altitudes. Stars glimmered over three stretches of field, eighty acres in all, that had lain fallow and dormant for years.

The three residents of the place kept busy with their separate pursuits. Meredith sat at her computer, browsing through UCLA MedNet and reading her e-mail. Burr crouched on the porch steps, making chords with his fingers on imaginary frets of a guitar, gazing up the way he liked to do, reading pictures and stories from the stars. Fiona worked in her sewing room, using her top-of-the-line sewing machine to make old-fashioned pillows to sell at the upcoming church bazaar.

Her hands ran over the fabrics, and she remembered where each had come from, a gingham cloth she'd kept on the table when the boys had been young, a hand-stitched handkerchief she'd carried in her Bible to church, a store-bought dress Ray had gifted her with so she'd have something new to wear to the dance.

She smoothed these out, laid each one upon another, until a pile six inches thick lay in her lap. As she ran her hands along the linen and gingham and chambray, Fiona found herself years into the past, a new bride, practically a child, so happy to have a husband and to be sure of owning land.

"Look at this dirt, would you, Fi?" Ray stooped between two turn rows and picked up a thick clod. "Best dirt in Fremont County, right here outside the barn."

"We picked a good place, didn't we, Ray?"

"Yeah." He'd wrapped his arm tight around her waist, squeezed her close, kissed her. "I've got a good way of picking. Both women *and* land."

"You think so?"

He answered fast, because he'd heard the sadness in her voice. "I know so."

"But the baby—"

"Can't help that you lost that baby, Fiona. You'll have others. You had Michael. And it's just been two years since he was born. There'll be others soon."

She'd stared up at stars that night, so close, so much like the stars she stared at out the window now. "I'll try. I know how you wanted a passel of boys."

He hoisted the dirt clod high. "I want a crop, Fi. And by God, we're going to get one this year. Barley we can use for feed and to plant and to sell. All that work, clearing out the sage. Who'd've known this land would be so rich and good. Who'd've known until we plowed into it deep and turned it over."

"It's good soil, Ray. You've picked good soil."

"I've picked a good woman, too, Fi. Don't want you questioning that anymore. I see you questioning in your mind when you don't think I'm watching."

"Can't help it questioning." Her voice, her strong voice that she'd used to coax him and support him and encourage him during this year, had clogged with tears.

He took her full in his arms and held her there, tight, as though he wouldn't ever let go. "You feeling like you want to go away? You want to take the train down to Casper and visit friends and go to a movie house? We've got money, if you need to get away."

"Who would feed the chickens if I went away? Who would keep that awful hog out of the garden?"

"That awful hog will be butchered and salted by Thanksgiving. We'll have ribs and salt meat all winter long because of that awful hog."

"No, I'm not going away, Ray. This is my place. On this land. Beside you."

"Anything happens to me, you promise me you'll stay here. You promise me you'll keep this land after all the hard work we've done." He released her just enough to hold up the clod again.

"By God, look at this dirt. Crops'll grow like the dickens, I tell you."

But she hadn't heard what he'd said about "crops growing like the dickens." All that time ago, he'd said those words. He was thinking about the dirt, and she was thinking what she'd do if she ever had to run the place without him.

She glanced down at the hands resting on the fabric in her lap, at fingers that were perfectly folded. She stared at them and remembered another voice, a precious voice, after Ray had gone. "You've done a good job of it since Ray died, Fi. That's what it is with you." Charles Burleigh's gaze followed the summertime stars as if he'd never known truly what he sought, or how he'd recognize what he sought for if he found it. "You see things clearly, Fiona. When I sometimes don't see them at all."

"You've taught me everything I know." She said it quietly, never lifting her eyes from his hands. "Charley, you're the pastor."

"No." She could remember just how he'd looked as he shook his head, how his green eyes narrowed and he'd sighed with a depth that told her he'd given his whole self over to her. "Something else has taught you, Fi. Something much bigger and different from me."

Her hands lay in her lap, perfectly folded, hands that had once been young and nimble, hands now gone pale as parchment and vein-ridden with age. She reached for the scissors. All these fabrics she began to cut apart, piece by piece, bits falling into her lap, bits of memories both joyful and sad. She arranged them, pinned them together according to shape, color, and size. Then she turned on the light above the shiny machine and began to sew the fabrics together to make fresh, unique patterns.

Meredith scrolled through her e-mail one last time before she began to delete them, item by item. She'd wanted to make certain she hadn't missed the response she'd expected from her faculty adviser at UCLA. She leaned back in her workstation chair, stretched her arms straight over her head, and sighed.

Of course, she wasn't a high priority to them now, being a thousand miles away.

Outside the window shone myriad stars. She threw her sweater over her shoulders and went downstairs. The light was on in her grandmother's sewing room, but she didn't call to Fiona. She used her rump to quietly press her way out the door. And found Mr. Colton seated on the very same step she'd intended to sit on. He sat with one arm outstretched, his fingers shifting in odd positions over nothing but air. With his other hand, he strummed air, too.

The dog at his feet lifted her head and emitted a low growl.

"Cy. Quiet."

Not one to give up territory easily, Meredith sat beside him, making sure she stayed exactly two paces to his right, and hugged her knees. "What are you doing out here?"

"Looking at the stars," he said, the first time she'd heard him light-hearted, and that set her a bit off balance. "Could've lain right in my bed and looked up at these same stars since there isn't any roof above me yet. Decided it'd make me sleep warmer if I came out and looked from the porch instead."

"You miss your guitar?"

He glanced from one outspread hand to the other. He dropped them both on his legs. "Guess so. Hard to get the full effect of stars without the strumming."

He was afraid to say anything else. Seemed like every time they'd started talking these past two days, they'd provoked each other into angry silence. He figured regular silence was better than the other kind.

The stars shivered and grew brighter, piercing the darkening azure of night sky. She hugged her legs tighter, propped her chin on her knees.

He propped his chin in his palm and said, "I know you don't want me here."

"You don't know anything about farming. And you picked a stupid place to learn. None of us know anything. We're biding our time."

"Your grandma knows about farming."

"Well, she's the *only* one."

"I'll figure out how to farm. I've done everything else. I can figure out a way to do that, too. You watch me."

"You'd better come up with something if you're going to pull this off the way you intend. You start making mistakes around here and I'll phone the sheriff. I'll have you booted off. I should've done that in the first place."

He picked up a stick and drew circles in the dust on the ground. Damn, but he was sick of hearing what everybody else thought. Damn, but he was tired of folks judging by what they saw and heard instead of what they *knew*. "You should've heard the things those folks were telling me this morning over at the co-op. Sugar beet people do this. Barley people do that."

"You went to the co-op already?"

"Thought somebody down there could tell me something to get me started." He found something interesting on the step right in front of his boot toe. And he made himself vulnerable for the first time to her, being brutally honest. "You're right on one count. If she wanted a crop, she should've asked somebody else. Usually when folks hear about my other jobs and how I got fired, they shake their heads and run me out."

"I'm surprised you didn't lie to her about that, too."

"Lied about the Jeep. Lied about working in Kansas. But that was to everybody standing around, gaping at me when I'd wandered into the dance. Didn't lie to Missus Trichak about my other jobs." Since he'd started telling her all this, he'd laid down the stick and started his fingers moving again, rippling them in patterns. "Gotten fired from everything I tried to do." His fingers, chording. G chord. C chord. And F.

She was just as skeptical as she'd always been. "You learn anything at the co-op that'll keep you from getting fired here?"

"Learned that corn people do something. Learned that wheat people do something else. And potato people always plant in the dark of the moon."

"Why were they telling you all that? About potatoes and the moon? That doesn't have a thing to do with barley."

"Folks always want to tell you how much they know. Even if it doesn't matter much. We talked about sheep and the zodiac and the corn and the tides."

"So out of all that, you decided you needed to plow."

"Yeah." She could see him in the starlight, gazing up as if the sky could give him answers. "I'll be out on a plow tomorrow, turning up earth. Of all the things I've done, I've sure never been a farmer."

"Mr. Colton." Meredith's voice. Soft and plush as this night. With a minor tinge of amusement. "If you weren't in Melody Flats right now, where would you be?"

"Wouldn't be anywhere else. Have to be here, is all." The night grew subdued around them. From somewhere far away, a dog barked. Cy raised her head, stayed alert for a moment, then laid it back down. A cow mooed from the Moleys' farm, some acres over. A breeze came up and they could hear rustling of grass and of the cattails that had overtaken the cattle trough.

He asked finally, "Is your grandmother as sick as she says?"

Meredith nodded. "Probably worse. Never known Grandma to tell a story about herself without gentling the edges a bit."

• • •

The next morning there came a tractor and plow, trundling up the highway.

He'd just come into view northbound on the road, jangling and clattering along at ten miles per hour while a row of frustrated cars wove in and out behind and tried to pass.

Fiona took the stairs two at a time, her hand splayed over her heart. "Burr Colton's coming in on a tractor. Can you hear him? He's clattering chains all the way up the road."

"Grandma, be careful. You mustn't excite yourself like this, and you know it." Meredith peeked out the window. He sat atop the machine with his back straight as a hoe handle, his Stetson cocked to one side of his brow, his shoulders the same wide, swaggery shape as the prongs on a pitchfork. His own dog, Cy, raced off the porch toward him in a tirade of barking.

"Oh, let me go get my camera." Fiona went off on a search through the hall closet. "Got to get a picture of this."

"Cy," Meredith called from the open screen door. "You get on back here, crazy dog. You'll do nothing but get in his way."

Burr turned in at the front cattle guard and commandeered the rig past the entry to the first field, past the entry to the second field, past the entry to the third. He drove the contraption clear up the driveway and into the dooryard, put the brake on, and jumped off while it rattled and clanked beside the front porch.

"Missus Trichak, Almer Moley said he didn't mind at all," Burr bellowed over the racket. "Gave me a demonstration, how to do everything, how to work the levers on the plow—" He banged merrily in through the door, looking for Fiona.

And came face-to-face with Meredith instead.

"Good morning," she said, sipping from her first cup of coffee.

He was going on sheer energy this morning, pumped on the exhilaration of making plans and seeing things go his way. He was a man free of inhibition, who'd driven three miles behind the wheel of a rattletrap tractor that would trench into the earth at his command.

"So you've gone and gotten a plow, have you?"

"I have." He couldn't decide whether to stare at her eyes drilling into him or at the checkered tea towel that hung on the rack behind her left shoulder. He opted for the tea towel.

Fiona came running in with an ancient camera. "Don't know how to use this anymore. Couldn't find a fresh flash bulb for it."

"Grandma, they don't make flash bulbs anymore."

"Merciful heavens. Wanted to make a picture of Burr on that tractor. Get on out there, now. Go on." She shooed him off as though she were shooing a fly. As he climbed back on, she hollered louder and louder. "I'm chomping at the bit for you to get started out there. You're wasting gasoline, letting Moley's machine idle like that."

"Yes, ma'am. I'm going." And so he did, rolling heavily away, starting right through the old gate in the north field, where she'd told him she had always begun. Burr took the perimeter of the field counterclockwise, lowering the lever to the plow blades, watching behind him as the blades skimmed the grudging earth, then dug deep.

Under the shares of Almer Moley's borrowed plow, Burr Colton went after the long-idle fields of the Trichak farm and easily split them asunder. The ripping steel brought up from Fiona's land the sort of good soil that folks longed for, dark clods and rich loam, strewn with broken roots, the same sultry color as overboiled cowboy coffee. The plow cut, tilled, and turned five furrows at a time, one acre an hour, ten acres per day, unbroken margins of ground that paralleled the lay of the land and gave the cultivated earth an appearance of splendid brown-waled corduroy.

"Look out there," Fiona would say every few minutes as she ran to a different window to see where Burr's tractor had gone. "He's gotten so far this morning. Three times across the field and he's barely started."

"Grandma. He's going to be doing this for days. Do we have to discuss it every time he rounds a corner?"

"I want to go to the field every day while he's out there, Meredith. I want to take sandwiches and sit down there and watch. I want to see him turn the earth."

And so they did. They spread a quilt each day and ate sandwiches in the fields while Burr Colton kept the machinery hustling, taking bites out of a thick gritty sandwich that he held with one glove. At the end of the afternoon, when he came to the house for supper, he'd scrub his hands for ten minutes without making progress. The dirt stayed with him as if he'd been marked with indelible ink, etching the moons of his nails and the folds of his knuckles with black.

One night when the fields were almost finished, Burr brought in an enormous clod. He set it in the middle of the mantelpiece, right between the photograph of Michael driving the tractor and Ray leading old Hi-Gal to the pasture. He said, "Look at this soil, would you, Missus Trichak? Best dirt in Fremont County, right here outside your own barn."

"That's just what Ray said when he'd dug up that field the first time. Almost the exact words." Fiona eyed the huge clump he'd brought in and said, "Oh, merciful heavens, Burr. How good it feels to cherish this soil again." She dug a tapered candle from the drawer, screwed it back and forth until it felt steady inside the middle of the clod, and lit it. "If we're going to have it on the mantel in the living room," she said, "the least we can do is make a decoration of it."


One afternoon, while Burr plowed the fields, Meredith took the Dodge into Melody Flats to run errands. She returned medical books she'd borrowed from the library, picked up groceries at King Sooper's, and filled the truck with gas at the Conoco station.

As she stood watching the pump tick away gallons

at the gas tank, she happened to glance at the pawn shop next door. In the lighted window stood the shop's newest acquisition, a beat-up guitar case with rusty hasps, its imitation leather torn and peeling around the edges.

Meredith seated the nozzle and turned off the pump. She paid for her gas purchase and parked the truck out of the way. She stood outside the pawn shop and pressed her nose against the glass. She'd seen it only once, the night he'd ridden home with them from the dance. But she recognized it.

Burr Colton's guitar.

The case had been propped open so passersby could inspect the instrument inside. Its soundboard was battered and covered with scratches, its bridge badly in need of repair. The brass frets had vague hollows, and the head was worn smooth, from hands fingering chords.

After she stood long enough for her nostrils to make two misty circles on the glass, Meredith opened the front door and walked inside. She'd never been inside a pawn shop before. Everything inside smelled musty and used, from the guns hanging on the pegboard behind the counter to the diamond rings and turquoise-and-silver squash blossoms in the locked counter beneath. She peered over the pegboard partition that lined the window. She tried to make out the price. An orange tag was tied out of reach, stuck into the soundhole so people would have to inquire.

"You interested in that guitar? I'll give you a good deal on it if you are."

"Not interested at all," she lied.

"Don't give out history on items," he told her even though she hadn't asked. The whole time he talked, he flicked a cigarette lighter with his finger, making it click and flame. Click and flame. "Wouldn't know about that one, anyway. Fellow dropped it off at the gas station on his way through town. Needed gas when I wasn't open and they swung a trade next door."

"I've never been in a pawn shop before." She walked around and perused his other cases, pretending she had other interests. "I thought you wouldn't sell stuff if people were coming back for them."

"Folks have a certain time to come back. We keep things in stock in the back room until the deadline passes. They don't return by the given date to pay the fee, item is in the window, priced, and out the door. That guitar's a hot item, too. I've had three or four people already in here giving it a once-over."

She knew good and well why Burr hadn't come to get his guitar by the given date. Her grandmother hadn't paid him.

"How much is that guitar?"

"Forty-five."

Fool thing to do, trading off a guitar the way Burr had done, something so much a part of himself that his fingers moved on it even when it wasn't there. A man would have to be desperate to give so much for so little. Desperate to stay somewhere. Or desperate to get away.

"Forty-five dollars?"

"That's what I said."

"I thought you said that a man traded it for gas. No tank of gas could cost forty-five dollars."

"Got to make my profit, little lady. That's what running a pawn shop is all about."


Burr never knew himself to be so hungry as he'd gotten to be on Missus Trichak's farm.

Oh, he'd been hungry like an animal before, starving and on the road, eating green apples or jerky from a jar in a Stuckey's, or sometimes scraping up enough change to buy a loaf of bread. But the hunger he felt now was different, a healthy hunger, the kind that came upon a man and hit him hard right before lunchtime, when his body'd say to him, "I've been working hard and I'm getting used to being filled up and being satisfied, and by heaven, it's time to start satisfying me again right now." Seemed these days he could always tell the time by his stomach.

From the roof of the barn, he could see eighty plowed acres surrounding Fiona Trichak's house with fine, dark margins.

What a job this fall plowing had turned out to be. Now all he had to do was figure out what to do next. Did he flatten the ground again before he planted? Did he pile up the ground more? How many seeds per acre did he need? By jiminy, he'd said he could learn anything, but for farming, he'd never thought he needed to know so many things. And all the while he tried to learn, that Meredith Trichak breathed down his neck, waiting for him to do something out of line so she could send him packing.

What was it about Melody Flats that his grand-father had thought so important? Why had he left that cryptic letter about seeking inside and seek-ing outside? Sure made no sense to him.

Burr turned to the sheet metal he'd laid, leveled off the heavy steel staple over the eave beneath the tin, and gave it one good *whack* with the ham-mer. The staple bit into the roof and rafter. He hit it again, sent it flush. He lowered his nose and sighted inches farther, making sure to position the next staple in a straight line.

Just as he raised his hammer, his dog, Cy, who three minutes ago had been lying placidly on the porch, gave out a warning bark. An unfamiliar car had pulled onto the shoulder and parked on the highway. A man climbed out of the driver's seat, stepped upon the bottom strand of barbed-wire fence, stretched the middle strand up, and made a hole to climb through.

Burr cupped his hands around his mouth and shouted. "Hallooo. What you doing out there?"

The trespasser either didn't hear him or chose not to answer. He balled his body as small as it would go and clambered through. Burr started down the ladder the moment the gentleman climbed back through the barbed wire and got into his car. The car turned in at the Trichaks' driveway. Fiona came to the front porch, drying her hands with her apron. "Now who could that be? And just when I've put out lunch, too. Meredith, set down that vinegar water and help set another place at the table."

"Let's see who it is first. You don't have to feed

everybody." Meredith gave a swipe at the glass on the porch side of the house, a smudge she must've missed when she'd been polishing windows that morning. "Seems an odd way to act, coming onto someone's property through the fence and snooping around the granary."

"When I was growing up, if anyone showed up at dinnertime, you threw an extra plate on the table. Didn't matter whether the folks were friend or foe."

"You stay on the porch, Missus Trichak." Burr left his tools in the grass. "I'll find out who this is."

"Invite him in, Burr. It wouldn't do not to be friendly."

The gentleman climbed out of a Chevrolet Caprice. Cy met him the way all dogs meet cars, making sure each tire got a sufficient barking before dancing around the fellow's legs. The man wore a London Fog bowler pulled low over his forehead, a crow feather stuck jauntily into the brim. On the left-hand rear bumper of the Caprice was a sticker that read "American Farmers Are Feeding You. Three Times a Day."

Burr strode toward him.

"I'm Harvey Keller." The fellow stuck out a hand. "It's a pleasure to make your acquaintance."

Burr had no choice but to extend his hand, too. "Burr Colton." And when the man offered no more information, Burr asked. "Is there something I can help you with?"

"Yes. I have a business proposition I'd like to make, Mr. . . . er, Colton. But I don't want to have to make it out here in the driveway."

"Oh. Of course." Burr stepped aside and led him up the steps to the porch. He held open the screen door and said, "If you've got business propositions to make, you'd best make them to Missus Fiona Trichak." He gestured toward his employer. "She's the one who owns this property."

Meredith reached across the table and laid a hand on her grandmother's arm. "A business proposition?"

Both Burr and Meredith were thinking the same thing. They both thought, Suppose he's come to make an offer on the property. Suppose he wants to subdivide it, or develop it, and pay her off with a nest egg that would keep her comfortable for the rest of her days.

When Burr suddenly lifted his eyes, he found Meredith looking directly at him. For the first time since they'd discussed how little he knew about farming and how she'd boot him off this land the minute he made a mistake, their eyes riveted, one to the other's, his gray and piercing, hers gone a deep green with concern.

*A business proposition.*

Meredith was thinking, What if he's here to make an offer on the old place? Michael and Barbara could finally see her settled. But this is Fiona's last year on the land, her last seasons on the farm, and she's decided to grow a crop.

Burr Colton was thinking, Please don't offer to buy this land today, mister. Not today, after it's plowed and I'm proving I can amount to something around here.

Meredith leaned forward on her elbows, patted her grandmother on the hand. "Well, Mr.—"

"Mr. Keller. Harvey Keller."

"Mr. Keller." Upon learning his name, Fiona immediately motioned toward the spread of beef and carrots and potatoes before them. "Why don't you sit down and have lunch with us. Been baking this meat all morning and it'd be a shame to have it go to waste. And I've got homemade custard in the refrigerator."

"Oh, no. Thank you. It's a simple question, is all. I happened to be enjoying the scenery as I drove by, and I couldn't help noticing these plowed fields."

He was taking a fair amount of time getting to the point, and Meredith couldn't bear it. "It's a beautiful piece of property, isn't it, Mr. Keller? It has belonged to my grandmother and been in this family since she and her husband, Ray, homesteaded on the Shoshone irrigation project. In the early thirties."

Harvey Keller's eyes danced with animation. "I hope you don't mind that I parked on the shoulder of the highway and took the liberty of walking down by the silo. I wanted to see it up close, to see if it was as good as it looked when described in my collector's book. It's a fine specimen, yes, sirree."

Burr cocked his head. "Your collector's book?"

"Decided there was no way to find you again except to drive up your driveway and introduce myself and tell you that I'd be interested in making you a fair offer."

Fiona asked, "A fair offer for what, Mr. Keller?"

He took a deep breath, as if his life depended upon Fiona's answer. "How much would you take for that old clanker parked out behind the silo?"

Burr Colton and Meredith Trichak spoke in unison.

"The old clanker?"

"The what?"

Fiona rose graciously from the table and extended a hand to him, smiling as if she'd just discovered someone of rare refinement, someone who recognized merit and distinction and value, too.

"So you're interested in my combine."

"I most certainly am."

"Been wondering when somebody'd come along who'd be interested in that old thing."

Burr sat down hard in his chair.

Meredith picked up a salt shaker and set it down again. Hard enough that salt vented straight up through the holes. "That combine?" she asked. "We'd probably give it to you if it meant you took it away."

"Oh, I wouldn't ask you to do that." He focused his attention solely upon Fiona. "I'm interested in refurbishing her for display and demonstration at the Midwest Old Time Thresher's Reunion next summer."

Meredith stared at him. "That's why you parked by the side of the road? You've been up close to have a look at it?"

"Sure have. She's quite a beauty. A combine made by Jerome Increase Case is hard to find in this day and age. Especially one in good condition.

A tractor-propelled combine, probably one of the first in this area." He stood taller, raised his chin. "I have the expertise to restore her. She'd be a pretty sight. It'd be a chance for her to travel all the way to Iowa."

Burr couldn't decide what about this conversation disturbed him the most, that they'd had no idea what the man was after in the first place or that they'd suddenly begun talking about a piece of rusted-out farm equipment as if it were a maiden aunt being given a chance to tour the country.

"That combine isn't in as good a shape as you might think." Fiona had an odd look on her face, as if she'd remembered something that seemed only fair to tell. "It's been through a fire."

"Piece of fine machinery like that, fire wouldn't hurt. I imagine you could put new belts on it and it'd keep right on going. I could see the places it had been scorched. What happened? A fine machine. Those things usually start when someone forgets to lubricate a bearing. You read the history of those things and you find out they started fires in fields all over California, before folks'd figured out how to lubricate."

Meredith didn't know about a fire.

She caught a glimpse of something in her grandmother's face she hadn't seen before, a depth of great sadness. She noticed Fiona took a seat again as if her knees had gotten weak. "No. That machine out there didn't cause any fire. It's just been involved in one."

When she told him this, her hand trembled against the table. A small motion of fingers, almost unnoticeable, like limbs trembling against a window.

"This was a fire of a different sort, started by matches. So much else was happening. We were getting people out of the way, you see. There wasn't anything we could do to move the combine out of the way, too."

"I'll pay two thousand dollars for it, as is. I've never been so excited to see something out in the field in all my life. It's quality. Sheer, old-fashioned quality."

Anxious to take attention from her grandmother and the glimmer of mysterious emotion she'd seen, Meredith said, "I can't believe you'd offer such money for that old thing. It's been sitting out there collecting dust and rust for decades. Somebody's been hanging political signs on it for the past dozen presidential elections. All the way since Thomas Dewey."

Harvey Keller gestured widely at Meredith. "Don't you know? Antique farm equipment has become something of a modern mania. I could list you dozens of shows where this thing could travel in Canada and the United States. They've got thousands of people who pay money to see old Johnny Poppers or something like this relic, lumbering across the field and chuffing their stuff."

"Two thousand dollars?" Fiona couldn't fathom the monetary figure. "I have to be honest with you, Mr. Keller. I only paid fifteen hundred dollars for it, delivered, when I ordered it from the Jerome Increase Case factory, and they sent it out brand-new. Maybe if it could still run—"

"I'll bet it *could* still run if the right gentleman could get ahold of it. I can see you're going to hold out for the right price. I can see that you are knowledgeable about the farm machinery market. So I'll go up on my price. How about twenty-two hundred? I'll offer you twenty-two hundred dollars, cash money on the spot."

Burr stood up and began to pace around. Seemed that was the only way to keep any sanity in this conversation at all, jumping up and down out of his chair, trying to keep his head about him. Twenty-two hundred dollars? For that rusty hulk out back of the granary?

He sat down hard enough to bruise his rump, though, when he heard Missus Trichak nix the proposition. "I'm sorry, Mr. Keller," she said. "I've enjoyed visiting with you today. But you'd best be on your way. That combine out there is not for sale."

# 8

T he e-mail from Meredith's faculty adviser
arrived on a Wednesday, two weeks after she
had sent the proposal and request.

It isn't that we feel you are not capable
of doing a research paper of this scope,

the computer screen read in its cold, distinct font.

The project you submit for consideration is
an admirable one, perhaps too admirable.
Since you are so far away, the staff is dis-
inclined to assign you the work at this
time.

We base this decision, as well, upon
the fact that you have completed only
two semesters toward your doctorate of

medicine at University of California at Los Angeles. We do request that you wait until a later semester, perhaps when you have established a firmer grasp upon student life, and resubmit this proposal at that time. It is a worthy project.

Sincerely,
Dr. Lou Pilcher
Faculty Adviser

Meredith punched the delete button and leaned back in her computer chair. Outside her window, a magpie had landed in a tree, its harsh *yak yak yak* ushering up an exact echo of her own discontented thoughts.

*Yak yak yak.* Yes, she'd resubmit the proposal when she had a firmer grasp upon student life. Yes, she'd resubmit when she lived on campus and could walk into Dr. Lou Pilcher's office and say, "I have a question about biomathematics in the micro-anatomy field and I'd like you to take two minutes of your time and discuss this with me."

She couldn't help feeling a bit disoriented this morning. She felt a long way from school, and from California.

Meredith shrugged into her coat on the way downstairs, pulled on knit mittens, and stepped outside. The ground had gone shimmery with heavy frost this morning, the fallen leaves curled and frozen like sparkling, contoured skiffs in the yard. She stepped off down the road toward the highway and was surprised to have Cy take up beside her.

"Well, girl," Meredith said, reaching for her ears. "Doesn't take much to make a friend out of you, does it?"

Unconsciously she shaded her eyes at the barn and looked to find Burr Colton. When she didn't see him, she felt halfway disappointed, then—just as quickly—halfway amused at herself because she'd gone to the trouble to look. The Jeep was parked. He'd be out wiring on a fence somewhere, or sweeping out the silo, or digging rocks out of the drive. Mr. Colton never went far.

Where she and the dog walked, Meredith saw signs of the coming winter. The frost lay in stripes on the shadow side of the furrows, leaving the fields the same salt-and-pepper color as an old woman's hair. The meadow chickweed had dried out and cured in curls in the ditch beside her. Some rodent, stashing away for the winter, had gone after a pinecone and left it where it lay on a rock, stripped bare as an empty cob, the red bits that housed the seeds left in a neat pile like stacked, fallen petals.

A cocoon had been woven and fastened with care upon a fencepost, its inhabitant already sleeping and metamorphosing toward upcoming spring.

Meredith took a breath of deep, clear air, so pungent and refreshing that it washed over her like water from a well, the kind so cold and perfect that it numbed your hands and teeth when you tried to douse your face or have a drink. Meredith took another breath and discovered a miraculous thing.

She didn't care a flip about the research paper.

She felt in a cocoon like the one on the fence where something quiet grew, something apparent and striking that burst forward when the weather cycled right, unfurling and beautiful. She was in that expansive mood when she felt that small things didn't matter. Big things mattered. And big things hid as small things sometimes, masquerading.

No matter what decisions her faculty adviser made at UCLA, Meredith knew she'd made the right decision coming to stay with her grandmother. As she came over a knoll, she paused. She saw Almer Moley's truck parked beside the granary. Four legs, each one of them garbed in faded, frayed jeans, laid out over cowlicks of old grass; four legs, two pair, each pair extending in a different direction from the hallowed underpinnings of that old combine and tractor.

Cy bounded forth and wriggled underneath the antique implements. Meredith sauntered to the contraption and bent over upside-down, until her hair hung with the grass and tangled with it. She asked, "Why aren't you working today, Mr. Colton? I thought you weren't finished yet with the barn."

"Needed a break from the barn," he answered carefully, as if this discovery of him beneath the old combine might prove his undoing. "Getting so I see corrugated metal when I close my eyes to sleep."

"Howdy, Meredith." Almer Moley waved from the other side of the tractor. Almer lay flat on his stomach, wrapped in a warm down coat too thick to display curves and valleys. "Good to see you. Haven't laid eyes on you since the harvest dance, and that's been a while ago." He reached with a wrench and tinkered with something right beside her skull. "When you talk to your dad, you tell him his old friend Almer says hello."

She was surprised. "You knew my dad?"

"We used to have a hell of a lot of fun, running around these acres, being boys together."

Burr Colton chewed on a long piece of stubble, tasting the bitter marrow of the stem, switching it from one side of his mouth to the other, as if the chewing of the grass could give him insight into the workings of this machine. His chin rested on the back of one hand, and he wore his hat pushed back until it lay flat against his neck.

"Don't let Burr fool you," Almer said, apparently unaware of the thin ice on which they trod together. "Him and me, we're not working at all. We're just laying out here thinking."

"You're laying underneath a combine and *thinking?*"

"And looking, too."

"What are you looking for?"

"Don't know, exactly." Burr answered this time. "Just got to wondering if that fellow who came by here the other day was right. Got to thinking, maybe while I'm working on everything else around here, I could take this thing apart and get it to working for Missus Trichak again."

"Started over this morning to help Burr put those two rafters up in the barn," Almer cut in.

"But I couldn't believe it when I heard this story. Couldn't believe it when Burr said a total stranger'd come up to the door and offered two grand for the thing."

"You ask me, you two'd be better off fixing the rafters and not wasting your time on this old thing."

Almer rolled all the way over, cupped his chin inside a greasy palm covered with axle grease. Sprigs of dried grass splayed out of gray hair the same texture as binder's twine. Despite the difference in Burr Colton's and Almer Moley's ages, they both looked like marauder boys, up to no good.

"This old thing, she's got quite a history. You should've seen me and your dad in Sunday school the week your grandma first ran this thing. We couldn't calm down, we were so excited about Fiona buying it and getting it going. Sunday school teacher kept saying, 'Now, boys. Now, boys.' Ended up having to change the whole lesson because of us. Ended up, she precluded her lesson on Jacob and tackled something entirely different, something closer to home. She made us turn in our Old Testaments to the Book of Ruth and read the story of the young Moabitess who gleaned wheat in the fields."

"What does *that* have to do with anything?" Meredith asked.

"Well, I kept asking her the same thing. I said, 'This is a dumb story about girls.' She said, 'It's a story about harvest. If you don't be quiet, I'll get the pastor in here and he'll give you the belt.' So I let it go at that."

Against Meredith's better judgment, she knelt and crawled under the combine, her head bumping against something sharp. "Ouch." When she crawled under, she noticed that Burr Colton crawled sideways a foot or two, as if he'd decided he'd better keep from getting in her way.

"Won't forget that day as long as I live. It was something to see, I tell you. The teacher let us out of school after lunch all during harvest week so we could help our parents in the fields. We were walking home through the draw, and your dad, he was more excited about this combine than he'd ever been in his life."

"My dad?" Meredith asked, incredulous. She couldn't believe Michael had been excited about farming, ever in his life.

"Your father hasn't told you what it was like growing up here, has he?"

"No." And here Meredith stared up at the underpinnings of the machine with the rest of them, as if she tried to decipher the machine instead of the way Michael had not only removed himself from this land, but had also refused to share the stories.

Almer picked up the wrench from the grass and began waving it to the cadence of his sentences. "The whole time we walked home that day, Michael kept saying, 'You coming over to watch, Almer? You coming over? We're cranking it up this afternoon.' But I wasn't supposed to go. I told him, 'Ma says we've got enough work to do around our own place without me taking time out to gape.' Darn it, though. I wanted to be there. My ma used to never back down for nothing. She wouldn't let my dad come watch, either. He told her at the supper table the night before that he wanted to be at that fence laughing when this thing wouldn't start up at all. If he said it once, he said it a hundred times. 'Whoever heard of putting gasoline in a farm implement, anyway? After the new wears off and Fiona Trichak goes back to sensible farm machinery, the price of good horses and mules'll go up by seventy dollars a head.'"

As Almer kept talking, they could see the scene, how the boys followed the trail until it broke out from among the trees and came to a place where they could see the rolling country and an array of unpainted farmhouses nestled squarely among upland swells that met the sky. "Something seemed to hang in the air that day," he said as he readjusted his weight on his elbows and tapped the combine's old exhaust pipe with the wrench, "something more than the chaff dust and the papery whisper of barley where it hadn't yet been cut in the fields. Trucks, motorcars, and mule-drawn carts parked everywhere. More kept coming, like everybody from Fremont County was coming to the county fair. That's when I saw Ma was there, and Pa, too. You should've heard folks talking about Fiona up and down the road. 'Oh, wonder of modern wonders.' 'A machine of ridiculous extravagance and incredible risk!' 'Fiona Trichak ought to have her head examined.' Folks all around the edge of the fence were saying, 'I heard they're doing it other places. I heard they've harvested on some of the big California farms with a twenty-horsepower steamer.' Somebody else said, 'Steamers ain't the same as tractors. Combustion engines ought to stay where God intended. On the road and out of trouble. Same as women.'"

"No *wonder* my grandmother turned Harvey Keller down." Meredith could almost picture Almer and her father, two rowdy, proud boys going out to help her grandmother, scaling the fence, paying no heed to the barbs on the fence or to barbs from the townspeople. She pictured two boys vaulting through waves of sun-cured barley, their heads bobbing atop the rippling grain like buoys atop a fantastic sea. "Nobody thought she could do it."

"You're right, Meredith. A woman less stubborn than Fiona never would've tried it. That new machine with the sickle bars red and gleaming, and the gray auger at its jaunty angle. 'J. I. Case,' it read on the side, right there. Look, you can still see the words." He pointed to the grain bin, where they could see the remains of the lettering now. "Your dad grabbed my hand and shouted, 'She's been waiting for me to get home, is all. You can help us, Almer. You can help us show everybody they're wrong.' So we did. Shut those people up once and for all. And when I got older, I understood something more than that. I understood they thought she couldn't do it because she was a woman. Most of all, because she was a woman. Because it was the 1930s and she was alone, because Ray'd already died.

"Once she started harvesting and the grain began pouring into the bin, everybody left.

Preacher from the church was the only one to stay and watch the whole thing. Funniest thing, like he was the only one in the county who'd thought she could do it. After all those folks had come, he was the only one who waited at the fence until sundown, until we'd gotten five times around the circumference of this field.

"I'll never forget. He had one of those hats, flat at the crown and brim, made out of fancy sennit straw. The sun just going down, and he climbed over the wire, came right up to us while we were still going, and looked up at Fiona where she sat. Funniest thing. He didn't say, 'I knew you could do it.' He didn't say, 'I've been telling folks they were wrong.' He didn't say, 'I'll get a good sermon out of this next Sunday.' He just looked up at her and said her name once. 'Fiona.' Then he pitched that straw hat into the combine, right where the grain was being cut and headed into the thresher, and that was that."

# 9

The third week of November, and winter
came on like a secret, stealthily encroaching,
threatening, then stepping aside to allow for
one more surprising, shirtsleeve day. As Burr finished roofing the barn, even the sunny days began
to grow colder. Clear days in Melody Flats gradu-
ated Degas-like into clear mountain valley nights;
temperatures bottomed out in single digits on
thermometers and gauges all over town.

Their friendship formed over the annals of
Fiona Trichak's unusual and collectible combine,
Almer Moley took to dropping by and helping
Burr with projects when he needed a hand. The
two of them lifted the new rafters high and
attached them to the ridgepole of the Trichak barn.
Almer helped, and Burr worked hard. The harder
Burr worked, the less Fiona and Meredith saw of

him. He went from sunrise to sunset, taking his meals on a plate in the barn, trying to beat the weather. More often than not, he cooked his own breakfasts on the rickety cookstove in the barn.

After those stories from Almer and the offer from Harvey Keller, Burr found himself getting serious about tinkering with the combine. He cleared out the barn, opened wide the double doors, and took the truck down to the granary to see about towing the old thing in. He hooked a tow strap from the rear axle of the truck to the front axle of the tractor.

He gave the Dodge as much gas as he dared, let it rev and labor, but the massive iron wheels wouldn't budge in the dirt. He checked the rearview mirror and decided he'd stretched the tow strap so taut, it'd snap in half and come back and kill somebody. No matter how hard he pulled with the truck, the implement wouldn't move. Aw, hell, he thought. Wouldn't be able to do much work on it until spring anyway.

As temperatures grew colder, clouds moved in, clinging along the high ridge of mountains to the west. When at last the sun beat through, cold wind began to winnow through crevasses in the Wind Rivers. The clouds unraveled like skeins of knobbly yarn, and in their place on the peaks had come a fresh, white powdering of snow.

In town, folks met at the Sarvisberry Inn or the Big Horn Co-op to lift a mug of coffee and salute upcoming bitter cold. "No snow yet," they echoed each other. "Not on the valley floor. Snow level won't hit us until just before Christmas."

They watched it coming with mindful eyes,

knowing each layer of cloud that came and drifted away to be a subterfuge, knowing each layer of cloud dropped snow inches lower, inches closer, to the fields. And on the counter of Sunrise Lumber where Evangeline kept the popcorn machine and the huckleberry candies, Taylor Kew set out a "first snow" jar, where men pushed dollars through a slot and dates they'd scribbled on the backs of their calling cards. When snow fell on the level in Taylor's parking lot, the card bearing the closest prediction date took home the entire kitty.

Every person who walked in that door saw the jar, poked another dollar in, and shook his head. "No winner yet. No winner yet." When the clouds crossed the valley floor they brought only cold rain, great scudding drops that moved in from the west and left nickel-size indentions in the loose dirt. At the Trichak farm, the raindrops pelted the barn's new roof, beating every bit as loudly as a drummer goes after a timpani drum.

The ancient siding on the barn soaked up the wet and turned black. When the skies cleared, the raw tin roof was laced with hoarfrost, when the sun hit it spectacular with color. And then another surprising day: a frontal system moved in from the south. The frost melted fast off the sun side of the barn.

Meredith Trichak noticed that Burr Colton was acting as secretive as the weather.

On the warmest days, he painted the roof of the barn. On other days, Meredith didn't see him much.

She took to walking out around the barnyard when her grandmother was napping. "Good afternoon, Mr. Colton," she said, very businesslike, on the days she found him outside. "What are you working on today?"

"The barn roof. Green, like Missus Trichak wants it." As if to remind her that she wasn't in charge.

"My grandmother is resting right now." As if to remind him that she'd come here to *be* in charge.

He'd splattered green all over the tattered jeans he wore. His curls scythed from beneath his hat. She stood watching with her feet spread apart, her arms genie style across her breasts, an employer overseeing an employee. When he climbed down the ladder to get a different brush, she noticed his stride had become even more angular these days after the hours he'd spent in the cast-iron seat of a tractor.

"What do you work on when you're not working on the barn?" she asked as he climbed the rungs again.

She saw his foot hesitate on one step. "Don't work on much else. Told you that before. I close my eyes at night and see corrugated metal." He got to the top of the roof, dipped the brush in paint, and dropped it. The bristles skidded down the pitch of the roof, leaving a wide green stripe in its wake. It landed not far from Meredith's feet and splattered paint on them. "You don't think I'm working as fast as I should be?"

*It wasn't different here from where it'd been anywhere else. Folks were always checking up on him.*

*Always watching him. Always looking for a reason
to find fault and send him away.*

"My grandmother is paying you from her retirement fund, Mr. Colton."

He climbed down wordlessly, picked up the
brush, eyed her shoes with green paint speckled
on them. He climbed up for the second time and
finally answered. "I'm working on a surprise for
Missus Trichak, is all."

An uncomfortable position, acting as watchdog
of her grandmother's finances. "If she's paying you
for your time," Meredith pressed, "there ought
not to *be* any surprises."

From that day on she noticed he made a point
to be outside and working during daylight hours.
On afternoons when he ate his lunch inside with
them, he sat grimly at one side of the table and
Meredith sat at the other, watching his hands lifting a knife, laying it down, lifting a fork, stabbing
meatloaf as if he'd like to stab something else,
speaking with false politeness to her grandmother as though Meredith weren't there.


Fiona Trichak insisted upon having a laundry day
on Thursdays.

As long as the temperature stayed above freezing, she insisted upon having her freshly washed
bedclothes hung out on the line and whipping in
the breeze, each corner of a sheet attached to the
corner of the next sheet to conserve clothespins.
Today, of all days, Meredith unloaded the washing
machine with some grousing. "It would be so

much easier to dump these in the dryer, Grandma. They'd be done and ready to put back on the bed in twenty minutes."

"I'll hang everything out myself if you think it's too much trouble." Just to prove she could, Fiona hefted a wet blanket from the machine and began to shake away the wrinkles. "They always smell so much better when they've dried outside. I'll have to settle for the other way the rest of the winter."

Meredith got the blanket away from her. "I'm hanging out the laundry, Grandma. That's what I'm here for, jobs like that. I'm just telling you it would be a whole lot easier if you'd be willing to have it done the other way."

"I like things to be done the way they've always been done."

"You can add a nice smell with a dryer sheet." Meredith hefted the basket to her hip, ashamed that she'd complained. Every time she tried to get Fiona to try something easier, Fiona volunteered to do the chore herself instead. Meredith carried the laundry basket outside and dropped it on the grass, and the sheets inside jumped in one big, wet clump. She tried to pick the first one out, but it was twisted together with the one next to it. By the time Meredith got the sheets separated, her hands were so cold that her fingers had gone numb.

She hung the laundry the way Fiona liked it, corner to corner, one pin, two sheets, moving down, disentangling, starting the whole rigmarole over again. Several times she threaded her fingers together and tightened them in front of her throat to keep them warm. She decided it must be thirty-three degrees. Any colder and these sheets would be frozen stiffer than cowhide by the afternoon.

As she hung sheets and blankets, she noticed the barn roof lacked a good six feet of being finished on this side. What was Mr. Colton doing today that he couldn't finish the roof? If it was warm enough for her to be hanging out wet laundry, it was warm enough for him to be painting, by golly.

Made more aggrieved by the fact that she could no longer feel her thumbs, Meredith left the last corner of the last sheet dangling and pranced across the yard to the doorway of the barn. From inside she heard an odd hiss. "Mr. Colton?" she called.

No one answered. She eased the door open a bit. "Mr. Colton?" she called again. She rapped with her fist. She could see a strange light coming from one corner. When he didn't answer again, she stepped inside.

It took a full minute for her eyes to adjust. It had been years since she'd been inside this old place, trouncing in the hayloft with her summer friends. Nothing had changed, from the rickety ladder that led to the hayloft to the succession of broken flower pots, from the rat-gnawed harnesses festooned over pegs to the spindly snowshoes or the wheelbarrow propped upright alongside the wall. Dust motes endlessly rearranged themselves in the shaft of light from the door.

Seemed odd, being in a place she'd known as a child, and also being unsure, suddenly realizing she'd brazenly intruded into Burr Colton's private dwelling.

He looked up from his project. His piercing eyes locked on hers. "What are you doing in here?"

She lifted her chin a bit higher than she needed. She felt the sudden disconcerting premonition that she had been wrong. She never should've walked in on him like this.

The hiss was gone. The odd light had been turned out. Burr switched on an overhead light, a bare bulb with a swinging chain that cast harsh, swinging shadows upon the knotty, splintered walls. He'd stacked paint cans, their sides scalloped with green, around the dirty oil drum in the nearest corner. He'd upended a wooden apple crate to make a table beside his bed.

His voice sounded rumbly and gruff, like rocks rolling together down a hill. "I don't remember inviting you inside."

Her chin raised higher still. "I came to find out why you aren't outside painting. It's warm enough to work out there, and you aren't working."

Two cots, one made, one with an ancient ticking mattress and no bedding, sat at affronted-looking angles to each other. The quilt on his cot had been provided by her grandmother. The woodpile beside the stove had been provided by Fiona, too. A portable cookstove crouched on the dirt in one corner. The lid of a cardboard box served double duty as a hamper.

In the box lay one pocket knife, one comb, a wooden cigar box that fastened with a metal toggle, and two threadbare flannel shirts. Except for the meager assortment of tools he'd brought with him in his Jeep and the extra pair of jeans he'd looped over the makeshift clothesline, she realized that he owned nothing.

Meredith couldn't imagine any dwelling looking barer, except perhaps for someone's jail cell.

"You going to fire me today because I'm not up working on the roof?"

"You know what I said, Mr. Colton. I'm looking for any good reason. What is that light I saw? What is that hiss I heard?"

She saw his shoulders rise and fall with discouragement. He disappeared into the old animal stall where he'd been concealing the evidence, the same stall where her grandmother had always stored the ancient disk plow. From the feed box he extracted something and shoved it at her, his abruptness a sudden giveaway of the tremendous importance he placed on this item. "Careful. It's warm," he said, his tone brusque. "I've just stopped working on it."

She held out rigid arms and was immediately overcome by its weight. He caught it and jostled it higher so she could get a better hold. "Come under the light. You'll be able to see much better over here."

Meredith stepped under the bare bulb. She looked down, and in her arms she held a weather vane, one of the most beautiful she'd ever seen. "Oh." Its silhouette was fashioned of black iron, a cowboy with his legs flying up astride a bucking bronco. Upon a dowel swung an ornate arrow, its wide tail cut to capture and point the embellishment in the direction of the wind. Below the arrow stood a round plate on which the directions of the landscape were marked and would be aligned, north, south, east, or west.

She whispered, "It's beautiful."

For the moment he'd forgotten her intrusion. He saw only the item in her arms that he'd labored over, the gift he'd made for the woman who had taken him in and insisted he take a job. "Almer let me borrow his welding torch to cut out the shapes. I was just finishing. See there, how thick it looks on this edge. It's because the metal had to be burned clear through."

She stared at it while he talked. Then she stared at his face, his hard-edged face in a young man's body, eyes that seemed not quite so hard now, only proud.

"Told Almer what I wanted to do for her, and he showed me how. That cowboy"—he pointed to the contour—"I copied him from the license plate on Missus Trichak's truck. That's the Wyoming State symbol. All I've got to do now is wait for the roof to warm up in the sun this afternoon so I can paint that last little spot. Soon as there's a day when the paint's dry and the frost burns off again, I'll install this thing right on top of the gambrel roof."

Meredith stood in the midst of perhaps the loneliest habitation she'd ever seen, holding this gift for her grandmother, a simple gift yet eloquent, something he'd hidden away here and had forged with his own hands. She stared at his hands. Thick fingers, rough work-worn skin, that had constructed such a beautiful thing.

"Used my first paycheck to buy the iron," he

said. "Took all of it, though. Next one, I'll get myself a coat."

She lifted her eyes to his again, not knowing at all what to say. "Oh, Mr. Colton. I am so sorry I barged in on you like this. I'm so sorry I doubted—"

She could see it in his expression again. He remembered suddenly that she'd come in on him. "You're going to tell her about this?"

She shook her head. "It isn't my place to tell her, Mr. Colton."

"I've had this picture in my mind all along, you know? I've wanted her to walk out on the porch and just see it on top of the barn, pointing into the wind."

Meredith was overcome by the recognition that, no matter how afraid he'd made her by coming, in some surreptitious way, this man was giving her grandmother something that she, herself, could never give. "Mr. Colton?" she asked at last.

"What?"

"Why would you do a thing like this for my grandmother?"

"Why?" And he looked worried for a moment, as if he thought she might still be trying to catch him at something. Then he decided to be brutally honest. "Because she's given me a place to stay for a while. Because she hasn't tried to run me off like most other folks did. It's been a long time in my life since anybody's made me feel *settled*."

Meredith smiled sadly, fragile lines etching the corners of her mouth. "I'm so sorry," she repeated. "Mr. Colton. I never should've barreled in here—"

She might have said more if they hadn't both

heard the creaking of the screen door and the hollow sound of Fiona's footsteps on the porch. "Meredith . . . ? Where have you gone? Are you finished with the laundry? The telephone's for you."

Meredith's and Burr's eyes locked in the sharp-shadowed light of the bare bulb. She saw, in that guileless, hollowed-out illumination, his narrow cheekboned face as if for the first time. The light held perfectly steady now and didn't swing. "She'll think I've been sloughing off," Meredith said. "I've left a sheet hanging by one corner onto the grass."

"You're her granddaughter." A slight, shy smile lifted the edges of his mouth. A slight smile that pleased her. "She's not looking to fire you, is she?"

"On my way, Grandma," Meredith called, and ran around to clip up the last sheet before she grabbed the basket and went in to answer the phone.


"I've sent you and Fiona a care package," Barbara said first off when Meredith picked up the receiver. "A new skirt I thought you'd like. Brown is the color here this year. I've also sent powder for Fiona. From Nordstrom's. Expensive powder. She ought to like it."

"Good," Meredith said. "I'll make sure she douses herself lavishly first thing when it arrives in the mail. The chickens and cows around Melody Flats love it when Grandma smells like Nordstrom's."

Michael, on the other line, apologized. "We're

sorry we haven't called to check up more often. We always plan on phoning, but things get in the way. You know how things get around here. Time disappears."

"Yes, I know." Her father had perfected the art of making time disappear. He'd retired from one company twice. He'd started his own consulting firm with two colleagues. No matter what happened, she didn't think he'd ever quit working. "I met a friend of yours the other day, Dad. Remember a boy named Almer Moley? He's been coming by to check on Grandma. Remember? You two used to play together when you were young."

"Your mother sent a care package yesterday. Did she tell you?"

"She mentioned it."

Then Barbara again, another apology. "We were going to ring you Thursday, but we had dinner with friends at Musso and Frank's."

Meredith said out of the blue, "You ought to come during the holidays. Grandma would love to have you for Christmas. And I'd love to see you, too."

"We'll have to think about that."

"At Musso and Frank's, we ate with the Stephensons. You remember them, don't you? Their son has gotten a job as a geologist with an oil company. He's bought himself a LoDo apartment in Denver." The location of apartments was important to Barbara, especially locations that gave a good impression.

Michael said, "I talked to Dr. Richtig last time I went into his office. He'd be willing to take another doctor into his practice when the time is right. Especially if that doctor might happen to be my daughter."

Meredith laughed. "Especially after all the money you've given to his congressional campaign."

"Don't laugh this off. He has a high-profile, prestigious practice. You could certainly do worse, Meredith."

"If you came for Christmas, you could see Almer Moley. I'll bet he'd love to trade old stories—"

He interrupted her. "Aren't you going to say something about Dr. Richtig? That's why we called, to tell you about Dr. Richtig."

"You should've seen Almer and Burr Colton. They got under that old combine of Grandma's one day and Almer couldn't quit telling stories about you. They tinkered with it some, but they couldn't get it running."

"What are you talking about?" Michael asked. "Who is Burr Colton? I've never heard of him."

Meredith glanced pointedly at her grandmother.

So Fiona hadn't told them. Meredith said it as smoothly as she could manage. "There's a man living here now. He's named Burr Colton."

Michael deciphered easily. "Not that stranger who came to the harvest dance."

Barbara echoed, "That strange homeless boy?"

"Good God. We told you what to do with that situation, Meredith. We told you to phone the sheriff and have that man removed."

Meredith said, "It's more complicated than that."

"No, it isn't. What can be complicated about a drifter who's going around taking advantage of tired old ladies?"

"He isn't taking advantage. She's hired him to work for her."

"Hired him?" This from Barbara. "How could she afford to hire him? She's on retirement income, for heaven's sake."

"She has hired him to do odd jobs, to fix things up around the farm."

For the first time during the conversation, Michael began to sound somewhat tolerant. "To fix things up?"

"Yes."

"Things that would enhance the property value?"

"Some. Mostly he's been plowing fields. He and Grandma are growing a last barley crop together."

"Not that," Michael said. "Good God. She can't be starting something as complicated as all that."

"It hasn't seemed to be complicated."

"You told us he was leaving. I thought that vagrant man had found a job elsewhere."

"He did. Grandma talked him out of taking it."

"Good God."

"Michael." Barbara broke in. "Can you please say something besides 'Good God?'"

With one sentence, in one afternoon, Meredith found herself in the new, odd position of justifying Burr Colton's presence on her grandmother's farm. "He's put a new roof on the barn. And painted it green."

At this point in every conversation, Barbara proposed the same idea. "Your grandmother needs to get to the doctor. Can't you convince her to stop by the clinic and see her doctor this week?"

And, always, Michael's retort. "Barbara, my mother's already had a physical examination. The doctor isn't going to tell her anything she doesn't already know."

"It's been three months, Michael. Conditions deteriorate."

"Dad? Would you think of coming at Christmas?"

Michael, evading both of them. "Is that man staying inside the house?"

"No. He's living in the barn now. In the farm-hand's quarters."

"So Mother has hired a farmhand, has she? Idiotic. Absolutely idiotic. She hasn't grown a barley crop since I was a youth."

"Dad." Meredith clutched the receiver with both hands. The time had come to ask him to be honest. She'd heard too many stories from Almer, heard too many evasions from her father. "What's made you not like it here anymore? Why don't you ever talk about the way things were when you and Almer were boys? Why don't you talk about the way your family used to be? There's something that's happened, isn't there?"

He paused, almost imperceptibly, but she heard it. "I don't know what you're talking about, Meredith. I like it well enough. Only it isn't my life anymore. And we never have the time to travel."

# 10

Two times driving past the pawn shop and back, and she hadn't decided what she should do. Three times past, and she parked the truck at the Conoco station.

She'd checked each time she'd driven by, had been dismayed to see that the battered guitar wasn't still displayed in the window. In its place stood an orange oil painting of a kokanee salmon, one mismatched barstool, and an artificial, bedraggled Christmas tree. Decided at last, she walked inside the door to be met with the same moldering, displeasing smell and the same fellow, who gave her a wry, knowing smile. "Back to have a look at that guitar, are you?"

"It isn't in the window."

"Moved it out yesterday. Had to make room for my newest acquisitions."

"It isn't sold?"

"Had plenty of lookers. It's a fine instrument, if I do say so myself. But, no. It isn't sold."

He picked it up from somewhere beneath the counter and handed it over to her, knowing she wanted a closer inspection.

"One fellow wearing a cowboy hat, he's been in here two or three times. Never seen him around Melody Flats before. He came in here and fiddled around with it so long one day, I thought for sure I'd made a sale.

"Funniest thing. He laid it back on the counter after a time, walked out of here without casting a backward glance at it, then drove up Main Street and bought a huge slab of iron from Sunrise Lumber instead. Funniest thing. I watched him through the window the whole time."

Meredith tapped ten fingers upon the pocked soundboard. She skittered her fingers over the frets, felt the sharp cut of catgut strings. She strummed it once without fingering it. It sounded to be in tune, but who could tell?

"You know how to play a guitar?"

She shook her head. "It isn't for me."

"Give you a good deal on it."

"How much?"

"Forty. Cash."

He picked up the cigarette lighter by the register. He fiddled with it, made it click and flame, click and flame, the entire time she made her decision. Meredith dug into her backpack, pulled out a her wallet, and came up with the money.

"I'll take it," she said with a beatific smile.

"Got yourself a bargain on this, little lady. A real bargain." He punched buttons on the register, bounced the drawer off his rotund middle, counted bills into the tray. He closed the register, laid the guitar roughly inside its case, fastened its clasps, and watched out the window as she carted the guitar away.

Meredith had changed her view of Burr Colton, in a matter of one afternoon, from a perspective of immense suspicion to one of begrudging tolerance.

In self-righteous indignation she'd blasted into his living quarters and accused him of unconscionably taking advantage of a woman who for, at that very moment, he was constructing a gift.

Despite Burr Colton's questionable presence on her grandmother's farm, Meredith had never felt so humbled or saddened in her life. Tonight, knowing she wouldn't enter the barn again unless invited and knowing she wouldn't be invited, she left the guitar she'd purchased in the truck, knocked at the barn door, and, when he answered, said, "Would you come out here for a minute?"

He settled his hat brim lower over his head, appearing duly suspicious. "What do you want me out there for?"

"Don't ask. You'll see. I've got something for you in the truck."

"You got no reason to need me out there."

"I do. You want to come with me, or wait here?"

His turn to be skeptical as hell about her. "Just as well wait here."

"Suit yourself." She walked over, yanked open the truck door with two hands, and carried the case at her side. She got to the barn and held the guitar out to him by the handle. Burr stared at it.

She swung it forward, as if she had to coax him. "Go ahead. Take it."

"That's my guitar."

"All the more reason not to stare at it like you've never seen it before."

"One fellow wearing a cowboy hat," the pawn shop proprietor had said, "fiddled around with it so long, I thought I'd made a sale." He took the case from her, reverently pressed a thumbnail against the fake leather stitching of the handle. "You bought it back for me?"

"I did."

"Why in heaven's name did you do something like that?"

She'd thought about that same question the entire time she'd driven up and down Main Street. Why did she have the urge to walk into the pawn shop and retrieve Burr Colton's guitar? She'd decided she was purchasing it as an apology, an ornate way of telling him how wrong she'd been when she'd gone barging in on him.

Meredith said simply, "If you hadn't bought that iron for Grandma's weather vane, you could've bought it back for yourself."

She didn't say, *Besides feeling sorry, I wanted you to have something to belong to you.* He hadn't any possessions in his life to speak of, nothing except the dog. The emptiness of his space in the barn had made her ache.

Meredith laughed to cover that aching now, the sudden realization that they were alone together making her shy. "I ought to tell you I traded a tank of gas for it. I ought to say that they brought out a hose and siphoned out the tank and gave me this perfectly good guitar instead."

He gripped the handle with both hands, uncertain as to what to say to her. "Thought I'd never see this old thing again." Meredith wondered if he might open the case and play it right there, but he didn't. Strange, too, that she'd almost hoped he would. He said, "Nobody's ever done anything this nice for me."

"I'll bet they have," she said softly, "only you don't remember."

"I'd remember," he answered. "No."

With the cold coming on and frost flanking the roof, it took almost a week before Burr Colton deemed the temperature suitable for mounting the weather vane. He climbed the ladder and slid along the apex of the roof, taking pleasure in the smooth places and the corrugated ones, the seams where sections joined, easier to slide over because of the green paint.

Burr had already been on the Trichak farm long enough to get his bearings, he realized, longer than he'd stayed in any other job. He aligned the iron "N" due north and the iron "S" due south. He checked to make sure the arrow swiveled freely, then bolted the whole thing down.

He sat back and watched the wind take the arrow. It swung south, southwest, and steadied.

Meredith and Fiona were loading a box for the church bazaar when Michael and Barbara Trichak phoned to say they wouldn't be coming for Christmas.

"We talked about it last week. You said you'd think about it, Dad." Meredith stuffed another festive pillow into the box.

"That's just it. We said we'd think about it, and we did. We've discussed it and decided we just can't be away."

"We waited to put up the Christmas tree so we could do it all together. You were going to cut it and Almer's invited and there's ornaments from when you were a little boy."

"My my, but you and Fiona are busy making plans for us just like everyone else. It's an impossible time to travel, Meredith. Everyone and their brothers are trying to fly into Jackson Hole and go skiing for the holiday. The tickets cost five times what they usually cost to fly into Wyoming."

"Money's never mattered before. You've always been willing to pay for whatever."

Fiona grabbed her arm and distracted her attention from the telephone. "Meredith. Look outside. Look what Burr Colton's doing on the barn." In the kitchen, Fiona pressed her nose to the glass. "Oh, just look." She threw open the door and bounded across the yard to the barn.

"Dad, I've got to go. Grandma's run outside."

"Doesn't your grandmother know she isn't supposed to run?"

"Dad—"

"If you wanted to fly home for Christmas, we would send you a ticket. That hired hand would be with your grandmother if she should need attention."

Meredith glanced out the window. Burr Colton perched high atop the roof, making final adjustments in direction. She saw Fiona directing him to push the "E" an inch toward his right, which was the exact direction of Ocean Lake. "No, Dad. We won't do that. That isn't what either of us wanted."

"The timing is fine for us. We can mail your gifts today and they'll be delivered on time."

A statement, not a question. "You've already got them boxed and ready to go."

"We do."

"What about us? We were planning different things, things we could give you here." Fiona was knitting a cowl-neck sweater for Barbara. There wouldn't be time for her to finish and get it sent in the mail. "Dad, I have to go. They're at the barn and I—"

"We never promised we'd be there, Meredith. We just said we'd *try*."

Out in the yard Burr stepped off the ladder and swept his arm in an ample motion from Fiona to the roof, a gesture that made his gift official. Meredith saw her grandmother graciously accept with a sideways nod of her head, the same masterful gesture with which a grande dame accepted an invitation to waltz. Meredith had missed it. She felt a melancholy twinge, as if she'd just been left out of something important. She asked her father, "When's your company Christmas party?"

Michael began to expound, something about the Rose in Santa Monica, Barbara's I. Magnin account, hors d'oeuvres and drinks, and Meredith didn't bother to listen.

"Well, it really makes no difference," Fiona told her while they drove to church to deposit the pillows and Meredith recounted what they'd said over the phone. "Phooey on Barbara's sweater. I'll send her powder from Nordstrom's, which she'll probably enjoy more because she picked out the fragrance herself. And never mind Michael. We'll have Burr cut us the tree instead."

They deposited the assortment of pillows with Evangeline Kew, chairman of the church bazaar committee. Evangeline set to work tilting the pillows at the correct jaunty angle, fluffing out the lace trim and the ruffles so they'd look attractive on the table this afternoon when the buyers began to arrive. Once the pillows had been properly oohed and aahed over by the ladies, Meredith drove them home and Fiona set to work, alternately checking out the window to admire her new weather vane and carrying down decorations from dusty boxes in the attic.

"Grandma, you've got to let me help you up there. The doctors would have a fit. You ought not to be climbing around on your hands and knees searching for things, much less be on this ladder."

"I'm the only one who can find them," Fiona insisted. "Oh, look. Here's the stuffed bear we put on the tree every year. What was his name? Harris? Henry? Oh yes, Herbie. I remember it was Herbie. We always saved Herbie to be put on by the youngest member of the family, whoever it was at the time. I remember when your father used to always do it."

The front door opened and in blustered Burr, hatless, a roll of barbed wire slung around one shoulder like an ammo belt. "You need me for something this afternoon, Missus Trichak?"

"Why, yes, I do," came the muffled voice. And while she was giving orders from the attic, Meredith thought, Grandma likes this. She's gotten accustomed to telling Burr Colton what to do. "Get Meredith to hand you five dollars so you can drive to the forest service and buy a tree permit. They'll give you a map there, too, and you can decide where to go cut one."

Burr's mind was on other things. After he'd mounted the weather vane, he'd been focused entirely on stringing fence. He'd been taking stands of barbed wire down one row, up another, down one row, up another, and he found himself slightly hypnotized by the endless row of fenceposts facing him. "Cut a tree?"

"Yes. A Christmas tree. Take a saw with you. There's a rusty one hanging on a nail in the barn."

It had been ages since Burr Colton had thought about Christmas. "You want me to cut a tree this afternoon?"

"Take the truck and it'll be easy. You just lop it

off and pitch it in the back. We always had our best luck up Mosquito Creek. But you might want to try the Old Pass Road, too, if you don't want to go that far." Fiona poked her head down through the square hole in the ceiling. "When you cut the trunk, leave another inch to cut off when you get it to the porch. They seal themselves up with sap, you know. You'll have to trim off a little more when you get home, and we'll start it soaking in sugar water. We won't wait any longer to decorate. It'll be a party for all of us, to celebrate the new weather vane. We'll just do it tonight."

He asked, "Are the keys in the truck, Missus Trichak?"

"Yes."

"The forest service office is on Main Street?"

"Yes."

Meredith opened the junk drawer and got him five dollars. When he took the money from her, their fingers brushed, her delicate willowy fingers again his rough-hewn ones. Their eyes met and held for one heartbeat, two.

He'd started for the door when Fiona poked her head out of the attic once more, her hair dangling in little wisps like the hair on angels.

"Burr. You haven't thought about Christmas much, have you?"

Burr reshouldered the roll of barbed wire. "No, I haven't."

"If you need time off, I'd be willing to give it to you."

"Don't need time off. Figure I'll work around

the place like it was a regular day. Got all these fences to fix, now that the barn is finished."

"Is that what you've done every Christmas before this one? You've worked?"

"Always been a good day for working. Other folks didn't want it. Usually got extra hours and got paid for them time and a half."

"You won't be going home to visit your family, then?"

He shook his head. "No, Missus Trichak. You know I won't be doing that."

"Well . . ." She righted herself and came down the ladder with a box of red Christmas balls in her hand. "You won't be fixing fences, either. You'll celebrate with us. I'll tell you right now, I won't bring you a Christmas dinner outside to the barn."

With a bit of delicate maneuvering, he switched the roll of wire from his right shoulder to his left. "You wouldn't want me to clean out the silo that day? Or work on those fences?"

"Merciful heavens, no." She'd come all the way down, left the balls on the table, and was starting up for another load. "I'm in the mood for a big tree, Burr. A spruce if you find one. The largest one you can manage."

After Burr drove off in the truck, saw and five dollars in hand, Meredith—who'd finally convinced her grandmother she could help—carried down the heaviest boxes while Fiona took a long call from the church. Evangeline Kew took personal responsibility for selling Fiona's pillows at the bazaar, each and every one of them, amassing a total of two hundred and thirty dollars for the new Sunday school wing.

"That's a good thing." Fiona went back to unpacking. "I'd've hated for any of those pillows to come back, although I could've sent one to Barbara in the box we're getting together for Christmas. Evangeline bought the pink one herself for her guest bedroom. They told me Lester Irons bought one for his wife for Christmas. He made the wrong choice. For her, I would've chosen the floral green and not the blue plaid."

"Maybe he knows his wife better than you do."

"Not by much."

They unrolled breakable ornaments from the tissue and reglued several that'd had their heads or legs or wheels knocked off while they'd been in storage. Several times during the unpacking and repairing and discussing the histories of things, Fiona glanced toward the road, checking for Burr. "I hope he won't go too far. I ought to've let him borrow Ray's old snowshoes. If he goes up Mosquito Creek, there's a chance he'll run into snow."

"I've seen those snowshoes on a peg in the barn, Grandma. They're too worn out to use."

Toward suppertime they heard the truck rattling up the driveway. The night had gotten much too dark for them to see anything except the truck's wavery yellow headlights. It seemed an eternity before Burr appeared on the porch amid flouncing limbs, he and the dog ensconced in the biggest spruce tree Meredith had ever seen.

"Oh, merciful heavens," Fiona said. "We'll have

to trim off three feet of it to get it inside the house."

He half kicked open the door with his foot and Meredith half let him in, and they stood looking out at each other through limbs. "I got one," he said with the same inflection that a hunter would use to say he'd gone out and blasted an elk. "Biggest one around."

"Oh, the tree stand. I forgot to bring down the tree stand."

Fiona started to the attic again, but Meredith stopped her. "I saw it up there, Grandma. I know right where it is."

After Meredith came down with the stand, Burr retrieved the saw and measured to cut more tree off the bottom. Fiona stirred a pot of stew on the stove. "You take off those wet boots and get warmed up." Burr stood in the doorway, gripping the jamb as if he needed to be steadied, glancing from the stew to the tree to the corner where it would stand.

For Burr, the thought came unbidden, a first herald from his past. It always happened this way, whenever he started to be invited to join in. He tried to be worthy of the good things folks did for him. Like working hard plowing the fields or building that weather vane. But one day, in one way, a line was always crossed, and he couldn't pretend it wasn't there.

*You don't want a fellow like me sitting around your Christmas tree.*

"Oh, I know you need to dry off, but I wish you would bring the tree in as soon as you can."

He retreated out the door and from the direction of the porch came the flutter and scratch of limbs, the zippery sound of a handsaw biting into wood. The sound stopped and started several times. At last he opened the door again. "Here it comes. You'd better move back some chairs." He brought it in, and it was so big and round and green, it seemed to take up the room. It revolved slightly as he carried it, Meredith's only indication that its weight burdened him. "That corner over there?" He motioned with his chin while Meredith moved yet another chair out of the way.

"Oh, perfect. Yes."

When Burr tried to set the tree inside the stand, it still wouldn't fit. "Aw, come on." First signs of frustration showing. "I thought I had it cut right."

"You did. It just isn't fitting." Meredith reached to help him stabilize it. She grabbed the trunk, and needles poked her in what felt like a hundred places.

The tree slipped into the stand. While Burr tightened the screws, Meredith saw the top of the tree way above her, its uppermost boughs grazing the ceiling. She felt overwhelmed by its size, as if seeing it from a child's point of view, looking up at the highest bough from the very bottom. She glanced below at the top of Burr's head, his cowlick a giant thumbprint atop his crown, his brown curls willy-nilly since he hadn't smashed them down with his hat. Something stirred in her, some gentle awareness of him she couldn't know but could only sense, as if he kept something hidden away that was tender and broken, something in him like a warrior that had been slain. She felt a yearning, even as she'd accepted the yearning a doctor accepted to heal patients, to find the thing that had been hurt in him, to heal it, to bring it back to life.

He worked the screws with broad fingers, his knuckles sticky with sap from the tree. His arms and the backs of his hands were covered with tiny red dots where spruce needles had jabbed his skin. Meredith closed her eyes against him, knowing his arms and hands were scratched and smarting, recognizing in the intimacy of the moment how far away he kept himself from them, realizing how far it was, perhaps, that she had pushed him away.

"Stew's on the stove," Fiona proclaimed without even dishing it up. "Anybody who wants to take a break from decorating can have some."

Fiona began to hang ornaments. She conveyed them from the table in their boxes and, one by one, began lopping their hooks over branches. Each one had its story, which she told with great vigor. "Oh, here's the Tin Lizzy Michael whittled when he was knee-high to a gander . . . the nest I found where the birds used a tinsel icicle . . . the skier made from clothespins Ray brought back from Jackson Hole." With all her excitement, the other two found it impossible not to join in. Meredith hung a jointed antique dog. She hung a newer ball, clear glass with a gold fiddle in the middle.

"Looks like Sam Grigg's fiddle," she said. "Makes me think of the dance."

"What's the story behind this?"

Burr held up a handmade ornament and let it hang from the tip of his finger. On one side was a yellowed printing from a Christmas card, three children singing in red coats with holly in their hair. Their mouths were pursed in typical Victorian fashion, their coats and holly gold gilded. The picture looked to be very old.

A photograph of a little boy had been pasted to the other side of the card. The writing had faded at the bottom but was still decipherable. "Luke 1," it read. The place in the Bible for the Christmas story. It had been handmade in Sunday school, then. "David T. 1938." He held it up to Meredith.

"Is this your father?"

She looked at it closely. "No. It isn't him. That's somebody else. Grandma? Who's this?"

Fiona's face was lost in spruce boughs. She peered around and saw. Her face, for a moment, lost its color. "Why, that's—" She sighed. Deeply. "Hang it up, Burr. Give it a good place. That one hasn't been hung on a tree for a very long time."

After all the talking, Fiona grew deathly quiet. She worked her way through the branches with total concentration, as if flouncing the layers of a wedding dress. She hung another ornament. And another. Then started on the box of candy canes. One. Two. Three.

"I kept another little boy for a while," she said. "He was up for adoption. A young girl in Melody Flats gave birth to him, and her father wouldn't let her bring him home."

"You *kept* another little boy? Was he *yours?*"

"I adopted him. Yes."

"But I've never heard anything about him. Not from you or Dad, either one. Where is he now?"

Tonelessly, while she dressed the branches: "He died." Candy canes again. Five. Six. Seven.

Burr hung the ornament on a prominent limb. The draft in the room made it spin. She'd said it with such finality, Meredith dared not ask more.

Fiona dusted off her hands. "We've made quick work of this." She stepped back, inspected the ornaments, and rearranged two of them. "How's that?" She cocked her head and eyed it for a long time, as if something weren't quite right. "It's a shame there isn't something of yours hanging up here," she said, not turning to Burr. "It's your tree, too, and there isn't anything—"

He stepped back and stood with her, shoulder to shoulder, touched beyond measure that she'd thought he needed to add something of himself. A memory of Christmas came, something that fought its way past all the accusations and the awful assumptions and the pain. He'd been a little boy, running across the floor, swept up like a puppy into the arms of his grandfather. "Merry Christmas." And a wet kiss on the nose.

Something wrenched in his heart, something unidentifiable and immense. If he'd known what hope felt like, he might've recognized it. But he didn't. It had been too long, with too many miles put between him and home. "I might have something," he said.

"Do you? Run and get it and put it on. That's all it lacks, Burr. Something of you."

He headed for the barn while Meredith stirred the stew. When he returned, he held an old cigar box in his hands. "It will need a hook or a ribbon bow or something to make it stay on." He unfastened the clasp of the box, opened it. "This? Would it be okay for a tree? It isn't an ornament, but my grandfather gave it to me."

Inside his hand lay a small, crude object, the aspen-wood whistle he'd carried when he'd first come into the dance. "Yes," Fiona said, taking it gingerly, holding it, feeling very close to who she had once been. "It looks like it belongs here, doesn't it?"

When Fiona finally slept after midnight, she dreamed that she walked through a fresh-burnt field. The barley stubble was covered with both smut and dew, frozen into a light frost that cracked when she stepped and covered her shoes with soot.

In her dream, she bent low because she'd found something, a charred piece of cloth like the shirt David had been wearing; only when she touched it, it hadn't been cloth anymore, it had been a photograph, one she couldn't see, charred pieces of it as translucent and brittle as a moth's wing. It crumbled in her hands.

She knelt on her hams in the stubble and the dirt and the soot, and wept.

Her second little boy. As if she'd had him and

never had him, had never gotten the chance to see his face. Yet his face might've been her own, she knew it so well, with its dark, spindly hair and pale blue eyes and the dusting of freckles so light, she decided God had said, "Oops, missed a spot here," and had barely swiped him with freckles on the way out.

He'd been her adopted child. And she'd stayed brutally aware during the raising of him that he'd been a gift from Kay Lee Wilkins, a brother for Michael to cherish, a new beginning in both their lives.

Somewhere during that night, as she dreamed of David, the dream lifted the way clouds lift, the memory gone from surreal to real. Everybody in Melody Flats had purchased a combine. She'd proven they could be run not only by a small group of men, but by a small woman and her boys as well.

The men came to her fields this year not to watch her harvest, but to converse. They stood amid her stubble as they'd stood everywhere, the sweet smoke from their pipes curling up like a smudge offering of Shoshone sage. They talked big and they talked long, talking over the same things again and again, the way everybody talked when details mattered. They compared quality of grain, the time it took to cut one acre with one combine, the going bushel price. When their pipes went out, they dug out a new batch of tobacco, tamped it down, dug matches from their pockets, and started talking all over again.

She'd told David not to bring her the matches

he'd found scattered in the field. She'd told him not to touch them. "You call me when you find one. You stand and yell 'Mama' and I'll come pick it up and throw it away."

There'd been a group of fellows, all of them dead and gone now, who'd been talking in the fields. And she'd discovered as they shared figures that she'd gotten more grain per acre than the others and that even though everyone else had combines now, she'd harvested faster. "I'll go to the house and make lemonade," she told them, because they'd stayed longer than usual, because they'd been amazed by the figures she'd given them, and she enjoyed hearing them talk about it.

Later after it had gotten over and the fire trucks left, someone told Fiona they'd heard David calling her. He'd been standing in a tall clump of dried grass, a ways off down the road, and he'd called out, "Mama. There's one right here. Mama."

She, in the house stirring lemonade, watching the spoon go round and round like a carnival ride in a crystal pitcher. And then, because she hadn't heard him and come immediately to take it away, he must've struck the match instead.

Such incongruous thoughts come at times like that. She remembered, when they'd turned away from his little body and looked up at her and shaken their heads, she'd thought without a feeling, "Oh, if only Charley hadn't gone, he could have done the funeral."

For Charley was gone, come to tell her goodbye in the middle of an afternoon last week when the boys had been playing. He'd said, "I can't stay in Melody Flats, Fi. I can't be close to you. It's six years of this and getting worse. I stay in this valley and I'll betray my God, my congregation, my wife."

She'd wanted to ask, *In what order*? But instead she said, "You haven't betrayed anything, Charley. You wouldn't, because betrayal isn't in you."

He said, "You're the only one who knows who I am. You're the only one who knows I'm somebody different from what people see."

She wished she could've been angry or in a rage at him, but it had never gotten that far, never gotten to a place where either of them thought she had right to rage. A person had no privilege to feel something when those feelings would affect a hundred other people or more, when it would affect people's *faith*.

He said, "Other folks have choices. We didn't."

"Or maybe other people don't have them, either," she'd said quietly. "Maybe they only think they do."

David had come running across the field to them then, the David of a week ago, alive and animated as a chipmunk. As they'd watched him coming, her eyes had been patient, but there were lines of strain along her face. "No love is ever lost, Charley. It comes around on itself, always for its own purpose."

"I'm going away today," Charley'd said as David bounded into his lap and gave him a hug. "Wanted to come tell you, because I'm going to miss you so much."

"Here's a present for you, then," David had said. "A going-away present so you'll have something to remember me by. My big brother, Michael, helped me carve my initials into it. See." He pointed. "D.W.T."

Pastor Charles Burleigh's broken voice said as much as his words. "You don't have to give me presents, little fellow."

"Aw, I want to. You've got to have this." And the little boy placed his precious hand-carved whistle inside the preacher's huge palm.

**11**

C hristmas Day, and their first warning of
the encroaching storm came from Burr's
weather vane, shifting and pivoting toward
the north, straight into a bitter wind. Squall
clouds came into view from over the mountains,
strewn across a sky the same color as Orient
pearls.

Fiona glanced at the clock in the hall when she
saw the first snowflake fall, then another and
another and another, until the swirls and the
tapestries of snow made even the green barn no
longer visible from the house. Seven forty-three
A.M. It would be today! Christmas morning and
someone would be pronounced winner of the "first
snow" contest out of Taylor Kew's jar. Finches and
chickadees flanked the little perches on Fiona's
window feeder, pecking at the millet recklessly, as if

it might be their last chance, their feathers tilted helter-skelter into the wind.

In a matter of minutes, the landscape of Melody Flats changed from its familiar one to something opalescent and exotic, every fencepost and wire, every harrow, every limb and sprig, etched with snow. While Fiona sat watching her birds, she saw the barn door swing open. The massive gate swept a distinct triangle in the perfect covering of snow. Out came Burr Colton with a collection of brooms, shovels, and a small canvas bag of chicken feed.

"Oh, he mustn't be working today, Meredith. Not on Christmas. What if he doesn't come in?" Fiona seemed frail and exhausted, pale, with circles beneath her eyes, as if she'd had no sleep. For the first time, Meredith realized how fragile she seemed. "I can order him to do chores, but I can't order him to open himself up to us. He keeps himself so *hidden.*"

Meredith wrapped her arms around her grandmother the way she'd wrap them around a child, consoling her, not understanding exactly why. "He'll come in, Grandma. He's doing chores that have to be done every day. Look, he's going to feed the chickens."

He wore a coat she knew he'd bought with one of his paychecks down at the Episcopal Church's Browse 'n Buy and his tattered sheepskin gloves. Beneath his Stetson, his ears were red with cold. His dog came out and stuck a nose in the snow, sneezed, and shook. The pair started off toward the chicken coop, leaving six footprints as they went, four small pawprints and two large boot shapes, blue indentions in the snow.

Meredith stroked her grandmother's gossamer hair. "All that time I thought he shouldn't be here, he fought back and stood his ground. Now something's changed in him."

"He needs us, Meredith. More than he'll ever say. More than he knows. He wouldn't have come here, he wouldn't've walked into that dance that night, if it wasn't so."

They ripped into their packages together, Barbara's perfect shop-wrapped gifts destroyed and cast aside in moments, the hand-wrapped ones they'd each gotten for the other taken slower and savored. Meredith folded back the tissue and discovered a tiered skirt that vaguely matched the pillows Fiona'd stitched for the church bazaar. Fiona broke tape with her fingernail, folded back the box, and removed a pottery soup tureen she'd admired in the window at the hardware store.

"It's beautiful."

"Perfect for church potlucks."

"It fits."

"Lots of soup will fit *in* it." A hug and a "Thank you," from one to the other. A hug and a "Thank you" the other way around.

Several packages remained under the tree. Grandmother and granddaughter looked at them and started to laugh. For neither had told the other that she had gotten a gift for Burr Colton. "What did you get him?" Fiona asked Meredith.

"A pair of polar fleece socks. And a wool hat to keep his ears warm. What did you get him?"

"Merciful heavens. I've wrapped up a shirt. A pair of polar fleece socks. And a wool hat to keep his ears warm."

"We've done it. What color are the socks you got him?"

"What about you?"

"You tell first."

"No, you."

That feeling came over both of them at the same time, that giggly satiated feeling of it being totally Christmas, when there's nothing left to do except be together and be loved, everything established, everything like the song, calm and bright. "Green," they both said. "Green to match the barn."

They practically fell off their seats, laughing so hard.

"What's going on in here?" Three fat fruitcake tins were stacked in front of Almer Moley's face, tottering at the same amazing angle as the Leaning Tower of Pisa.

"It's Christmas, Almer." Fiona stood and rescued him from the fruitcakes. "Welcome."

"Come in, Burr," Almer called over his shoulder. Then, to Fiona: "You ought to see all he's done out there this morning. Fed the chickens and shoveled the walk and swept the porch and salted the steps. You ought not let him work like that on Christmas morning, Fi."

"Fiddlesticks. Don't you go blaming Burr Colton's work ethics on me. Our first snowstorm, wouldn't you know, and it's on Christmas Day."

Burr had no choice but to be shooed into the house with Almer, and he felt shooed into the merriment, too. They cut into one of Almer's fruitcakes, and he donned a pair of his new green socks, and he measured the new creased flannel shirt against his shoulders. He held the warm hats together in his palms, turning them the way he turned the brim of his Stetson. He heard himself saying, "Why, this is something. This is really something."

After dinner they settled in for a game of Shanghai rummy, and Almer coaxed Burr into the game. Meredith sat right beside him and tormented him every time she held a card he needed. "You could lay down if you had the three of spades, couldn't you?" she'd say. "I've got the three of spades right here." All this hoopla for a farmhand at Christmas. She'd expected him to laugh, or relax, or at least have some fun. And she'd turn the card sideways, baiting him, tapping it on the table so he'd be sure to see.

"Leave him alone, Meredith." Fiona, laying down a set of three and a run of five with a little slap onto the table. "He's just learning how to play."

Almer said, "Don't let it get to you, Burr. She's been figuring what everybody needed and holding their cards since she was ten years old."

In defense of herself, Meredith said, "I didn't do it at first. Grandma taught me everything about holding cards. She was the one who always watched what people saved and figured out what everybody needed."

And Burr, laying his rummy cards on the table in spite of the rest of them: "That's it. I think I've won, haven't I? Add up your scores and tell me."

That afternoon, after they'd finished their third game, an unfamiliar car rolled into the driveway. "We've certainly been having our share of visitors lately," Fiona said as she went to the porch.

"Might be someone else to buy the combine." Almer tamped the playing cards on the table and slipped a rubber band around them.

But it became clear the moment the woman climbed out of the car and gathered her young daughter into her arms, they'd come because they needed help. "Meredith," Fiona called over her shoulder, "I think it's someone for you."

Burr ran outside, took the child and a bloody towel from the woman's arms, and brought them to the house. They didn't have to trudge through deep snow because of the path Burr had already shoveled.

"For me?"

"They told me at the emergency number I'd find a doctor here," the woman said as Burr carried the little girl inside.

"But I'm not a—"

Burr deposited the little girl into a chair beside the fire and helped her hold the towel to her forehead. Meredith could tell by the child's long black hair and dark eyes that she was Shoshone, that she'd come from the Wind River Reservation a good distance away.

"There's no one to help who lives close by," the woman pleaded. "It's Christmas Day. The doctors from the Tuesday clinic are all home with their families in Riverton."

Meredith knew the rest without the woman explaining it. The clinic doctors had known she'd

come from med school to stay with her grandmother. They had directed the woman to come
here.

"I'm not a doctor yet." Meredith stooped to the
child's level and took the towel in hand. Half of it
was wrapped around her arm and half used to
soak up a good amount of blood from her forehead. "I'll do the best I can."

"She may need stitches," the mother said.

Fiona made sure the mother was sitting in a
comfortable chair, too, because she looked in a
much worse condition than her daughter. "I'll go
up and get the first-aid kit."

"What's your name?" Meredith asked the child.

"Hallie Antelope," the little girl answered, her
tearstained face wincing with pain.

"What happened, Hallie? Can you tell me?"

Between sniffs and sobs, the little girl started to
tell. The mother added parts, too, until they told
the story back and forth, the uncanny way all
mothers add to stories and make children feel like
children.

"I was playing outside—"

"Building a snowman with her brothers . . ."

"—and I had the carrot for the nose—"

"Hidden behind her back so she could be the
one to stick it on . . ."

"—and he tried to wrestle it away from me, so I
ran. . . ."

"And he jumped on her, twisted her arm
underneath her, and ran her right into a barbed-
wire fence, all for a carrot. . . ." Ms. Antelope kept
going the entire time Meredith examined Hallie's

forehead. "Christmas morning, you know. They'd had so much sugar from their stockings. They were running wild."

"We've been running wild here, too," Meredith said, taking alcohol from the first-aid kit Fiona had brought her and using it on a cotton ball to daub the wound. "There. I can see it much better now that it's cleaned up." She saw immediately that the cut had been bloody but not deep. She had just the thing for it in the kit. A butterfly bandage. That put in place, Meredith said, "Now, let's have a look at that arm."

Gingerly the girl proffered her arm, elbow first.

"Have you tried to move your fingers at all since you fell?"

Hallie Antelope shook her head.

"I want you to move your fingers slowly. Cup them and open them like this." She demonstrated. "Okay? You try."

In slow motion Hallie closed her fingers and opened them again.

"Now your thumb. Don't move anything else but your thumb. Poke it straight up like you're giving someone the 'a-okay' sign."

Hallie gave her the "a-okay" sign.

"Does it hurt when you do that?"

Hallie nodded.

"Is this sore?" She poked.

Hallie nodded.

"And this?" Meredith prodded.

On they went, checking muscles and bones, until Meredith determined Hallie didn't have anything sprained or broken. Presently she glanced at

Hallie's mother. "I'm going to splint it and wrap it in an Ace bandage, just to be safe. She doesn't have anything broken, so there's nothing the hospital in Riverton would have done for you today."

"Thank you." The woman began to fumble in her purse.

"Keep ice on her wrist for twenty-four hours. After that, change to heat. And it's okay for her to have a half tablet of ibuprofen to take down the swelling. She shouldn't wrestle with her brothers for the rest of the week. Tell them to treat her gently, no matter how much sugar they've eaten."

"I will do that."

"If she still has any soreness in her muscles by next Tuesday, I'd take her to the clinic and have a doctor look at it."

"Can I write this down?" the mother asked. "I'll never remember everything."

"I'll write it for you."

Meredith tore a sheet off a notepad and jotted her list of instructions. She underlined "No wrestling for the remainder of the week" three times.

Not until the woman had pulled out her wallet and offered to pay, not until Burr Colton had carried Hallie to the car and placed her on the front seat, not until Fiona and Almer had waved the Antelopes away, did Meredith realize she'd just treated her first patient.

"I didn't expect to be treating a patient today," Meredith announced so she'd make certain they all noticed. She latched the first-aid kit and turned to find Burr directly behind her.

"Oh—," she said.

And he said, "I was just—"

They both broke off.

"Was just going to tell you, is all. Was going to tell you that I think you're awful good at that." He spoke in a tone that made her glance quickly up at his face. "You're going to make a good doctor when you get back to school."

"Guess I should have been nervous about it or something. I didn't even have time to catch my breath."

Outside, evening light had finally broken through and fringed the snow clouds with gold. Cars passed by in the distance, the slush on the highway making them sound deceptively nearby. It seemed as if they both noticed at the same time that the fire had burned down in the stove.

"Better stoke up the fire," she said, reaching for the poker.

"Better go bring in some firewood," he said, heading for the door.

"Burr." She stopped him when he had his hand on the door knob. "Would you bring in your guitar tonight? Would you play for us, since it's Christmas?"

"You'd want me to do that?"

She nodded.

He didn't answer until he came in from the back stoop and dropped an armload of wood with a loud, splintery clatter into the wood box. "Could bring the old thing in. Could give it a whirl, if everybody wanted."

"Oh, yes." Fiona carried in a tray of hot chocolates and set them on the coffee table.

"It'd be a treat," Almer agreed.

Burr used old coals to reignite the fire. In no time at all, a warm yellow glow leapt against the glass. Flames curled over the logs and sparks glimmered like small storms as they lofted into the chimney. Meredith sat across from Burr Colton and tapped her knees together. Firelight reflected in his eyes. Flames colored his face amber.

"Well, you all really want to hear some music? Guess I'll go get my guitar." He slapped his knees and stood up. He was gone to the barn for a few minutes. He came back with his guitar just as Meredith broke a stick in two and thrust both pieces into the stove.

Burr laid the case open on the floor, where it would be safe from the heat. He pried open the latches and lifted the instrument from its case. He propped the curve of the box across his right leg and stretched his hand like a spider to finger his first chord.

In the glimmering light Meredith saw his hands as if for the first time, the calluses on the caps of his fingers and the rough thickness on the thumb. His eyes shone luminous, mythical light that reflected in his gray pupils as he played. He thrummed the strings once, let the chord reverberate away like a whisper. Then, unsatisfied, he began to pluck each string, turning each peg tighter, tuning by ear.

The flames snapped and danced. Fiona and Almer sat side by side on the sofa, nibbled more fruitcake and sipped hot cocoa. Meredith moved to the hearth, laid her hands uncertainly in her lap, as if something remarkable were about to happen.

And then he began to play. Picking and strumming, ever so often a slap on the soundboard, a break, and a change of key. Burr let his music speak for him. It soared. It wept and frolicked. It recollected and foretold.

When Burr finally spoke aloud, he spoke not to anyone in the room, but to the stars outside the window. "My dad taught me how to play just before he left town."

"How old were you?" Fiona asked.

He thought awhile. "Can't even remember an age. Couldn't've been older than eight, though."

Meredith watched him picking and strumming, watched his eyes paying homage to the stars, saw his foot tapping to the rhythm of his heart. The thought came, fleeting as a breeze, as she watched his hands claiming his instrument, to wonder what it might feel like if his hands claimed her, too.

"Did your dad give you that guitar?"

"Nope. He taught me on a different one. He carried it off with him on the day he left town." He tilted it up to have a look at the pocked soundboard. "I bought this one after he'd gone, when I got a hankering to play."

"You're good on that thing," she said. "Real good."

"Ever' so often, I get to worrying this thing's going to break wide open in my hands. But you can't patch a guitar or glue it together or anything, else it'll ruin the tone." He lowered the instrument to his legs, laid it flat against his knee as he looked at her. He said the same thing he'd said at the barn. "Thought I'd never see this again when I walked out of the pawn shop that day."

"Just wanted you to have it, after I went running into the barn like I was going to—"

Meredith stopped. They each glanced at Fiona. She'd been laughing at something Almer had told her and so hadn't heard. They realized Fiona didn't know the whole story of it.

She didn't know Burr had spent his first paycheck from her on iron for the weather vane.

She didn't know Meredith had gone to the pawn shop to rescue Burr's guitar.

Their eyes met. They shared a secret between them. That seemed nice, pleasant. Burr felt more comfortable, more disguised from her, and therefore more open to her in this soft darkness, than before. In the firelight Meredith's hair shone the same color as molasses. Without thinking, he reached with one finger and threaded one strand of it behind her left ear. He felt Meredith catch her breath.

It was his thumb that he brushed against her cheek, the broad thumb that had gone callused from roofing barns and stringing fences and plowing fields. Yet he'd touched her as lightly as webs would brush skin, so lightly that she wanted to grab his hand and hold it within her own, to capture the electricity that thrummed between them and reverberated as surely as a note from his guitar.

She touched his arm, felt the featherweight of

the fabric slip beneath her fingers. Cold night and warm skin. Warmer still the cotton at his elbow, smelling burned like linen that had been ironed because he'd held it too close to the fire. Their eyes met and held.

Almer asked all of a sudden, "Why'd you stop playing the guitar? We were listening."

"No reason," Burr lied. "No reason at all."

He picked up the instrument from his lap and began again. He closed his eyes against the low firelight as his music drifted skyward with the embers.

**12**

O ne thing that could be fairly said in Meredith Trichak's favor was that once she began to believe in someone, she let them quietly know.

Once she'd seen the feeble, cherishing eyes of her grandmother on Burr Colton as he fed chickens Christmas morning, once she'd seen the reserved, almost secluded manner Burr accepted and yet held himself away from their family celebration, she knew the time had come to allow him entrance into their lives. No matter how odd this draw seemed to be between an old woman and the young man she'd hired, Meredith realized it had become too important to Fiona to disavow it any longer.

There, too, was the matter of the fireside and the magical music he created on the guitar and the thumb that had gently, reverently, brushed her cheek.

Meredith could not put these things out of her mind.

Shortly after breakfast, which Burr Colton had eaten alone in the barn, she saw him working along the east field, stringing barbed-wire fence. She donned her Columbia coat and flopped her ponytail over the rim of her new wool headband. She started up the driveway and called to him, "Good morning, Mr. Colton." She waved her gloved hand.

He raised his eyes, and she saw he wore the wool hat Fiona had given him yesterday. He nodded. "Hey there," he said through his teeth. He took a staple out of his mouth and started hammering it into the post.

"Your ears look much better this morning," she said, referring to his new hat. "Much warmer than they did yesterday."

"They are much warmer." He unrolled a length of wire and headed for the next picket. She followed him. "I'll wear the hat you gave me tomorrow. With two of them, I'll be able to alternate."

She stood beside him in the snow, shoved her hands in her pockets. She watched, saying nothing, as he aligned the wire from post to post, sighting low with his eyes to find the plumb line. He positioned the wire where he wanted and hammered only once. The staple bit into the wood.

"You want some help or something?"

That stopped him in his tracks. "You'd want to help me?"

"Sure would." She clapped her gloves together. "It'd be a great skill to know how to fix a fence. Never know when something like that would come in handy."

Burr stood straight up for a minute and looked as if he might say no. But instead, "We could do two strands at a time, if you'd like."

"Okay."

He taught her how to jimmy out the loose staples from the old pine posts, how to check for sagging wires, how to leave old wire in place if it was holding. He showed her how to string new wire, watching out for the barbs so she wouldn't cut her hands. He let her measure a wire from one pine picket to another, pounding in the staple so it held the wire flat against the wood. When they walked to the next post to start all over again, he didn't say, even though she'd noticed, that she'd hammered in the wire just a smidgen crooked.

He also didn't tell her, even though she noticed, that they moved twice as slow, now that he'd let her help.

After lunch, which he ate inside the house with Fiona, they got a system going. She pried out old staples with one hammer, he hammered new ones in with the other. She checked for loose lines, removed them, and rolled them up when they were sagging. He measured and strung new wire when he found an empty place. Sometimes, if the wire wasn't too far gone, she'd unstaple sagging wire, pull it tight, and pound it in again.

They worked in silence for a long time. He said finally, "That was quite a day yesterday, wasn't it?"

She was right in the middle of jimmying out a staple. She removed it and tucked it inside her coat pocket. "Yes. It was a good Christmas."

"Did it make you sad that your parents didn't come?"

Meredith tightened up a length of wire and decided she could use it again. For a long while she didn't answer. Then, "Yes. But no."

"Why both answers?"

"I'm a grown woman. I've gotten past the point of expecting these big family shindigs where we all fly in and spend a week together. It's just . . . "

"It's just what?"

"It was Grandma's last Christmas in her house. I've wondered if she thought about that. I wanted it worse for her because of that, I guess."

"Wonder if Missus Trichak thought about it that way."

"I wouldn't ask." Meredith gazed at the sky for a moment, clinging to the tightened fence wire. "And I'm sure they haven't thought of it that way, either. They live this fast life, and they don't stop to see who they're running over along the way. Barbara and Michael are always so willing to be involved as long as you'll let them be involved on their own terms. Or as long as you'll change your own life to accommodate theirs."

She looked up to find him watching her, his hammer idle. "There's been times you've been that way, too, haven't you?"

"Yes," Meredith answered, meeting his eyes with honesty. "I am very much like them. It's taken me spending this time with Grandma to see it in myself."

Sitting at her computer one night late, sending a halfhearted e-mail to her faculty adviser at UCLA, and Meredith had an idea. She thrust arms in her coat and ran to the barn to find Burr Colton. She knocked on the door. When he answered, he didn't invite her inside.

"What are you doing out here at this time of night?" he asked.

"Farming," she said, jumping up and down. "Have you ever figured out what to do about farming?"

"I'm figuring out as I go along."

"You ever done anything on a computer?"

Burr said, "Never had the chance to touch one. Doubt I could even turn one on."

"You could find out about farming on the Internet, if you wanted to try. I'm hooked with a modem to UCLA. We could look up barley through a search engine and you could learn what you need."

He made a little tent of his hands over his lips as if he weren't certain he should accept.

She coaxed him. "It'd be just like you've taught me to string fences, only now I could teach you something, too." Just as he'd started thinking her idea didn't seem so farfetched, she added, "I'll show you. Come upstairs with me to my room."

"I don't—" He stopped. It had been months since he'd ventured upstairs in the Trichaks' house. And that had only been in the midst of an evening when he'd been too exhausted, too starving and lost, to object. Something hard and bitter and fierce knotted at the bottom of his gut. I can't do this, he thought. "Meredith, you don't know—"

But she'd already left him behind. She'd gone running and laughing across the snow in the moonlight, her dark hair flailing out behind her like a flag. He had no choice but to follow her, past Fiona where she snoozed on the couch to the accompaniment of the Weather Channel, past the guest room where he'd once slept, past the bathroom with its silent toilet, to another room, Meredith's room. With a white desk in the corner, lined immaculately with standing folders of notes, each labeled in her firm, slanting script. With a row of cubbyholes that held pens, paper clips, and a selection of needle-thin leads for her mechanical pencil.

He tried not to look around him. He tried not to touch anything. She motioned for him to have a seat. He did.

"This is my workstation," she said with the same authority as a travel guide, the same voice he remembered from a lady who'd toured them through the state capital in Pierre. "This is how you turn the computer on."

Burr couldn't help seeing her personal things, that funny striped bathrobe slung over a chair, a case halfway open to reveal gold necklaces strung on hooks. A framed photo of friends, California Generation X's at the beach, eight or so of them attired in bikinis and trunks, sunburned and robust and covered with sand.

Meredith's voice droned on about the computer.

But in his mind, he'd traveled miles away to another girl's bedroom like this one, with pink things on a dresser and a Cabbage Patch doll on the cedar chest and their clothes slung across chairs. He'd been on the road awhile then, but he kept going back to Belle Fourche to see her, kept thinking he could convince her to come with him. "I shouldn't be in—"

"Aren't you listening?" On the nightstand beside Meredith's bed, he saw a cut-glass vase holding one china rose. He made himself focus on the sound of her voice, on the hard chair beneath his bum, on the one petal of the rose that had a tiny chip in it. "You aren't going to learn anything about the computer if you don't pay attention."

He stared at the keyboard. He scooted back and forth in the chair until he felt reasonably situated. Each instruction she gave him, he repeated as if he had to force himself to think.

"You push w-i-n to bring up Windows."

"W-i-n for Windows."

He hunted and pecked on the keyboard until he located the w, the i, and the n. The screen flashed from black to a petroglyph of icons and an hourglass.

"Now that you're in Windows, click your mouse on Netscape, like this."

"Click the mouse?" He picked up the mouse, turned it over, and looked at the little ball on the bottom. "What part of it clicks?"

She reached around his right arm and took it from him, getting close enough to feel her breath in his hair.

"You lay it on the pad like this. The roller moves around and takes the arrow with it. See? And that flashing line is called a cursor."

"Why is it called a cursor? Is it because it makes people curse?"

She laughed softly, wondering why he seemed so disoriented and afraid since she'd brought him into her room. It couldn't just be the computer, could it? "You just try it and see."

He accidentally clicked the mouse on the scroll that came down, "Favorite Places." A whir sounded, and before either of them knew it, he'd connected them to the UCLA MedNet. "What's this?"

"My med school stuff."

"What is it, though?"

"My schedule last semester."

"Let's see it."

"You're supposed to research farming, not my class schedule."

He clicked again and ran down the list with his finger: Microanatomy & Cell Biology; Clinical Applications of Basic Science; Doctoring 1; Gross Anatomy; Laboratory. "You're studying all this?"

"I've already finished with that. Next year, I move on to the hard stuff."

Not a little overwhelmed by what he saw before him on the MedNet screen, he repeated the instructions she'd given him. "Go to the search engine." He moved the mouse to the correct icon and clicked. With no further prompting he typed "Farming."

As Burr began his search on the computer, Meredith realized how much he'd already taught himself from his visits to the Simplot warehouse and his quiet moments listening in over coffee at the Sarvisberry Inn. For long into the night, Burr Colton sat in Meredith's chair in her bedroom and executed searches on the computer. Meredith finally stopped prompting and watched him, intensely aware that he'd already taught himself plenty. He knew exactly what questions to ask. Within two hours, he had printed lists of twenty different varieties of both spring and autumn barleys. He discovered the best varieties of malt barleys versus the best varieties of seed and feed barleys. He knew how to order insect-resistant barley from Great Britain and insecticide from Simplot. "This is telling me everything. Who'd've thought anybody could do this?"

"It's amazing, isn't it? Thought it would help you."

"It does. Oh, it does."

He'd been instructed in three different forums that he ought to wait no later than mid-February to start plowing again if the topsoil had thawed. He knew he ought to order Gallatin barley from the co-op, the seed that would grow well in a Wyoming climate, and he knew to purchase a hundred pounds of seed per acre.

From an agri-net homepage, he'd read that he'd have to use Missus Trichak's old disk plow the second time around, to break up any remaining clods and furls. He knew to fertilize with nitrogen. And he knew to roller harrow the field, smoothing it just a bit, before planting time.

If he tried to plant after mid-April, he'd be

starting too late. If he tried to plant in mid-March, he'd be starting too early. He found out the barley sprouts began to send up shoots a week to ten days after they'd been planted, especially if they were irrigated or got enough gentle rain. And he'd left three questions e-mailed to a barley expert, a farmer from Australia with a homepage who said he'd be thrilled to answer inquiries.

Burr printed out the last five pages, then played with the mouse and the icons enough to figure out how to disconnect. The screen went black again, with white letters. He found the on/off button. The machine flickered off.

"I'm sure the fire's gone out in the barn. Should've stoked it up before I left." He gathered the last of his printed documents and tamped them into a pile. "Can't hardly absorb it all. Have to read everything over about five times so I can remember it all."

When Meredith didn't answer him this time, he turned and found she'd gone sound asleep, her arm draped around a knob on the footboard, her dark hair nested in the crook of her own shoulder, one miniature gold loop lying against her ear, and her legs curled up beneath her. "Meredith?" For an instant the feeling came again, fear that struck him fierce and hard, like a blow. "Hey." He gripped her shoulder and barely shook it. "You want to wake up? Hey."

She didn't move. He stood over her with his papers in both hands, measuring the balance between trust and fear, approval and accusation, gain and loss.

"Meredith. You've gone to sleep sitting up."

Her head lolled to the other side, revealing the other earring lying against the other jaw. It seemed he had no choice but to lift her and put her in.

From looking, he could tell Meredith slept on the left side of the bed, her head on one thick pillow and one thin, beneath a sheet and a worn blue coverlet that wasn't half as nice as the one Fiona had given him when he'd spent the night in her guest bedroom. Burr set his papers on the computer. He scooped one arm beneath her bent knees and wrapped one arm behind the small of her back.

She wasn't heavy. When he lifted her, her head flopped sideways against his chest, her ear and her jaw and her pulse square against the crux of him that held his heart. Meredith's dark hair bunched beneath his chin, its texture as fine and light as cashmere.

*Don't think of the other in Belle Fourche. Don't let this make you remember. Don't let it, or it'll chase you down in this place, too, sniff you out like a dog.*

Only once before had he seen lashes so close, so intricately wrought, like brunette lace against cheeks. And Meredith's face, the same flawless color as the china rose that sat at her bedside. As he carried her, she snuggled close against him, a woman in a protector's arms.

The innocent, subconscious motion, that motion alone, touched him deeply, blindingly. He felt as if he might never breathe again.

He laid her lengthwise on her bed, found a quilt to drape over her on the back of the rocking chair. He bent to remove her shoes, loosening the strings one eyelet at a time, until he could slip each sneaker effortlessly over her heel. As he wiggled each of them off, a shower of collected things fell out, wood chips and little rocks. He set her shoes on the floor by the chair, wiped the debris into his hand, carried it over to dump in the trash. Meredith shifted sideways, buttressing her neck and arms with the thin pillow.

Burr did his best to spread the coverlet evenly over the peaks and wanes, the helix, of her body. Tugging the quilt farther this way. No. Too far. Over that way. And all the while hating himself for his fear, hating that since what had happened in Belle Fourche, his hands felt rawboned and clumsy around a woman. He stood for a moment, watching her sleep, remembering how weightless she'd felt in his arms. He turned out her light, retrieved his pile of farming papers, and went outside to his cot in the barn.

Days went by, deep gray winter days, and despite the dormancy of the land, with each of them, Burr began to feel a sense of time rushing past. Now that he'd learned so much about planting, with each week he began to consider it more. *Soon it will be time to begin.*

Every snowstorm that moved in, Missus Trichak made a point to tell him. "This is just what we want, Burr. A deep snow that will lie long and keep the ground warm. Snow to leave the ground soaked when it melts away."

He gave up on the endless barbed-wire fences, because every time he started another length of fence, Meredith came bounding out to help. He began to sweep out the silo instead, using the shovel to edge the ancient grain up from the funnel-shaped floor. And he decided he'd found another job as endless as stringing fences. Every time he got a shovelful aimed to go out the door, half of it would fall out and roll to the bottom again instead.

Mid-January, and he drove to Big Horn Co-op to order new barley seed for Missus Trichak. He strolled through the door, tinkling the brass bell overhead, and found a gathering much similar to the one he'd found before, valley farmers sitting astride bags of grain, coffee cups in hand, shooting the breeze.

"Howdy," he said.

"Well, if it ain't Burr Colton, come to ask advice again." Several of them readjusted their stance atop their burlap bags. The farmer named Darby started right in with his moon theories again. "I hope you haven't scheduled your planting until the moon is waxing."

"You fellows getting ready to plant, too?" he asked, slinging one foot over his own bag and getting himself settled as though he belonged there.

"Yep. We're all thinking about it," someone answered. "This time of year, you always get antsy waiting for the snow to melt."

"Seems like you're making some progress out at the Trichak place," the fellow behind the counter noted. "Heard you borrowed Moley's plow. Didn't have to rent one from the implement dealer after all."

"Missus Trichak lent her combine to the Moleys a couple of times. Seemed like a fair trade."

A snort came from the back of the room. "From what I hear, she lent it out a half a century ago."

"Favors are favors," Burr said, straightening himself on the seed bag a little, sitting taller. "They don't go away."

None of them could sit still, they were all so curious about him. "You here on business this morning," somebody asked, "or just wandering in to shoot the bull?"

"Here on business. Too much work to be done out on the Trichak place to be coming to town and wandering."

"What sort of business you doing?"

"Well"—and here he faced the farmer named Darby—"is there a certain time of the moon in which I ought to be ordering my seed grain? Don't want to do it today unless you tell me it's right."

Darby sucked on his bottom lip and thought hard for a minute. He shook his head. "Off the top of my head, can't think of one rule that applies."

Burr turned back to the counter. "I'm here to order Missus Trichak's seed, then."

The proprietor got out an order form, poised his pen. "What kind of seed would you like?" The whole roomful leaned forward on seed bags the way folks leaned forward on theater chairs when an exciting scene was coming.

Burr said, "I'll have Gallatin barley seed. Figure I'll need a hundred pounds per acre out there. Trichak's got eighty acres under the plow. Figure that adds up to eight thousand pounds of Gallatin seed grain."

They all looked just a little bit disappointed, as though in some way he'd spoiled their fun.

"You been studying up somewhere?" somebody asked.

"Been conferring with experts," he answered.

"Let's see . . ." The proprietor started punching numbers into a calculator. "That'll be—"

"I figured $16.53 per a hundred pounds."

The proprietor made several notes with his pencil. "You figured right. To the penny. Here's the total, plus tax."

Burr stood from the bag, walked to the counter, and picked up his receipt. "Be back to pick up my seed grain in mid-February," he said, and he headed for the door.


On the farm and shoveling out the granary again, a whole shovel out, old grain rolling back in. Burr Colton leaned in the doorway of the corrugated metal cylinder, staring out over a steel gray sky and furrowed land that seemed to disappear at the edges, the same color as the sky.

He shoved his glove in the pocket of his secondhand coat and fluttered the edges of the sales receipt from the Big Horn Co-op. With Meredith's help, he'd ordered the right kind of seed, the right amount at the right price.

*With Meredith's help.*

Burr leaned his head against the corrugated metal and shut his eyes against the sky. Every time he closed his eyes, he thought of the feel of her asleep in his arms, the way her head had crooked against his arm and made him feel like her protector.

And every time he reveled in the feeling of touching Meredith, the old fear, the hated dishonor, returned. He was taking the stand in his own defense again, recognizing the line of accusing faces filling the courtroom, trying to make people he'd known his entire life see past the accusations.

The combine and tractor sat against the metallic winter sun, its shadow a hazy gray coming toward him, every sickle and wheel and cog looking different to him from the way it had before, each horizontal line drawn dark and pronounced with snow. As harebrained as that Mr. Harvey Keller's ideas had been, Burr figured this was as good a project as any to keep himself busy and away from Meredith until it came time to start plowing again. He'd discovered the key hanging on a nail beside the barn door, tagged with a bead key ring and a paper inserted into a thick slab of plastic. In scribbled pencil it read "Case 1938."

Burr brushed snow off the contoured iron seat, climbed up, and inserted the key into the ignition. He turned the key and stepped on the starter. Nothing happened. He went to the silo and retrieved the broom. He swept off the combine and the rest of the tractor, feeling snow veiling through the air and melting against his skin.

Meredith wouldn't remember how she'd moved against him, how she'd shifted close into his arms when, since the trial, everyone he'd known had pulled away.

He swept out a hollow in the snow and situated a tarpaulin he'd brought over it. He burrowed into the snow, felt the cold sun on his face, felt the ice freezing his buttocks, and he decided it'd have to do.

*If Meredith knew about it, she'd pull away, too.*

Burr found some amount of solace in the feel of the tools in his hand, the steel unbendable and cold, a raw extension of a man's own muscle. He whaled into first one bolt and then another, each of them welded into place by years of dirt and chaff and rust. Nothing would budge, no matter how hard he forced. He'd have to try a different method.

With sheepskin-gloved hands, he fiddled with the oil cups. He took the wrench to one, bared his teeth, and got it disconnected. He found it empty. He checked several belts and found them brittle. They'd snap the minute they moved.

He checked the sickle bar, the blades, the tractor carburetor. He poked and jabbed in what seemed like a hundred different places inside the greasy carriage.

Once he'd made the decision to tear the thing apart, Burr felt urgency overtake him. He strode to the barn to retrieve an oil bucket and carried it

grimly back to the field. He went after the wing
nut with pliers, once, twice, three times before it
finally gave way. He took off his glove and finished the job with bare fingers. Oil began to run
down his arm while he unscrewed the cap. He
watched while it drained in a silent stream.

"Burr?" Even though she'd said his name softly,
it made him jump and stab his hand on something. "You're tinkering with the combine? You
still think you can make it run again?"

He yanked out his hand. Blood began to ooze
evenly from a gash on the back of his knuckle.

"Oh, no. You've cut yourself. Let me see." She
reached in to take his hand.

"No." He yanked it back from her. "Don't." He
put his fist to his mouth, sucked off blood, and
tasted oil, too.

"Don't what? Don't touch you?"

He focused on making one revolution per bolt,
concentrating on getting the oil pan off evenly.
How was he supposed to answer a question like
that?

*Don't make me want to be a part of your life,*
*Meredith. Because you'd never want to be a part of*
*mine. You're bringing something of me alive that it's*
*best if I let die.*

"Just busy down here, is all," he lied, gazing up
at the undercarriage of the tractor as if it were the
most fascinating thing he'd ever examined in his
life. "This thing needs gaskets. Needs a battery,
too."

When he finally did glance in her direction, he
saw in her eyes a measuring of him, a calculating

of him. She said, "Grandma told me you ordered Gallatin seeds down at the co-op."

"I did." In frustration, he ran his fingers over his face. Only then did he remember that he had oil all over his hands and he'd probably just made himself look like some sort of exotic zebra. "Ought to thank you for that. Meredith, I found out everything I needed to know to help your grandmother. I couldn't've gone any further without what you did."

"All the same"—she knelt on all fours and peered closely beneath the huge metal wheels at him— "you're keeping away from the house. Grandma said you'd told her you wouldn't come in for lunch today. Or supper, either."

"Don't know why you think I'm staying away from the house. Tried to tow this rig and get it into the barn, but it's so heavy I couldn't get it to budge."

"Is it me you're staying away from? If you aren't staying away from the house, is there a reason you're trying to stay away from me?"

From upside-down where he lay, Burr unwadded a piece of paper from his pocket, pulled out a pencil, and wrote, "gaskets" and "tractor battery." "Why would I do a thing like that?" he lied. He shoved the paper into his pocket again, felt it wrinkle.

# 13

Mid-February, and the plowing began all over
again. The sun flared down upon the fields
without much warmth, but the nights didn't
plummet any longer. The clouds moved in overhead; everything on the farm felt moist and rich.

Snow melted almost as quickly as it fell, the
water running in rivulets between the furrows.
Fiona requested that Meredith begin to hang the
sheets on the line on Thursdays again. Burr
drove the truck to the Big Horn Co-op, signed
off on the Trichak account, brought home eight
thousand pounds of barley seed, and stacked it
in the barn.

Almer Moley and Burr traded off days on the
plow. Almer plowed his place Monday. Burr plowed
Missus Trichak's place Tuesday. Almer plowed
Wednesday, Burr Thursday. Between the two of

them, they prepared the soil on both farms immediately after the first thaw.

For the disking, Burr used the old disk plow that had been kept stored away in the barn, the plow Fiona Trichak had sat upon when she'd first offered him this job. The disks severed deep into the soil, knifing away clumps of roots and clods and furls. Burr and Almer each took their turns with the whirlybird spreader from Simplot, fortifying the dirt with nitrogen. When the land was ready to roller harrow, Burr began that, too, smoothing the soil to receive the seeds.

"It's like a romance," Fiona said one afternoon while she and Meredith walked the rutted front road. They'd both taken to walking out more, had gotten used to whistling and finding Cy trotting beside them, the dog's wet, heart-shaped nose raised to the level of a glove.

"Romancing the dirt," Meredith said, almost sadly. Getting it ready for—"

"Insemination."

"Grandma!"

"It's why men love planting time so much," Fiona said broadly. "It's like sex for them."

"Grandma."

"Don't you see? The land is for giving birth, a continual process. Farming's always been that way. The animals reproduce. The fields reproduce. It's the closest thing a man could ever do to bearing children."

"But it all has to die to work, doesn't it?" Meredith asked, catching her jist. "The land has to be harvested. The animals have to be sold off or eaten."

Fiona took her granddaughter's hand and they swung arms as they made their way to the house. "That's the way it is, child. The woman is the only thing on the farm that never ceases. From sunup to sundown. What did Ray used to say? Something like 'Joy in springtime, companion in summer, worker in autumn, comforter in winter. From baby to baby, something to show for it instead of selling it away—'" She took the first step to the porch, and suddenly she didn't seem quite so merry anymore. Her feet paused on the steps. She seemed to have journeyed. Meredith wondered if she was thinking of that little boy named David.

"Grandma?"

More often lately, Fiona drifted away to a place that left a gentle, sad expression on her face. When Meredith raised her voice these days, it wasn't so much to make Fiona hear as it was to capture her attention from someplace far away.

"Oh, I'm daydreaming again, aren't I? Sorry. It's awful when you remember things from so many years back and can't remember what blouse you wore yesterday." She looked suddenly weary, as if she'd been on a long hike instead of just to the cattle guard and back. She patted her granddaughter's hand and squeezed it. "I'm going up for a catnap if you don't mind."

"I don't mind. I'll do some studying and get lunch ready."

"And take something to the field for Burr? He's said he isn't coming in again."

"I'll take something to the field for Burr." *I'll*

*take him a sandwich and I'll hand it to him and I'll walk away without saying much. Because, for some reason, that's what he wants from me.* "Go on up and have a good sleep."


Meredith rang up her father at the office while Fiona took her catnap and the cheese dogs baked in the oven.

"Dad. Hello."

"Why have you gotten me at the office? Is it an emergency? Is your grandmother okay?"

"No, it isn't an emergency. Yes, Grandma's okay."

A silence at the end of the line and a little pop, when Meredith knew for certain Michael'd lit a cigarette and taken a deep draft. "You frightened me for a moment, calling me at the office like this, Meredith. I thought it might be bad news."

"I've been wondering something ever since Christmas, something I was hoping you could shed some light on."

"We didn't come because we couldn't get plane tickets."

"This is something different altogether."

From her end of the line, Meredith could hear a door opening, a whispered question, a whispered response from her father. "I've got a meeting in a few minutes," Michael told her. "Something I was preparing for."

"Don't hang up. This won't take a minute." She felt slightly underhanded, calling about a thing like this. "Unless I drive into town and use a pay phone, I never have a chance to call and ask you questions when she doesn't hear."

His interest perked up a bit. She heard it in his voice. "What?"

"Can you tell me about that little boy, David?"

And the longest pause of all. "David? Who said anything about David?"

"When we decorated the Christmas tree, Burr found an ornament with his picture on it."

Meredith heard his chair creaking and imagined him leaning forward, snuffing the cigarette out again, half-smoked. The edge to his voice made Meredith uneasy. "Well, she slipped up, didn't she? I can't believe there's a picture of David left anywhere in that house. I thought she got rid of all of them."

"Dad?"

"Meredith, I have to go. There's nothing I can tell you. Do yourself and your grandmother a favor and forget you ever heard anything about David. Mother's getting so elderly, isn't she? Please. It's best at this point to let sleeping dogs lie."


Burr drove in proudly one morning with the grain drill, a perfectly engineered contrivance that bored seeds at regular intervals into the ground. The operation was precise but simple, hundreds of pounds of seed grain loaded into a hold and dispersed methodically two inches apart, followed by a cloak of thin chains that wobbled back and forth of their own accord, filling each hole with loose dirt from the furrows.

Burr checked the phase of the moon just to be sure. It was waxing. Darby What's-his-name would approve. He worked acre for acre, hour for hour, the machine's touch upon the soil so unequivocal and vague that only if you knew what you looked for could you tell if a field had been planted.

In a fit of zeal, Meredith went with Fiona to church and they made a game of sorting fields as they fanned past neighboring turn rows. "That one's planted." From Meredith.

"That one, too." From Fiona.

"Not planted."

"Not planted, too. Merciful heavens. I'll ask Muriel today why they haven't finished. They don't hurry and get their seed in the ground this week, they'll get caught in next year's freeze."

"There's another one. Not planted."

"You're wrong. See the patterns in the dirt? That's planted."

The church service, thank heavens, was not unbearably long. By the time they returned to the house, they found Burr carting old rusty things out of the barn, throwing out rakes and shovels with broken handles, pitching hay bales to one side as if they were hotel pillows.

"What are you doing now?" Meredith slammed the truck door twice because it had trouble closing.

He seemed as disconsolate as a boy who'd been left behind by a playmate, or an artist who'd completed a masterpiece. "Nothing. Because there's nothing left to do."

"Oh, Burr." Fiona rushed at him and hugged

him. "It's finished, isn't it? Eighty acres of it all planted."

"Yes, ma'am." He took his hat off for her and turned the brim. He'd taken to wearing his Stetson again just as soon as the weather had gotten warmer. "Took the grain drill back this morning. There's nothing left now except fix more fences and wait for rain."

On other farms in Melody Flats, they irrigated. "No need to do that," Fiona assured Burr. "It'll rain. It always rains in April. I know this country. I promise you one of those slow, deep soakers. Not a hard rain that makes a crust."

"How can she not worry about the rain?" Burr asked Meredith one evening when she'd come out to bring him his supper. "There's so much at stake. All the money she's put in. All the time and effort on this crop. How can she stop now and just *trust?*"

"Maybe it doesn't matter that much. It's her last crop, after all."

"But that's it, too, don't you see? It's her last crop. If that barley doesn't sprout on time, she'll never have the chance to do it again."

Meredith handed him his plate through the door. "Here's your supper."

"Thanks." He opened it a little wider and took it. Then, "You want to come in for a minute?"

"Into the barn? I didn't think you wanted me around."

*I didn't. I don't. Oh, but I've missed you. After being on this farm, I'm out of practice at being alone.*

"I've got it cleaned up a bit now, is all."

Meredith stepped inside, bundled her sweater tighter around her shoulders as if she felt the need to hang on to something. The guitar case sat propped against the wall by his cot. She pointed at it. "You been playing that guitar a lot?"

He nodded. "I have been. Keeps me company out here, you know?" He peeled a splinter from one of the unplaned old beams for lack of anything better to do. "Don't know as I ever said a proper thank-you for going to that store and getting my guitar back."

"You did. You did when you were playing for us on Christmas night."

Back to the barley and Missus Trichak again. Safe subjects. "Maybe when you get as old as Missus Trichak is," Burr said, "you see things happen over and over so many times, you don't question them anymore. Maybe that's a kind of faith I never thought about before."

"There are plenty of elderly residents in Melody Flats who believe in irrigating."

"Almer does." Burr had finished his supper. He set his plate aside so she could take it when she returned to the house. "He's soaking those seeds right now."

They each sat on a separate cot, he with his boots set firm and square like the legs of a chair, she with her ankles crossed, slender as a Thoroughbred's hooves.

"Grandma wants everything to be the same as it used to be. Guess that's more important to her than anything. It's why she still hangs the laundry on the line—"

She entwined her fingers and stowed them between her knees.

He braced his forearms on his thighs and studied something interesting on the mattress.

From the corner of the barn came the scuffling of a field mouse running over last autumn's leaves. A big-horned owl landed on the roof above them with a thud and a wieldy flapping of wings. Pure moonlight filtered in between warped boards, no rain clouds in sight.

He groped for a topic of conversation. "Still been working on that combine when I get the chance." He looped two forefingers together. "Even chucked a rock at it, that old thing made me so mad."

"Bet you've been doing more than throwing rocks. Bet you've been cussing at it, too."

He looked at her with new regard. "You're getting to know me pretty well, aren't you?"

"I am."

Only she couldn't figure out why he stayed away, and what was wrong between them. She felt electricity humming whenever he stood close. She recognized it in the way he colored faintly when she surprised him, in the way he never met her eyes when he spoke but always found something interesting on the wall or on the floor.

"You ought to hear what I've done to the combine." Like what he was doing now, ticking off things on his fingers instead of meeting her with his eyes. "Put new plugs in all the way around. Filled it up with gas. Put in new gaskets all the way around. Put in a new battery. And WD-40'd everything that moves. I've come to the conclusion that fellow was an idiot to offer good money for a junk heap like that."

"Why do you keep working on it, then?"

She had him there. He couldn't very well say, "I keep working on it because it's the farthest thing away from the house and you." Instead he said, "Maybe because it's the same thing to your grandmother as the irrigating. A way to get things back to what they used to be. I don't know, maybe if I'd do better at it, if I could get it inside a garage, or had an extra set of hands to take the bearings apart—"

Too late, he realized the door he'd opened. She said hopefully, "I could be an extra set of hands."

"You?"

"I could fix Hallie Antelope's arm. Maybe I could fix a combine, too. I'd help," she said, forcing the issue, "if you wanted me around."

The sun warmed the turn rows at the Trichak farm, and no rain fell. Cracks began to splay across the coffee-colored dirt. Land carefully turned by plow, cut by disk, and smoothed by roller harrow began to lump up, dry out, and blow away.

"Almer's already got sprouts coming," Burr told Meredith as he maneuvered the socket wrench inside the tractor and freed the closest bolt. "So do the McMurtrys, just across the way."

"I know." She scooted with her elbows and climbed farther beneath the tractor. "Saw it yesterday morning when I took Grandma to the clinic for her checkup."

"I should've talked to her. I should've tried to convince her to irrigate. Never mind the money, Meredith. If she'd've been willing to sell this old rust relic, she'd've made enough profit to water her land."

"No wonder the combine won't run, with you calling her names like that every time you get the chance. Where do you want me to hold the flashlight?" She beamed it directly at him.

"Not in my eyes, if you don't mind."

She shimmied the light all over before he knocked on the oil pan with a pair of pliers. "Here. Shine it here."

"How's this?"

"Perfect. Would you help me with these fittings? With just one hand, reach in and grab hold. Right there."

"Here?"

"Yep." She grabbed, and in no time her hands were as oily as his. "Now." He pitched the pliers toward her. "See that bolt on your side? See if you can work it loose. Once you get it to the point you can unscrew it with your fingers, we'll lower the sides of the pan at the same time."

She laid down the flashlight and used both hands for leverage. The bolt loosened. Not until the pan began to slip sideways did Meredith realize she had it off balance. The pan began to topple and fall. He grabbed her right wrist and guided it where it should be, smack in the center. "There. Keep your hand right there. It works best if you'll support it like this."

Their greasy fingers slid together, entwined like

the teeth on a comb. Late afternoon sounds, spring sounds, the incessant dripping of water, the treble cry of a red-winged blackbird, the pipe song of a distant meadowlark, encircled them in the brittle grass. Although the sun delivered the spring's first gentle warmth, the soil lay still holding winter's chill beneath them, an indolent cool that would remain long after the fleabane and the clicking grasshoppers and the earthworms laid their summer claim.

He dropped her hand faster than a hound dropped a porcupine, his ears coloring faintly.

Burr's grip had left an interesting bracelet of grease where he'd first seized her arm, black daubs on the knobby bones of her wrist. He swallowed. Hard.

"Sorry. Didn't mean to do that." And he thought her voice sounded ragged, too. "Won't let that pan fall again."

"Wouldn't want to lose anything in the grass. No loose bolts or cotter pins or anything."

"No," she agreed. "We surely wouldn't."

He focused on the fascinating underpinnings of the tractor. He pried loose a length of metal and rolled it between his thumb and forefinger. "Looks like something got really hot."

He held it over so she could see it, then secured his wrench on the bearing bolt. When it didn't loosen easily, he hammered the wrench with the butt of his hand. The bearing came off and the connecting rod, too. This is my last try with this," he said. "The Case dealer found a replacement lying on a back shelf. If it won't fit this model, he said I could file something down. This is the piston. See? It runs up into the cylinder like this."

She handed back the part he'd disassembled very carefully, making certain as he took it that their fingers didn't touch. He reinserted it, and Meredith saw the new piece swing with ease. He wouldn't have to file anything at all. He jiggled something else and quickly began tightening.

She sensed, as he squared up the bolt holes this time, an urgency in him that had never been there before. "Just might work this time," he said with each revolution. "Just might happen." She laid down the light and moved in to hold the pan for him without being asked. He picked up the flashlight and played its beam over the ground, making sure they hadn't left spare parts around.

With strange assurance, Burr showed her where to dump jugs of fresh oil in the motor. He showed her where to inspect the gasket for leaks. He showed her how to check the compression of the piston and how to wiggle the blades on the header to make sure it was ready to spin.

"Now. Let's see what she'll do." He crawled up into the seat and put a foot on the starter. The starter buzzed. The motor jostled once, twice, then quit.

"Darn," Meredith said, giving up already. "After all that work, I thought it might stand a good chance of going."

"Shh. Wait." He held up one hand, and he'd gone pale as the foam over on Ocean Lake. "Before, it's never gotten far enough to shake. She sounds different, Meredith. I'll swear, the old thing sounds like she almost caught."

"Maybe you're hearing things." But Meredith ran to his side. Perhaps. Perhaps. Suddenly she was just as excited as Burr, after all the months of work, thinking he might've heard the engine start to grab.

"Please," he whispered to the combine, almost not daring to hope. He went through the routine much slower and more deliberately this time, turning the key, stepping on the starter. The machine huffed and chuffed, once, twice, came harder.

"Burr?" Meredith stood beside him, not realizing she'd gone ahead and clutched his leg. "It's going to go, isn't it? Isn't it?"

"I think so," he whispered. "I think so." The engine rattled. It sputtered and caught. Cylinders spit and thundered to life. Blue smoke puffed from the exhaust pipe. For the first time in sixty years, the motor had turned over. Burr sat astride it like a soldier returning from war on a tall horse, his chin lifted, letting it idle, listening to the beautiful standard of the plugs making their rounds. After the first two or three revolutions, the engine wasn't even missing.

"See if she'll move forward," Meredith hollered. "See if we'll be able to do the harvest with her."

He nodded down at her. For the first time in sixty years, Burr moved the gearshift forward and Fiona's old tractor slipped from neutral into first gear. The massive farm machine lurched forward and seemed to crawl over the ground, heavy wheels biting into the dirt.

"You did it, Burr. You made the thing run. We can surprise Grandma this summer. We can bring her out and give her a ride."

He jumped off almost before he'd gotten it parked, too overwhelmed by the miracle of the combine to think of anything else. And when he saw the drops running down her cheeks, he'd thought maybe she was crying until he felt something on his hand, too, and his shoulder, and his nose, and he glanced up at the sky to see the rain.

Sometime while they'd been working beneath the combine, somber clouds had silently crept in over the valley. They hung low against the mountains, the sort of clouds that let you see a rainstorm from a distance like a tattered curtain blowing past or a petticoat that barely brushed the land in a waltz. Burr and Meredith stood together for a moment and looked up at the sky. Water began to pelt their faces, penny-size drops, cold and thick. From somewhere far away, thunder rumbled and echoed off the Wind River Mountains much closer by. "It's going to be a good rain," he said. "A good soaker, not a hard one that forms a crust."

She looked at him, and this time he knew it for sure. Her eyes were watery. "You said Grandma would know. You said it was a sort of faith."

The days and weeks of running away, the times he'd convinced himself that needing folks hurt him worse than not needing them, the parts of his spirit that had become so entwined with grief and defeat, so distorted and grim, that he'd had no way to find his way out of them, these didn't matter in the least as he stood next to Meredith and the rain splattered their faces.

He did the unthinkable.

Burr drew her against him and soaked up the feel of her the way the soil soaked up the rain, the way a parched man drew water and slaked his thirst. She came into his arms gladly, triumphantly, reveling in the heat of his body and the clamoring of his heart next to her own.

His shirt hung in wet folds over his chest.

Her hair hung in wet ribbons down her cheeks.

She splayed her hand wide against his shirt buttons. He splayed his hand wide against the rivets of her jeans pockets.

Rain dropped off his lashes and dripped from her chin, wove through their fingers as they touched each other's skin.

Gray eyes locked on green. One stood straddle-legged and square, his legs planted firm as the legs of a chair. The other stood on tiptoe so she could gain full purchase within his embrace. Burr inclined his mouth down toward hers. Meredith lifted her face toward his. Wet lips sought wet lips. One tongue delved for the other and danced when it found its mark.

"Burr Colton. Who would've thought . . ." She whispered his name against his mouth as eagerly as if she were a little girl wishing. She brought up his one hand from between them and spread his wet, rough-hewn fingers. She made a bowl of their hands together, as if their hands intertwined could hold the fullness of what she'd begun to feel for him. He accepted her touch, closed his eyes,

found her hands and his need, her spiritual doctoring, too compelling to deny. And she traced
the leathery folds of his hand with her own
thumb, laid the callused pads of his hand against
her cheek, cradling his work-worn fingers gently
there.

# 14

That night, Burr Colton lay in his cot and listened to the light, soaky rain skittering on the new barn roof, the fire gone out in the stove, his guitar packed away in its case. Every time the wind came up, he imagined it might be Meredith, come to the barn to find him. Every time the rain came harder or the door creaked and the old barn shifted or Cy lifted her head, Burr lifted his head, too.

When he wasn't imagining sounds he was staring at the rafters above him, the old ones and the new ones, thinking how hopeless it seemed that the rotten wood would collapse soon and the two beams he and Almer'd replaced would remain.

As he stared at the decaying wood over his head, he felt as weatherbeaten and detestable as the primitive lumber he'd tended. No matter what he'd tried to do, no matter how much he'd tried to repair, he was like this wood on the barn and the fenceposts that lined the lane, rotten and worm-eaten underneath, falling away.

*You never should've let it happen.* His mind became its own living thing, roaring at him, indicting him. *You never should've touched her.*

He lay on that cot, staring at the pine knots on the fresh beams above him, remembering how it'd felt kissing her and needing her and watching her hands as she'd gently doctored up that little girl.

He thought how being on Missus Trichak's place had made him feel hopeful again. How it'd made him start wanting things.

Things he didn't deserve.

And he thought of the work left to do after the seeds started to sprout, the insecticiding, the weeding, getting the equipment ready, the harvest. All this time, too, he'd planned on painting Missus Trichak's porch when the weather turned nice. Last week, he'd even talked to a co-op fellow who'd said he'd stop by and maybe contract for a price on Missus Trichak's grain.

All this, and he'd gotten himself a schedule to live by, apportioned his days in cadence with the seasons, always making plans of what he might accomplish tomorrow.

"Shouldn't've trusted me," he wanted to rail out at Missus Trichak, the lady who—for some unknown reason—had offered both faith in him and friendship.

"Shouldn't've trusted me," he wanted to shout to Meredith, who'd been right from the beginning, who'd told her grandmother he could be someone who could hurt them, whom they ought to order away.

*You'll find out about me and you'll be like the others. You'll find out what I've done and you'll want me gone.*

Damn, but he ought to leave now.

It'd be simple enough. He could go into the house, take something. One of those gold chains off Meredith's dresser or money from the drawer. Just like he'd taken the money from the motel room in New Mexico.

Burr hadn't any idea what time that night he finally fell off to sleep. He didn't have a clock in the barn to go by, only the sun and the moonlight and the awful emptiness grinding in his stomach. Could be he went all night and didn't sleep at all. He shut his eyes and tried to drift off, and he was taking the stand in his own defense again, recognizing the line of accusing faces that filled the courtroom.

His own mother sat on the third row.

The lawyer's question, "Did you, Burr Colton, knowingly invite Miss Susan Maplehold to accompany you to a movie on the night of Friday, November seventh?"

His answer, "Yes, I did."

The lawyer's question, "Is it true that you've returned to Belle Fourche on several occasions to see Miss Maplehold? To try to convince her to come with you?"

His answer, "I have."

"And when you initiated sexual advances on

Miss Susan Maplehold in her bedroom on Friday, November seventh, did she tell you that she wanted you to stop at that time?"

"She . . . I—"

"Objection, Your Honor. Leading the witness."

"Sustained. Don't answer that question, Mr. Colton."

No matter who jumped to his protection, the one person who should have and didn't, the one who'd mattered most and had kept her place stoically in the third row, had been his own mother.

He'd focused on her during his entire testimony, as if instead of having to defend himself to a room full of people, he had to defend himself only to her. *Guilty as charged*, her eyes screamed at him the entire time he clenched the witness chair for leverage. *That boy takes right after his father.*

Before daybreak, he watched through the ancient knotholes in the barn wood while the velvet darkness faded to the cool watercolor blue of early morning.

He got up, folded his extra clothes, laid them in the box with his comb and his contorted toothbrush. He wrapped up the old cigar box in one of the shirts. He pulled out the sack of dog food from beneath his cot and tucked away Cy's bowl. He hefted the guitar case and glanced once around the barn.

It had taken him less than five minutes to pack up everything he owned.

Stealthily he carried the box and the guitar case and piled them inside the Jeep. He instructed Cy to jump in. He stood for a moment, the driver's door open and the keys in the ignition, giving off their little hum, taking stock of the wet fields that surrounded the farm. He imagined he saw a tinge of green. He'd accomplished most of what she'd wanted him for. The fields were harrowed and planted. Nothing left much for the seeds to do. And the combine was running, although she didn't know.

Maybe he'd go inside and say something to Missus Trichak, something awful that would make her let him go. Or he thought about the money in the junk drawer. He needed extra money. He hadn't saved anything. For some crazy reason, he'd been thinking he might stay.

Burr left Cy in the Jeep, opened the screen door, and started for the junk drawer. Silently he slid open the drawer. The money was gone. Nothing left except a packet of gum, a handle to one of the kitchen pans, and assorted screws and thumbtacks. He hadn't decided what he'd do if he actually found any money. He rummaged around, making certain it was gone.

And then he heard Missus Trichak's voice.

"This is always how it is with you, isn't it?"

She stood in the shadow of the stairwell, a stack of dollar bills in her hand, the money from the drawer. She'd been expecting him.

"I've known this about you ever since we talked that first morning at breakfast. You stick around one place just long enough to start proving to yourself that you might be worth something. Then something always happens to make you think you're protecting somebody else if you'll make them push you away."

He eyed the fistful of dollars, his heart pummeling because, when it came down to this part of it, he always knew what he could expect to happen. He said, "I was gonna steal all that money from you."

"Ten dollars? Like hell you were. You wouldn't've done anything like that to me."

Burr couldn't believe Missus Trichak had said a word like "hell." He froze where he stood.

She said, "I can see what's happening as clear as I can see the nose on my face. I didn't just fall off the turnip truck yesterday, Burr Colton. You're running from something, something that caring for people brings out in you, something that makes you scared."

"You think I've started caring about people here?" he asked defiantly.

"You've started caring about Meredith." No "think" involved. She'd seen them skirting each other like brown bats skirted the light. She wasn't blind.

"It's better this way, don't you see? It's better if I leave with her thinking I was somebody I wasn't, than with her finding out who I really am."

"Could be different from that," Missus Trichak said. "Could be we're the ones who see who you are, and not the other way around."

"You don't know," he said. "You don't know how bad it is, or what I've done."

"No, I don't know."

She stepped toward him and laid the pile of

bills back in the drawer, daring him with her eyes to take them.

"And don't think there wasn't any way of me finding out. Our Dinwoody Municipal Library carries every issue of the Belle Fourche newspaper. I could've gone and looked it up any time I'd wanted if I'd've gotten nosy enough. But I'm not. And it doesn't matter, anyway. I've lived long enough not to give up on people, to know that it doesn't matter a fidget what other folks say."

"You don't want me around here, Missus Trichak. Your granddaughter's been right about me all along."

"Are you wanted, Burr? Are they after you to throw you in jail?"

He squared his chin. "Not anymore."

"But you're still running away."

He didn't answer that question. His Jeep was all packed and Cy was waiting in the front seat. That seemed evidence enough.

"You mustn't run," she said. "You must give Meredith the chance to accept or deny."

"It doesn't matter what happens between us. She's got her whole life ahead of her. She's going back to school. To be a doctor."

"And you? Where are you going?"

He plopped down hard on the chair and buried his face in his hands. "Nowhere. Fast."

And here she stooped beside him, the skin on her face as fragile and old as papyrus, when she made him lift his face. She lopped one old hand over his knee. And when she spoke, he couldn't know it, but she spoke as much to herself as to him, and to a young girl she'd known forever ago, a girl who'd entrusted her with a tiny son, Kay Lee Wilkins. "You got to learn that no matter what you're running from, once sorry is enough. There isn't a need to rise up every morning repenting for the same thing you repented for yesterday." *I should've raised him to be a man, Kay Lee. I should've watched David closer. I should've never let him out of my sight once you entrusted him to my care.*

*I'm sorry, Kay Lee. I'm so sorry.*

Burr didn't understand why tears splayed from the old woman's eyes. "It's taken me a whole lifetime to let myself be forgiven. Don't want to see that happen to you, too."

He gripped both of her feeble hands, trying to figure out how on earth she'd understand something like he felt.

"No matter how sorry you were, Burr, or what you did that was wrong, you've got to find a way to get on. You've got to find a way to fight yourself through."

"I could've changed it, though."

"That's the most awful part, always thinking you could've done something different, isn't it?"

"Yes," he said, still sitting on her kitchen chair, his fists clenched over her hands, the skin over his knuckles white and stiff as leather, tears starting to drip down his face, too. "Yes."

He sniffed and wiped his nose generously on the shoulder of his shirt. They held on to each other for the longest time, fingers intertwined, old ones and young, loving and forgiving, needing and giving, the present and the past. At long last she asked him the question she'd been longing to ask since he'd first walked into the dance.

"Will you tell me one thing, Burr? Will you tell me why you came to Melody Flats?"

He nodded. And then began his own story softly. "My grandfather wrote me a letter one day before he died."

"Your grandfather died?"

Burr nodded. "Just last month. Me and Cy were back there for the services. That's the only reason I'd ever go, was for him. Never went back after a while unless I had to. Never even stayed in my own house again, after the trial."

And Fiona said very softly, as if it might be too much to ask, "Do you mind if I see it? Do you mind if I read what he wrote?"

"I'll go get it. It's in the Jeep."

Outside, the sun had barely risen over the eastern fields and over Ocean Lake. A magpie landed on the railing of the porch, fluttering its wings in the first morning light, feathers so black as he ruffled them with his black beak that they sheened blue. Burr let Cy romp out of the front seat. He reached in for one shirt, unbundled it, and took out the cigar box where he kept his treasures.

"Here." He flipped open the toggle and pulled out a blue onionskin envelope. Fiona opened the flap, pulled out a letter written on blue onionskin paper, and unfolded it.

She didn't read it at first. She held the open paper in her hand as lightly as if she might be holding crisp butterfly wings. She inspected the script a long time before she began reading his words.

"Dear Burr," his letter read, "I have set these things aside so you, and only you, can have them when I'm gone. If you're reading this now, I know that time has come. I have not often had the time to tell you I was proud to have you as my grandson. You have much promise in your heart, promise that—because of your mother and father's confrontations—has never been allowed to surface and grow. Your mother is my daughter, Burr, and I do not always agree with things she has done. She has not always been right. But then, I have not always been right, either.

"You have been brave in my eyes, braver than I ever could be, because you have gone on a search that everyone could see. And I have always been on that same search, but kept it so people couldn't see. We are very much alike, you and me, and I wanted you to know that, and to know that I have found pleasure in it.

"The little hand-carved whistle is one a young boy gave me many years ago when I and your grandma Delia packed up and left a pastorate we served in a town in Wyoming called Melody Flats. Should you ever get the chance, I believe you should go there. It is in the central part of the state, I believe with a good paved road now that puts you within driving distance of the county seat of Riverton. I've watched it on the map from time to time and have wondered how it is growing. My whole life, I have searched to find something the same as what I found in that little town. But it was never to be again. A man leaves friends behind him, friends who have become such a vital part of his existence and such a vital support to his soul that there are times he feels that, without them, he has no breath, no fortitude, no courage. You might say, 'Well, Grandpa's a preacher. He ought to rely on God for those things.' But I believe God sends people along, too, to let us know that He is in His place.

"I may be an old man now, a codger and a fool. But I found something in my life there, very early on, when the timing wasn't exactly right. I believe you might go searching there now, and find what I found as well. And thus I leave you

"Your loving and proud grandfather,

"Pastor Charles Burleigh."

Fiona stood from the stoop and handed the letter back to Burr. "Are you named short for him? Burr short for Burleigh?"

Burr nodded.

"Well. How about that?" She slapped her hands against her knees and dusted them off, and he gave her a hand up. "There's your answer right there, isn't it? You'd best go unpack your Jeep before Meredith wakes up. And for me, guess it's time I got around to fixing breakfast."

When the barley fields on the Trichak farm began to sprout, Meredith had the feeling that she could stand in the middle of the dirt, looking over it, and could almost see a constant movement of the soil. Bent backs of greenery pushed their way up out of the darkness. Almost like animal activity, it was, the growth so noticeable that it reminded

Meredith of the raising up of something that had been asleep, the stretching of an arm, the nodding of a head, like the time-lapse films she'd seen in school, where everything seemed to be unnaturally sped up or slowed down.

She hadn't known what barley would look like. When it came, it was green, a good green like grass, first sending up one spear, then a second, until it became taller than grass and began to wave in the wind.

Folks from the co-op and other farmers from miles down the road took to stopping and shooting the breeze with Burr. "Crop looks real good, Burr," one said. "What sort of fertilizer did you say you put in? Know you've been conferring with experts, and I wanted to hear what they said."

"You been insecticiding much?" someone else asked. "Doesn't seem like you've got many bugs out in those fields."

Once, the farmer named Darby drove over. "Could tell driving by that you planted in the wax of the moon. Your foliage is greener than McMurtry's across the way. Taller, too."

As the days grew hot and the grain grew tall, Meredith noticed her grandmother watching whenever she was together with Burr. She said to Burr one day, "It's like she's watching us, waiting for something to happen."

"Maybe she's watching us for this to happen," he teased, and he bent over and carefully kissed her. "Or this," and he kissed her again. But that was just it. He'd gotten to where he kissed her often, took her hand, and touched her easily as they walked along. But never again had he held her so tightly against him, never again had he showed her with his embrace that he was broken and thirsty without her, that he'd give his soul to have her in his arms. That afternoon they'd gotten the combine running, the afternoon of the first rain, she'd thought about him loving her.

But she'd thought too soon, she decided.

In a different way he'd closed himself off completely from her, like a distracted parent who looked you in your eyes when you spoke but was thinking of something else. He still shielded himself from her. If she hadn't seen him so totally open, so totally exposed and selfless that afternoon, she would never have known.

The morning came when, together, they decided to surprise Fiona and give her a ride on the combine.

"Have we got a surprise for you, Missus Trichak," Burr said as he took her arm, his flannel shirtsleeve linked to her green polyester-clad one. "Something we'd like you to give us your opinion on, out beside the silo."

Fiona had been sewing again, never one for being long away from her machine, fabric book-covers for next year's church bazaar. "That way," she'd explained to Meredith earlier, "nobody'll be able to figure out whether you're reading a romance novel or the Bible."

"You want me to drop everything and come just like that?"

He snapped his fingers, knowing exactly how to treat her when she'd decided to be exacting. "Just like that. I'll drive you if you feel like riding. Or walk you all the way if you feel like walking."

"In that case,"—she patted his arm, a simple show of great possessiveness—"I'll come walking with you. You keep your hand on my elbow, Burr Colton, and I feel like I could walk clear into Melody Flats and back. I've never felt so fit as I do today."

"You look good."

She winked up at him, and he found himself endeared by the childlike fervor in her face. No matter what she said, these days she always seemed ready for adventure. "Being around you two young kids makes me feel good."

Cy waited for them on the front porch. As they stepped off down the rutted front driveway, the dog zigzagged beside them, stirring up dust on the road for a while, then going belly deep through the edging of tangled, broken grass. Every growing thing along the way wavered in the breeze and greeted them with summer-golden joy, the wheatgrass top-heavy with its beards, the goldenrod lining the ditch as far as the eye could see, like saffron ribbons.

It seemed Fiona couldn't help chuckling as they walked along. "Look at all this," she said. "And to think I'd given up after the years. Should've known better. Land doesn't deserve giving up on, does it? It always holds its own."

It seemed funny that he'd never noticed it, how each seed of each species came armed with some appliance of dispersal, so perfectly designed to escape and fly that he doubted a well-trained mechanical engineer could come up with anything close, much less better. Twisting darts and parachutes for the wind, miniature spears and hulls of tiny thorns, all waiting for the movement of animals or breeze, all waiting for the cuff of a man's trouser, the hem of a skirt, the trotting passage of a dog. "Look how well planned everything is. And we think we know what's best." Fiona stared into the crystal bowl sky as if she could see parts of yesterday and tomorrow all at the same time. "We think we can make decisions and change any of it. When everything is so finely ordered as the seeds." She picked a dandelion, blew at the fuzz, and watched as a hundred perfect-balanced pods lifted upward like so many paratroopers. She patted his arm again, gazing up at him with some concern. "Have you talked to her yet, Burr? Have you told her what it is inside you that's made you afraid?"

"No," he told Fiona. "Not yet." He understood that he must. But the deep fear remained, although it had become muted with Fiona's gentle ministering, less potent because it had been shared. "I'll tell her and she won't want me anymore." It was the first time he'd said it aloud to anyone. "I'll tell her and she'll want to send me away." *Not to mention what you'll think of it,* he could add.

"You give her a chance, Burr. That girl has a good head on her shoulders. You know that as well as I do."

"Yes, ma'am. I know."

Burr knew the moment they crested the hill when Fiona could see the combine. He and Meredith had parked it a ways from the granary at a different angle from where it had always been kept. He felt Missus Trichak stiffen beside him. He said easily, "There's the old rust relic now."

"It's been moved, hasn't it?"

"Yep."

"Has that Harvey Keller fellow been snooping around here again? I've already told him this combine isn't for sale. The nerve of him, walking in off the highway and expecting me to accept money from him while we sat around the table, enjoying dinner. And I've never heard of anything called the Midwest Old Time Thresher's Reunion."

"No. That fellow hasn't been back around. This is something much different."

But she'd become too maddened by the thought of Harvey Keller's return to hear Burr's gentle reassurance. The whole time she talked, her fingers moved through the air, fluttering like starlings. "To think he'd think he could cart off to Iowa a farm implement that shaped the entire farming history of Melody Flats, Fremont County."

"Hm-m-mm." Burr couldn't help it. He had to tease her a little bit. She came out as so cackly and hard about it, when he knew she got all soft and sentimental about that old piece of farm machinery. "If it's as important as you say, maybe you ought to donate it to a museum. Do something with it to make sure it never leaves this area. Seemed a good deal of money he offered you just so he could 'cart it off to Iowa.'"

"Is that what you're bringing me down here to show me? That you've moved my Case combine and gotten it free of the mud and mire so I can take it into the museum and get my name hung on a plaque? I don't want a plaque. I hate plaques. All plaques are good for is making somebody polish them."

"Not hardly. This isn't so you'll get a plaque." Burr couldn't stand it anymore, couldn't wait until she shared the secret that they'd been harboring. And at times, when the old machine had been balky, he'd wondered if they would ever get there at all. The ripening heads of barley threshed the air in constant, competing waves, catching the sun with their grain whiskers and changing, in one swift, ivory motion, to a deeper hue of apricot, a color he'd seen hinted at in dancers' gowns and in Wyoming sunsets. "It's still too early to harvest. But it's certainly not too early to get the combine out and take her for a dry run." At her blank expression, he kept up. "You know. Give it a couple of good turns around the field. To work the kinks out."

"What are you talking about?"

"The combine's working, Missus Trichak."

Meredith heard them coming and waved. He caught his breath at the sight of her, her eyes wide with the magic of the farm and its growing crop, her dark hair pulled back from her face with a pretty tortoise-shell barrette. Burr paused. He wanted to capture this one moment, this one sight of Meredith, and preserve it for always. If he never owned anything in his life, if he never did another bit of good, he would have this moment, this memory of Cy bounding ahead, the dog's body arcing through the barley to meet Meredith. Meredith cupped her hands around her mouth and shouted, "Thought you'd never get here. Took you long enough." Cy rolled over and poked all four legs in the air so she'd get a tummy rub.

"Meredith. Child." Fiona stood staring up at the combine the way she'd stare up at a replica of ancient bones. The lettering had almost gone off of it by now, but she could still make out where it had once read "Case" around the grain bin and along the sides of the massive straw racks. She laid one hand upon the steel flanks of its tractor and stroked it. "Who'd've thought . . ." She whispered the words, never taking her eyes off the huge farm apparatus. "Who'd've dreamed . . ." And then, as if she'd drawn herself back down into reality, she pivoted toward Burr and grinned at him. "Turn it on, would you? I'd like to hear the thing running again."

He grinned back and dusted his hands off on the backside of his jeans. "Not going to start it up just yet. Me and Meredith thought we'd get you sitting on it first. Thought we'd let you tarry a spell and have a look at the countryside."

"I'm an old woman, Burr Colton. I can't climb up on that thing. Now, that'd be a damn fool thing to do."

"Seems to me you've been telling us lots of stories about the damn fool things you've always pulled off."

She said pointedly, "Last fool thing I did was to invite some no-'count stranger into my house for a decent supper and a night's sleep." Then she grinned, a wide enthusiastic grin that reached clear into her eyes and beyond. She looked like a kid given her own choices in a candy store. "Oh, I'd love to get up on that thing. Seems to me, if I remember right, everything looks pretty good from that angle."

"Seems to me it's about time you refreshed your memory." Burr put his sheepskin work gloves together and made a stirrup of his hands, while Meredith supported one shoulder of her grandmother's and one hip. Cy leapt about their feet. Even the dog seemed to sense something unprecedented taking place. Fiona placed one foot on Burr's hands and tested him for sturdiness. She glanced at Meredith. "You ready?"

Meredith nodded. "Ready as we'll ever be. Go ahead, Grandma. I've been waiting to see this."

Fiona reached high, higher than Burr had guessed she could, and grabbed on to the huge metal steering wheel for leverage. "Okay. Here goes nothing."

She swung her leg up over the tractor with attack and style. She situated herself in the curved iron seat, her chin raised, her posture slightly military. She took in one sweeping view of the waving barley that surrounded her, her crop, and it could have been Ray's and David's and Michael's crop, too, as it grew rich and bounteous around her.

Fiona did not speak. She sat motionless, and with exuberance, taking in the whipping of the sheets on the line, the rustling of the birds and barley, all that one heard when one developed a liking, a subtle taste, for silence. She seemed to hear voices of wizardry, the land speaking. The wind lifted the grain heads and lifted Fiona's hair, lilting past as the barley performed a papery dance to its melody. Burr and Meredith saw she'd become transported by something far more powerful than earth and distance and time.

"Sh-hhh." Meredith touched Burr's arm when she thought he might speak. "Just let her be."

A whisper. "Thought she wanted to start up the engine."

"She will, in due time."

"I've never seen her quite like this. She's remembering, isn't she?"

Her remote expression had come again, that wistful sense of distance measured not by miles, but by time. She gazed beyond the fences to the dirt road, as if she saw Pontiacs and buckboards lining the way, as if remembrance of them brought her wisdom, and wisdom brought her strangely moving significance and peace. A whisper again. "Yes. She's remembering. And hanging on. This will have to last her a while."

As quickly as she'd journeyed, Fiona came back to them. She reached down with one hand and touched Burr lightly on the shoulder, as if to remind herself that he wasn't an apparition. She smiled at both of them, reassured, her eyes clear and calm. "I can see clear up the Riverton road from here." She took a long, deep draft of air. "Oh, and just smell the farm."

"I've developed a pretty good nose for dust myself." Burr reached a hand up to her. "You ready to drive it?"

"Drive it? Why, Meredith won't even let me drive my own truck."

Burr scrambled up on the platform behind her. "Turn the key. Step on the starter." He climbed onto the seat behind her as plugs fired, the carburetor sputtered, and the tractor started off. It lumbered forward in low gear along the ground, and all that was attached to the Case combine, the auger and the sieve and the sickle bar, bounced. Fiona took the steering wheel and promptly steered them toward the fence. She hit the brakes in a panic, jouncing them both, jostling the auger and the sieve and the sickle bar. Their heads jerked back. The combine pitched forward as she steered them safely around from the fence and into a gully instead.

She'd gotten all giggly. "Take the wheel." When he did, she covered her bosom with one widespread hand and couldn't stop laughing. "I'd've driven it clear over to Almer's place and mashed down the Moleys' chicken coop."

"I don't care a flip about Almer's chickens," Burr teased her, "but I have spent all winter rebuilding these fences. It'd be awful to watch you run a combine over those now."

Burr guided them back to the granary, turned off the key, and jumped off. But Fiona stayed atop the parked combine for a while, looking out over her land reborn. The Absarokas stood in the distance, great buttes against the sky, arrested in motion as if they'd once been gigantic rocky waves breaking over some prehistoric shore. He said to Meredith, "She looks good up on that thing, huh? She hasn't just been telling us stories. Makes me wish to have seen this place in its heyday. She belongs up there, Meredith."

Meredith said, "In its heyday, it couldn't have seemed better than this."

He didn't answer.

"Though I don't know what will end up being harder in the long run—growing this crop for her the way she's wanted, or having her leave now, when everything's producing the way it is. If we've made a mistake, it's that one. It's in not letting things stay dead the way they've been. It's in reminding her of how much she has to leave behind, right when it's come time for her to let it go."

"Yet, we've given it to her again. For one last time. That's how she looks at it, you know."

"If it was you"—Meredith broke off a stem of ripening barley, held it high so the grains reflected apricot light—"how would you have it?"

"Me?" And he knew the time had come, because of her question, to be brutally honest, to tell Meredith the truth the way he'd promised Fiona he would. He would tell her this now, and soon, maybe tonight when he got back from his errands, he would tell her the rest of it. She deserved that much, and he knew it. Fiona had convinced him. Meredith deserved to make her own choice.

"Would you want to go back to where you'd been one last time, to see it the best way it could be, before you left it completely?"

The wind blew her hair across both their faces, smooth as linen. Burr said, "Before now, there hasn't been any place I wanted to come back to."

# 15

Burr drove into town that evening to pick up the Simplot whirlybird fertilizer spreader again. When the car turned into the driveway that evening, Meredith and Fiona both thought it was Burr returning. Either that, or another farmer come to tell him he'd done a good job and ask advice. They came all the time now, turning off the highway and bouncing across the cattle guard in their trucks and cars at odd hours of the day and night, asking him about the moon and the fertilizer and the depth of plowing and what angle he'd driven the tractor when he'd roller harrowed.

But when the car pulled up and someone hopped out, it wasn't a farmer at all, but Evangeline Kew, chairman of the church bazaar committee, huffing and puffing as if she were an old artifact of a tractor herself. Fiona raised her arm to welcome her.

"Evangeline. What on earth are you doing out running around visiting at this time of night?"

Without preamble, Evangeline announced, "This isn't a pleasure visit, Fi. Get your suitcases, the both of you. Pack enough for an overnight stay. You'll be safe over at our place."

"What are you talking about? We don't need our suitcases. We aren't going anywhere."

Evangeline kept looking over her shoulder, as if a posse were following her. "Oh, yes, you are. Don't dawdle. I'm afraid he's right behind me. That dangerous, awful man."

Meredith asked, "What dangerous, awful man are you talking about, Mrs. Kew?"

"Oh, you don't know what a perilous position the two of you have been in, and all this time. Fi, that any of us ever allowed you to bring that man home with you in the first place. And you let him sleep in your guest bedroom upstairs. And the Hesters almost hired him, too. We ought to have run him out of Melody Flats that first night he was here. And the men would have if they had known."

Fiona stood now and placed a hand on her friend's shoulder. "Evangeline. If you'd just calm down—"

"I won't calm down about this. No one ever ought to be calm about a thing like this. An abomination to women, that's what he is. And to think he's been under our noses all along, living with two women in our very valley that were out here *alone*. To think we'd let this *happen*."

Perhaps the best way to figure out what Evangeline accused him off would be to try another tack. "How did you find out about this, Evangeline?"

"My cousin lives in Belle Fourche. Everyone there knows who he is and what he's done. During the trial, they ran his picture on the front page of every newspaper. They're on their way through Wyoming on vacation, spending time with us, and she was at the hardware store a while ago when he came in. She told me everything immediately. Please, Fi. Pack your suitcases quickly."

Meredith asked the question quietly, but Evangeline didn't hear her. "The trial? What trial was there?"

Fiona took Meredith's hand to silence her. She turned to Evangeline and said in a calm, clear voice, "He doesn't frighten us, Evangeline. He's told us all about it."

"He has? And you let him stay?"

"Of course we did. Look what good he's done around this place."

"But he was accused of *rape*." When she said the dreadful word, she let a whole rush of air come out with it. "A girl named Susan Maplehold. Of going into an innocent girl's bedroom and holding her down and *forcing* her—"

Fiona heard Meredith gasp. She held her granddaughter's hand tighter, tighter, past the point of pain, past the point when either of them could feel their fingers any longer. "Yes," Fiona lied calmly. "He told us." A pause. "And what does your cousin say about his conviction? Was he convicted of raping her, Evangeline?"

"No. He wasn't convicted. But you know how

those things are. Men are always getting off on technicalities, good lawyers who say the woman asked for it, things like that. My cousin said he probably got off because his grandfather was the preacher. And just to be *accused* of such a thing. Why, they say his own *mother* thought he was guilty at the trial."

Pinpricks of light turned in at the end of the driveway. Burr Colton's Jeep, towing the whirlybird fertilizer spreader. Fiona said, "Go in the house, Meredith."

"Grandma," Meredith whispered, shattered.

"Do as I say. Now."

Meredith went only inside the screen. She turned back, once inside, to hear what her grandmother had to say. Fiona turned to their irate, frantic guest.

"There is much injustice afoot in this world, Evangeline. There isn't a sure way to know who is guilty and who is innocent, who is telling the truth and who is lying. The court system, by all means, is not infallible. But we've been safe here with Burr Colton since the last harvest dance.

"If he'd wanted to take advantage of either of us, he could have done so many times. There's money, there's jewelry. And there have been two women here alone, one of them young and beautiful and kind, whom, God forbid, I may have placed in some sort of danger. Nothing here has been touched in dishonor since he arrived.

"You are a God-fearing woman, Evangeline. And Burr has got to start his life again some way, no matter how shattered it has become. Grant the man that one dignity, if you please."

But it was too late for that now. Burr pulled up to the barn and hopped out of his Jeep unsuspectingly while Evangeline stood between them. The dog, too, jumped to the ground.

Evangeline turned to face Burr, her teeth bared with the same hateful effect as a wolf facing another over fallen game. "They won't come with me to safety no matter what I say," Evangeline warned. "If anything happens to them tonight, I'll have the sheriff out here to arrest you first thing tomorrow." She turned toward her car, kept her hand on the handle, and viciously added the rest of it. "*Rapist.*" She spat the word at him. She slammed her car door shut, made a show of locking it, and drove away.


Burr stood in the driveway beside the fertilizer spreader, his fists knotted at his sides, his chin hanging low, the brim of his Stetson hiding his eyes, the great heaviness of fear and shame overtaking him. He waited for her to tell him to disconnect the fertilizer spreader from his Jeep. He waited for her to tell him to clear out his things from the barn and take to the road.

Fiona stood without speaking. But even in this desperate moment, her eyes conveyed great wisdom. So this was the thing, she seemed to be saying, that you thought would frighten the both of us, that you'd thought would crush Meredith away.

He'd been right to be afraid.

He waited, a stone-broken silhouette in the barnyard, while she turned from him and went to the house. Meredith stood just inside the screen, her eyes streaming with tears. She might have been ten years old again. "Grandma, what should I do? What should I do?"

Fiona made a slight motion back over her shoulder with her head. "Seems to me there's somebody you care about standing in the barnyard. Someone who's been angry and accused and afraid. I imagine he's wondering what to do, too."

"I can't just go out to the barn like that, in the dark, to find out about him. Evangeline Kew said—"

Fiona touched her granddaughter's arm. "Never mind Evangeline Kew. Think about the times he's taken care of us, when we've been safe."

"Why didn't he trust me enough to tell me?" Meredith cried.

"You're going to have to ask him that, won't you?" A second touch on the arm. "Go, child. In this case, it must be you. After what she's said, he won't be the one to come in explaining. I know him well enough. He'll be out of here by morning, thinking to protect you."

He hadn't turned on the sharp-shadow light of the barn. They saw each other in the moonlight that filtered in through the old rickety boards, moonlight that became ample and potent as their eyes adjusted. She stood in the exact place he'd once handed her a weather vane and she'd taken it in her arms, astounded. He said, "All those things you said to your grandmother that first night, all the things you said I could be. You were right."

"No." She wouldn't believe him. "No."

"Never should have stayed here. Never should've let your grandmother convince me to come."

Her heart quickened when she heard him condemning himself. She wouldn't accept it. Not any longer. "I've seen you since you've been here. You think there's been hiding, but there hasn't been. I've seen someone who's a good farmer, who's caring for my grandmother, a protector."

"Not me," he said, his face gaunt and pale. "I'm a no-good drifter. Go from job to job. Never can hold anything down." He dropped to the cot in the corner and hid his face in his hands, his shoulders stretching the seams of his shirt, rising and falling with each shudder of his body. "No one would ever want to—"

"Don't be running from yourself. For God's sake, you tried to hide it from the both of us long enough."

She knelt beside him, lifted the brim of his hat from where it lay against his back. She laid the hat on the barn floor and slipped her slender hand through his hair, combing it, feeling it fall with cool silkiness between her fingers. She drew upon all her strength, all she knew about this man. Not what she'd seen or been told, but what she *knew* of him. "Tell me, Burr. Tell me what they accused you of."

"It isn't . . . I can't—" His big shoulders, rising

and plummeting again. His body tremoring with hurt.

"Why did you ever leave town in the first place? Why did you leave your home?"

"My dad left when I was a little boy. Me, I stayed with my mother. And everybody in town expected me to be a preacher like my grandfather. To take over his ministry, Mother said. There was this service when I was a little boy and a missionary came to town to speak, and he saw me and said, 'This boy has a preacher's call on his life just like his grandfather.' And they all laid hands on me and prayed. Well, I'm no preacher. But it was all my mother could talk about from the time I was seven."

"So you left because you couldn't be what she wanted?"

"More than that," he said, his voice breaking, and still not looking at her. "Different from that. She didn't want me around because I'm not what I was supposed to be. It got easier to hitchhike and go on the road than it got listening to her tell me how disappointed in me she was. Got picked up and arrested and spent the night in jail the first time when I was thirteen. My grandfather drove over and picked me up. In everybody's eyes, I was a preacher's grandson gone bad. I'd gotten to be 'just like my father.' And pretty soon, it was too late to be any different. Things in a small town take on a life of their own."

"Did you do it?" Meredith asked point-blank, not wanting to say the awful word.

She couldn't even fathom the brokenness she

saw take rise in his expression. "Meredith, no. She was the only thing that kept me going back. Never would've done anything to hurt her."

Had Evangeline said her name? Oh, yes. Susan Maplehold. "You were in love with her, then?"

He stared at his own knee. "I thought so. Wanted her to come with me, you know? I don't know, to find a place we could get away from everybody's talking and make a life for ourselves. But she'd never believe me that I'd be willing to settle down. She'd never listen when I told her I'd find something and settle down."

"Why did she say you'd done it, Burr? Why would she ever accuse you of such a thing?"

With one hand he clutched the other, as she knelt at his knee and made him face everything that had chased him away from home. "Everything she said we did, we did. I took her to the movies. Then I took her home. Then we went up into her bedroom because her parents weren't there and she said it'd be all right. She let me take off all her clothes, one layer at a time, all these little pink things, and she had earrings like yours . . ." He trailed off, needed a minute to get his composure. "Later she told me she'd decided she wouldn't go with me. I, like a fool, didn't leave her alone. I thought that time together, what we'd done together, had to mean something. I wanted her to leave town with me. I wanted her to marry me. I kept calling. I kept going to her house to see her. And that's when she called the police."

Meredith sang out his name like a song. How he loved the sound of it. "Burr."

"Only thing I could think of, they wouldn't do anything unless she filed criminal charges. After what happened between us, to Susan, I guess that seemed like the easiest thing."

"How could she do such a thing? How could she accuse you like that? How could she do it?"

"After it was all over, I was on my way out of town and I saw her walking along the street, happy as if nothing had ever happened. I stopped and asked her why. And she said, 'To get rid of you. To make you leave town again and leave me alone.'"

"You might've spent time for it in jail."

"What would it have mattered to anybody? I'd been in jail for wandering and getting picked up on the highway a few times before. By that time, in her eyes, it was a simple thing to add that to all the others."

"But they found you innocent. They had to understand she charged you for something you didn't do."

"You heard Evangeline Kew, didn't you? The jury found me innocent. When you're in a trial like that, folks don't remember if you're guilty or innocent. They only remember that you've been accused."

"Why is it that you act as if you are guilty of the crime?"

"It's like everything else in my life," he told her. "I could've done it differently. I should never have gone with her to her room or touched her, not in love or in need. I should have left town when she told me to go. Ought never to have trusted her. Ought never to have trusted myself." And that, his one last sentence, made Meredith understand the significance of what they'd shared here, the delicate way he'd opened himself up for Fiona, the difficulty for him, the lingering doubt, when he'd sat close beside Meredith or edged her hair behind her ear or kissed her in the rain.

"That's it, then, isn't it?" she asked. "You've decided it was your fault, either way."

He nodded.

"Surely somebody stuck by you, Burr. Surely your family—"

But he bit his lip like a little boy and shook his head. "My grandfather stuck by me. He was the only one. Not my mother. She'd gotten to seeing me all wrong somewhere along the way. She told everybody in town she thought I was guilty as charged."

He gazed down at her, his face colorless, his body stiff, his soul held in abeyance as though something could be about to shatter. She laid a hand upon his knee, touched his jaw, traced it as if she needed to be reminded of its form. Then she laid her head against his knee, laid it there with her pale neck revealed to him, as if he were sovereign, she his subject.

"You believe me." He didn't say the words as a question or even as a statement. He said them only as if he needed to feel their possibilities for the first time, as if he needed to consider for the first time the realization that there was someone besides his grandfather, that Meredith could be someone, like a princess who'd believed the odd, awful life of a frog or a beast or a wolf, a princess who might release him.

For so long he hadn't trusted himself, hadn't thought anyone might know the truth of his story and trust him, too. But she nodded against his knee, nestled her chin deeper against the fabric through which she could feel his warming skin. "I believe you." He saw the strands of muscle in her neck, the throb where her pulse ran, ebbing and flowing with each heartbeat like a tide. He saw her lift her face to his. Without a word she unzipped her coat, unfastened the snaps, and freed the toggles. She cast it aside herself, where it lay like a sleeping child on the floor of the barn. She unbuttoned the top buttons of a sweater until it spread wide at her collarbone. She lifted it over her head, cast it upon the dirt as well.

He didn't move. Still she knelt before him, the skin of her breasts as flawless and fair as milk glass. "Burr," she whispered. "Please. Look at me." It was the first time he lifted his head, the first time he'd met her gaze. And the expression of pure trust in her eyes brought him hopefulness he hadn't felt for two years or more, a journey inside him from darkness into daylight.

She guided his hand to her heart, placed his rough palm in the lacy valley between her breasts, where he could feel the even, strong beat there beneath her rib cage. "I'm not afraid of you," she said. "I'm not afraid of what's happened or what people have said."

"How could you not be?"

He felt her very body throbbing beneath his touch, her heartbeat rhythmic and sure. "It's nothing I have to convince you of, is it? It's already something where I've seen you do the convincing."

He breathed deeply, the breath coming from such a depth within him, that depth within a soul where excavation must be total and devastating, disentangled, swept clean with admittance and pain before it can become fresh and raw, to heal. When he didn't draw her into his arms, she knew the other chapter of the story between them. She knew that she beckoned for his touch in trust, and that he could return it only in trust, that he might not be able to reciprocate. But when he removed his hand from where she'd placed it, it was to take both of her hands within his own. He held them there, widespread, so he could drink in the sight of her the way the ground had soaked up the thick, precious rain.

During the past month, even as he'd taught her his worthiness, she had taught him hers. In caring for her, in needing her, in watching her care for Fiona, he'd known colder darkness, deeper emptiness, because his very presence here had jarred and freed that darkness, that emptiness. He reached for the lacy straps of her bra, and his memories were gone. All that remained was the presence of Meredith, opal glass skin, the shining green eyes of his healer, his friend, his love. He eased the straps down off the curve of each shoulder. The fabric folded and fell away, revealing her nakedness, her trust, a gift. And he touched, could have closed his eyes against the power of his burgeoning senses, but didn't because he wanted to see her. Oh, how he wanted to see her.

She unfastened her bra for him. It fell away onto the floor with the rest of her belongings, discarded, forgotten.

She moaned as he looked at her, a sound not a barrier between them, but a beckoning. And said his name again like a melody. "Burr. You see. Please."

He took her breasts within his hands. She buried her face upon him, her hair cascading against him, the fall of it liquid upon him, like water. Her tears wet his skin, anointing him, soaking into the roots of his soul.

He said, his voice as soft as a breeze, "If I made love to you, it would be different."

"Yes," she said. "Different from anything."

"And it wouldn't be something to run from or hide against."

"Or anything to be accused of."

"A gift," he said.

"Of trust," she finished.

"Would it be because you want to heal me?" he asked. "Or would it be because of something more?"

"Because of something more," she answered. "So many things more."

His shoulders shuddered again. A last release of pent sorrow. A new realization. Beginnings where before there had been only endings. Harvest.

She unbuttoned his shirt. One button. Two. She pushed it off his arms and revealed the well-honed muscles she'd watched as he'd worked on the barn roof, tanned arms she'd known and measured for their shirtless self-sufficiency. She realized she could close her eyes and know the shape of them, the graceful movement and power of his torso, the smell and sight of him, his arms, the muscles of his back, even as she knew the shape, the characteristic movements, of her own limbs. Sometime during the past months, he had become this much a part of her.

She had not been wise enough to know it as it happened. She knew it now.

"You are beautiful," he said, and his words made her feel slightly dizzy, off balance.

"I want you to make love to me," she whispered. "I want you to see how I trust you." For she knew he trusted her. She could see that, too, in her new wisdom, in the way he looked at her in the moonlight of the barn. She laid her hands splayed against his bare chest, felt the hair there, too, curled and coarse between her fingers.

He picked her up and carried her to his cot, the one that had sat in the corner even when she'd been a little girl. He laid her there on the bedding, made with linens that still smelled of cedar, the way they always smelled when they came from her grandmother's closet.

Fiona knew, from the moment Meredith charged out to the barn and Evangeline Kew squealed her tires turning out onto the highway, that she would not sleep that night. She dozed, fell halfway into dreams, rose out of them, and saw the ceiling, the moonlight over it in a wash, pale translucence, the color of a woman's exposed opalescent skin. She wondered if Meredith had come in from the barn yet, knowing she'd be brokenhearted by what must have happened to Burr, yet knowing in her heart of hearts that her granddaughter would be safe. She stared at the clock's harsh green phosphorous-lit face.

After the happiness of driving the tractor and combine, to have such a despairing visit from Evangeline Kew. "You ought to have stuck with plumping pillows and selling them feverishly at the church bazaar," Fiona wanted to say. "You had no right to trod where two such precious children are fighting to find happiness in their lives." For she understood that Meredith had long been as lonely and lost, in her own particular way, as Burr Colton.

She supposed they'd be offended if they heard her calling them children, when they were both well on to being thirty years old. By the time she'd been Meredith's age, she'd married Ray and had given birth to Michael and had homesteaded the farm. She'd been taught lessons of the land and lessons of the heart. She'd been taught that each followed no bidding except for its own. Like farmland itself, when one's heart ranged where it could not be followed, perhaps it ranged, too, where it must be followed always.

Meredith and Burr were not children. She only saw them that way.

Fiona stood from the bed, drew the curtains aside so she could see the moon. It hung low in the sky over the farms, waxing into fullness, its face a daintily carved cameo, ancient and benevolent. It seemed tonight to be the only thing in creation that had the wisdom to mete out proper justice.

As Fiona gazed out at the moon, she wanted nothing to separate herself from its presence. She wanted to be outdoors, not hidden behind glass or wood or linen gauze, so near to the earth and the moon that she could taste its lemon bitter light. She wanted, as she watched the night sky, to be closer, to touch and be a part of the earth the way a woman touched her husband's body, so completely, so tenderly, that with a gasp and a cry the communion becomes primal, a physical, breathless coupling.

Burr ought to have told Meredith about the trial sooner, she supposed. She wondered as she gazed up into the moon what events had transpired in Burr's life, why a girl had seen fit to accuse him of such a crime. Fiona knew she'd done the right thing by pretending to Evangeline that they'd already known. Who'd've thought Meredith would find out about a trial in Belle Fourche in such a precarious way. But perhaps it couldn't be helped. Perhaps it had been something destined. As all things were supposedly destined. Perhaps.

All this seemed too much for her suddenly, too much to try to manufacture excuses and detours for other people's lives. Maybe she'd been selfish to have Meredith here, to let her take a year out of med school. And then perhaps it had been selfish of her to want to live her life again through the two of them, to have things turn out a different way.

Despite the ruckus Evangeline had caused, Fiona felt peaceful. She pulled a quilt from her bed and wrapped it around her shoulders. She lifted her elbows and braided her hair without having to see a mirror. She took pleasure in the weight of her hair roping against her neck. She left her feet bare on purpose. She loved digging her toes deep into the dirt.

She'd just started out the screen door when she saw Meredith closing the door of the barn, bare-footed, her shoes in her hand, carefully making her way back across the stones and the thistles in the dooryard. "Grandma?"

"You've been with him a long time, child."

"Yes. I needed to be. What are you doing shuffling around out here on the porch? It's the middle of the night."

"You knew I wouldn't sleep. Not after all that, not after what Evangeline said."

"Were you watching for me to come out of the barn?"

"No. I was watching the moon. I thought you might already be up in your room."

"Do you mind if I stay out, too? Don't think I can sleep for a while, either." Then, "You ought to have worn a robe, Grandma. You'll get chilled. You know the doctors wouldn't want you to get chilled."

"I've got my quilt. That keeps me warm. Of course I don't mind if you stay out here with me, if you don't bother me about my robe."

"You don't have slippers."

"Slippers are good for nothing. They keep your toes from feeling the good earth. You've got no right to lecture me, Meredith. You don't have slippers, either." And at the same time, they shared a downward glance at the tennis shoes, the crumpled socks Meredith held in her hand.

They found places side by side on the steps, hugging their knees, lost in the silence, their eyes voyaging into the heavens the way a sailor voyaged a home coast. They were quiet a long stretch, hearing only the sounds of the brown bats diving for their supper, the whistle of duck wings as the birds flocked and exercised for autumn flights to the southland.

At last Meredith said, "Remember what you told me that one night about people on the farm, Grandma? Remember? Because I've never forgotten."

Fiona shook her head and rumpled her granddaughter's hair. "How am I supposed to remember what I've said on one night? I've said a lot of good things over my lifetime."

"You talked about why you didn't feel alone here. About the light of the land. That this moonlight was the sort of light that revealed things about people, not the kind that made it easy for folks to hide away."

"I said that?" Fiona asked.

"Yeah. You said it. A long time ago." They rocked like two girls, their chins braced on their knees, their fingers clutched around their ankles. Fiona draped the quilt, made it into a shawl across both their shoulders. Meredith said simply, "I'm in love with Burr Colton, Grandma. I have been for a long time."

"He's had a hard time in his life, Meredith. I'm happy that you love him. He's a good man. I have been glad to find that out, too."

"You had to find it out? From the very beginning, you've acted like you already knew."

"No." Fiona turned her full face up to the moon, and in the milky light, Meredith saw that she looked young. "I didn't know for a while. But I hoped."

They rocked a little while more. Meredith said, "Except for you and his own grandfather, I don't think he's ever had anyone to have faith in him."

Fiona reminded her, "You have had faith in him, too."

After a long while, Meredith said, "I'm going upstairs to bed. One of us ought to get some sleep. You can be late in the morning. I'll make breakfast for Burr." She draped the quilt around her grandmother's shoulders. Fiona gripped it with both hands.

"You ought not to stay out here too much longer. Don't want you to get chilled."

"I won't. I'll come in soon, I promise." But Fiona lifted an arm and called her when she was halfway in the door. "Meredith?"

"What?"

"Come back for a minute." Meredith let the screen door shut and went out, bending so her grandmother could hold her face in two parchment hands. "You're going to make a fine doctor one day."

"I hope so."

"I know so." Fiona kissed her on the lips. "I love you," she said. "Got to make certain you know that."

Meredith gave her an absentminded smile. "I

know that. I've always known that. I love you, too, Grandma."

"Good night."

"Good night."


Of course she wouldn't go inside just yet. She'd been out in worse weather with the boys, working in the silo and shoveling feed when this dark ground had been frozen harder than a cast-iron skillet. Fiona waited patiently until Meredith's light went out above her. She stayed sitting on the stoop and leaned her head against the post and shut her eyes. Funny the way dreams switch and turn, the way they tease a person into them and become shape-shifters, like life itself, befuddling and revealing until the dreamer becomes something different from what he was before.

She knew even as she began to drift away that she was being silly. She smelled ripening grain in her field just as she'd smelled it riding with Burr Colton, only she'd just come around the back of the straw spreader, her hands covered with grease, her short curly hair not gray anymore, almost exactly matching the sunny color of Michael's. She mopped sweat off her face with the length of a sleeve and resettled her cap. "High time you boys made it here. What've you been doing? Chasing jackrabbits?"

"Almer had to poke his feet in the water."

"Sorry, Missus Trichak." She remembered that Almer had lowered his head a mite. "Didn't know there'd be so many people. Guess I was looking for a reason to keep from helping at my own place."

Fiona pointed at the crowd standing at the fence. "Your ma and pa are standing over there." She nodded her head toward the road.

"I know. I saw them."

"Seems they're looking for an excuse not to be working, same as you."

"We've been cutting and binding for three weeks. Seems we could be in that quarter section from now until the cows come home and still not finish. Harvest is endless." He jammed one hand inside the bib of his overalls and started scratching again, just thinking about the misery. While he scratched, he looked up dolefully at the machine. "Pa says the darn thing looks like a tin can. You suppose it'll cut and thrash this whole place by Friday?"

"By Thursday." Fiona winked at her son. "We'll have our granaries loaded and be driving the last wagons to the elevator by Friday noon."

The crowd outside the fence showed symptoms of restlessness. Bits of conversation wafted with the wind across the furrows. Somebody said, "A tractor doesn't spook and run away."

Somebody else said, "A mule can be balky, but nobody ever had to buy a new turbine for a mule."

"Perhaps it'd be safer," someone suggested, "if we still used a cradle and a flail."

Jake Weinauer ducked under a strand of barbed wire and strode toward them. He cupped his hands around his mouth and bellowed, "Yahoo, Fiona. Need any help? Everybody outside the fence thinks you're having trouble getting started."

She planted her hands on her hips. "I'm not having trouble. By all means, tell everyone there not to worry themselves. I'm getting these boys indoctrinated. Michael's going to be my header tender."

Michael straightened to attention. "I am?"

"Yep. You are. Now David here, he's going to be my engineer, and help drive this thing like a train." She grinned down at her youngest son, the one she'd taken in from Kay Lee Wilkins, as he hid halfway behind her knee. David kept tickling her leg with a barley whisker and giggling for all he was worth. He was covered with dust from the top of his overalls to the soles of his little brown Scout shoes, which was understandable since he'd been busy turning somersaults in the grain.

"And Almer's going to walk beside the tractor. I'm going to spend the afternoon teaching him to be a Cat skinner."

Almer smiled. "Yeah."

Jake didn't let it drop. "Thought you might need a man's help, is all. You got nobody here to help you but kids. With me being your neighbor—"

"I haven't had a man's help in a good while, Mr. Weinauer. Don't know why you think I would begin to rely on that now."

He straightened his shoulders and returned to the spectators in a disjointed prance, one that reminded her of a sage grouse strutting past and puffing up his gullet.

"Time to get started," she said after she'd finished watching him swagger across the field. She showed Michael how to adjust the header so the sickle bars cut at the desired height on the gentle surges and troughs of the land. She showed Almer how she would push the throttle forward to keep the tractor moving at just the right speed. David stood with one foot on top of the other while she explained to him that he must stay with her at all times so he'd be safe.

She'd already brought in the fuel wagon and filled both tanks with white Gilbarco gasoline. One last time, she checked the grease cups and settled the old coffeepot of crankcase oil behind the seat. She wiped the grease from her hands with a rag, then poked it inside her jeans pocket.

"Here goes nothing."

She took one deep breath and stared at the tractor.

"You scared, Ma?" Michael asked.

"Yes. Scared to death."

Almer said, "Never thought to *see* this thing, much less walk around with it."

"You make it sound like it's got legs."

"Might as well. It has everything else."

Fiona hefted David onto one hip and balanced him there, while he locked his legs around her middle. She swung up with him and settled him in her lap. She nodded to Almer. Michael took his place on the platform, made ready to keep guard over the glistening red bars.

A perfect day for reaping, one so dry and clear! No moisture remained from the morning. Each barley stalk bowed its head, obeisant to the heaviness of its bounty. The tractor lurched forward, its metal-cleated wheels piercing thick roots and earth.

"Those folks ought to be cheering or something," Almer shouted over the chugging. "We're showing them now, aren't we?"

"Not yet," Fiona said. "We're not yet started. But we *will* be." She turned around and bellowed to her son, "Michael."

Michael worked the lever atop the platform, and the blades quivered to life. The sickle bar knife began to oscillate, glittering with fresh oil and just sharpened edge. Fiona lined the tractor out at the corner, and off they went, opening the field in a clockwise direction.

The combine took its first bite of standing grain.

Everyone at the fence eyed the spinning bars. Despite Fiona's confidence, most everyone else expected the doomsaying to come true. They halfway expected the barley heads to shatter before any grain made the bin. They halfway expected the tractor, so stinking and noisy, would pound over the land like an elephant, leaving earth and plants trodden in its destructive wake.

In rhythm to the chugging of the machine, Fiona Trichak began to sing. "Am I the one? . . ." She belted the words loudly enough to be heard over the clanking of the combine. She saw Michael shake his head. She saw Almer grin. Alongside her, David poked his fingers into his ears. She couldn't blame any of them. If they'd heard this song once, they'd heard it a hundred times. It was her favorite, and printed to play on the piano with a picture of Rudy Vallee on the cover.

She sang while she made the circuit. Sickle bars skimmed low against the stalks, setting up a whisper all the more theatrical for the banging of the huge steel machine that caused it. She'd already passed halfway down the draw. Behind them lay a swath of straw cut and strewn beside the fence. Grain poured into the bin like water. "You oughtta see it in here," Michael hollered down to her. "Tons of barley. And we're getting together a nice collection of grasshoppers, too."

She swiveled back, tilted her face victoriously toward the sun. As she came upon the corner and made the first sweeping turn, folks along the way began to flail their arms and to applaud her.

"Knew Fiona could do it," somebody shouted.

"Darn thing's working just like we expected it to," somebody else joined in.

Lined along the fence, their motorcars and the harnesses on their horses flashed in the rich autumn sunlight. Their words rang out across that cured field. "She'll have her place harvested in two days if she keeps up at this pace, won't she?"

As they veered around the second corner of the field, they passed an assembly of folks from Melody Flats Community Christian Church. Pastor Charles Burleigh stood watching them as though he were watching a parade, his boot propped on the lowest strand of sagging wire fence, his fancy sennit straw hat slanted at such a jaunty angle that, in a more conservative clime than Wyoming, it would have set people to complaining that it wasn't right for a minister.

Charles Burleigh raised his hand and waved.

Fiona lifted her chin elegantly as they passed by him. She whispered in David's ear. David waved back.

They rounded the third corner and David wriggled around so he could get something out of his back overalls pocket. "What are you scrooching around for?" Fiona asked, trying to concentrate on driving the tractor.

"Got my whistle in my back pocket. Wanted to blow it while we were driving around."

"You been sitting on it in your back pocket the whole time we've been doing this?"

"Yep."

He stood up on the tractor and fished the little aspen-wood whistle out of his overalls. He held out a small, grimy palm and showed it to her. "It's something, isn't it?"

"It's been carved out by hand."

"Yep. Whole time Michael's been teaching me to whittle, this is what we've been working on. Couldn't get it to make any noise for the longest time. Now it does. See?" He put it in his little mouth and blew so hard, his cheeks puffed out like a bullfrog's. The thing tooted all right. It made a nice airy sound.

"That's something." Fiona headed the combine toward the fourth corner, the first square finished in the field. Now she could start doubling back. "Glad your brother was willing to help you like that. Sure does work, doesn't it?"

"Michael helped me get my initials in it, too. See? D.W.T. For David Wilkins Trichak. He said he thought that'd be good. He said if I ever lost it, folks'd find it and see my initials on it and they'd always know it belonged to me."

"David." Fiona started awake and realized she'd been dreaming. Merciful heavens, where was she? The porch?

*Got to go inside, like I told Meredith I would.*

Her feet were so cold, she couldn't feel them. She wiggled them, got the blood to flowing back into her toes. She wrestled with the quilt, gathered it around her, and stood. But the struggle with the quilt seemed too much. Her head went fuzzy and she couldn't catch her breath. She felt so disoriented, she thought she might fall.

She felt below her with her hand to find the step where she'd been sitting. She found it easily. She found it still warm. She lowered herself onto it and looked up at the night sky. She tried to call Meredith's name, but nothing came. A pain shot up her arm, a searing pain, like standing too close at the opening of a hot oven door. It clamped around her chest and claimed her, pulled her into it, becoming larger and larger, until only it and she remained.

Fiona kept her eyes upon the gentle orb in the sky, the moon that beckoned her toward it with its puppeteer hands. She gave herself over to the moon, and to the clenching pain that seemed to go tighter and tighter around her chest until, at last, the pain became so immense, it could not be pain at all.

She felt a current flow over her from some far-away place, blowing toward her and compelling her like an exquisite, generous kiss. In an instant she felt nothing, gloriously nothing. And she felt everything, reborn and wholly loved, a free spirit, verdant, like the fields that lay naked and yearning beneath the moon.

They'd be waiting for her. She'd long been certain of that.

There would be the three of them. David, who'd still be a boy. Her Ray, who'd gone so many years before. And Charley. She would see Charley.

And it would be good.

# 16

The Trichak farm. Burr rummaging around on the other side of the barn almost at dawn, peeling a fencepost to replace one that had rotted and worked its way out when the rain had come. A meadowlark singing by the road, its song flutelike and melodious. Chee chee chit chit-er-ee. Chee chee chit chit-er-ee.

And Meredith, coming downstairs in her bathrobe, planning to start breakfast so her grandmother wouldn't have to fix it. A glance out the window, and Meredith saw Fiona still there, sitting right where she'd left her last night, with her head leaning on the post. "Grandma? Grandma." No matter how many times she had imagined this moment, no matter how many times she'd practiced it in her mind, the practice didn't make her ready for it. She had thought she'd be able to practice CPR, to keep

Fiona alive until an ambulance came. But her grandmother must've been gone for hours. She must've gone just after they'd had their talk on the stoop last night.

Only later did she remember that she'd screamed out his name. "Burr. Help me. Please. Burr." Oh, thank heavens for Burr. Oh, thank heavens for when he'd come running. She didn't know what to do. All the planning and all the training, and she felt entirely helpless. Meredith sat on the stoop and gathered her grandmother into her arms. Burr phoned the appropriate officials. Burr phoned the church. The coroner came. Michael and Barbara were notified. When they phoned from LAX, Michael said they'd thrown a few possessions in a bag and were on their way on the next flight. Meredith and Burr had never eaten any breakfast. The fencepost still lay in the yard where he'd dropped it.

They began a stunned watch in the house, sitting beside each other at the kitchen table after the coroner had taken the body away. Food began to arrive from church members. The house seemed as mystified as they were somehow, paused on a brink of something, everything in its place where Fiona had left it yesterday, the fabric for a blue plaid bookcover still strewn beneath the needle of the sewing machine.

Fiona's presence was supremely linked to this place, from the mud prints her shoes had made on the floor yesterday to the old clock that kept the time today as it had always kept Fiona's time of day, precise, relentless. The weather vane pointed to the east and Ocean Lake.

They held on to the only thing each of them could hold on to. They held on to each other.

"Meredith. Dear God, Meredith. She's gone, isn't she? What will happen without her?"

"I don't know. I don't know." She nestled her face against his neck. Her tears trickled into the hollow at his throat. Their bodies fit together as if they'd been hewn to fit together, hewn by a Creator, as he held her and she drew strength from him. The broad angles of his chest aligned with the gentle expanse of her shoulders. The cradle of her hipbones swathed the firm plane of his abdomen. How good it felt, how achingly necessary, to give credence, to know that while Fiona's life on earth had ended, theirs lay before them. Each stood tall and firm and solid for the other; they matched their very breaths. One inhaled as the other sighed. One exhaled while the other's lungs filled. Their hearts clattered like hammer irons against each other, fierce and strong and violent. As they hung on to each other, they hung on to life.

In Meredith's mind, as Burr kept her steadied within his arms, he shored her up against those hours the way a jetty protected a coastline. He kept deep rocky parts of her from washing away in grief. She clung to him, to loving him, with her entire being. With him holding her, she became strong enough to collect the moments she remembered with Fiona and with Burr, too, their time together during the past seasons, touching them tentatively, not opening them fully, only making certain of their presence.

Just after noon a nondescript rental car turned

in off the highway and ground to a halt beside the house. Burr released her, stepped back. "That'll be your parents, won't it? I'll go out and work at peeling those fenceposts. Need to keep my hands busy. It'd be better if I found something to do."

They parked in front of the house, and Meredith opened the screen door. Michael Trichak climbed out of the driver's side and sorrowfully gathered his daughter inside his arms. "Dad." And before she could say anything more, Barbara had rushed up, too, hugging her so tightly that she could scarcely breathe.

"We got here as soon as we could," Michael said. "The airline schedules into Wyoming are awful."

Barbara added, "We didn't want you to be alone here for any length of time. If we could have called and gotten someone to drive over and stay with you, we would have. How terrible that you were the one to find her gone."

"I wasn't here alone." All morning she'd been wringing a tea towel, and now she held it in the direction of the barn. "Burr was here. I couldn't have—"

"Oh, yes," Barbara said, as if she'd just remembered. "The hired hand."

"And it wasn't awful, finding her. She was right where she'd've wanted to be. Sitting out on the stoop with her head against the post, watching the moon. It'd be a blessing to go that way, in a place you loved so much, don't you think? We'd just had a good talk—"

"That reminds me," Barbara interrupted. "I've

got to phone the retirement center in Valencia tonight. I'll get them to refund my deposit. I've had a deposit on a room for her there so she could be close to us. To get on the waiting list, I had to make a deposit. Can you imagine a place so popular, they take money from you just so you can wait in line?"

Burr came around from the fenceposts and moved forward to meet them. He'd extended his hand before either of them turned his way. "This is Burr Colton," Meredith introduced him. Michael and Barbara and Burr shook hands all around. When they were finished, Burr took a piece of baling wire out of his pocket, folded over a third of the wire, spun it between his thumb and forefinger like a toy. For a long time, nobody said anything. Michael cleared his throat. He made a show of surveying the yard.

"My mother told me what a fine job you've done around the place. And I can see it. Thank you for all the work you've put in, Mr. Colton. Had my mother paid you this month? I'll certainly see that you get your paycheck for your last month of work."

"Thank you. But don't think of that. Missus Trichak's—"

Michael didn't stop to listen or to catch his breath. "Yes, you've done a good job around here. Except for the green roof on the barn, the old place looks"—he jutted his chin forward, took assessment of the surroundings without a trace of sentiment, as far as Meredith could see—"just like I left it." He took Barbara by the hand and led her up the front steps. "Is that coffee I smell?"

Meredith climbed the steps behind them. "I put some on when I saw you coming up the drive."

Barbara stopped before they entered and ran one fingernail, a red fingernail as shapely and hard as a beetle, over the wood. "The porch has been painted recently, hasn't it? Several coats."

Meredith went on inside and took mugs down from the hooks in the cabinet. "Burr just did that last week. He gave it three coats since it's on the west side and bakes in late afternoon." Barbara went to the door and pushed aside the curtains to have a look. "Between all of you, you've made it into a dear little house." She tapped on her teeth with one of the hard red fingernails. "Michael, what do you think about this? All the work Mr. Colton has done around here has to have increased the property value somewhat from the last time your mother had this place appraised."

"And the fields," Meredith added. Oh, how she wanted to make sure they noticed the fields. "Burr got the old combine going again. After borrowing Almer's tractor so many times, we're going to do this harvest with Grandma's old Case combine. People all over town have been coming by and asking Burr questions. The land is so productive after lying dormant—"

Michael sipped his coffee with an air of sedate satisfaction. "Oh, yes." After his third airy sip from the mug, he glanced up quickly. "Barbara, I'll phone Andrew Jacobs first thing after we get settled in. I'd like to talk to him before Mother's funeral and make sure we've set the price right. I don't want anything to get in the way of the deal we've made. I also don't want to give this old place away without recognizing its full value."

Meredith frowned. "The deal you've made?"

Barbara went to the kitchen suddenly, as if she'd decided she no longer wanted to be treated like a guest. She thumbed through the old spoons in the drawer until she found one she considered acceptable. "Oh, yes. Isn't it exciting? To have a buyer so quickly, and a cash offer so we can close. Of course it wouldn't have come together like this if your father hadn't already been sending feelers out. We knew we had to plan for something like this when his mother would leave this place. A California businessman has had his eye on this property for several months. Michael called him from LAX to let him know the property would be coming on the market. He made us a nice cash offer, right there at the airport. Won't be near the amount of money that a property of this size in California would have brought. But it's respectable."

"And it's fast," Michael said. "That's the best thing. At a time like this, when everyone's mourning someone they've loved, its best to get business matters taken care of quickly."

"When is the closing?" Meredith stood stiffly beside the table where they'd made themselves at home. Out the window, she could see Burr peeling new fenceposts.

Michael answered, "You know how these things are. Everything ought to go well, if Mother's got her will in order. We've got to see how fast we can get the title insurance pushed through. But as soon as possible. Before the end of next month, if possible."

"Next month?"

"Yes." Barbara rose again, this time going to pour herself a second cup. "It's best for all of us if we get the place cleaned out and it doesn't sit empty for too long. And hasn't it worked out better than anyone thought it could? We can all get back and get on with things. Your father might not have to take more than four days off work. And just last week I talked to your faculty adviser at UCLA. He says that you can come to campus any time and register for your next classes. He thought you ought to do it as soon as possible. Cell and Tissue Biology is filling up. And you've got to have it next semester. It's prerequisite to Physiology and Biological Chemistry."

"I know about those classes. I'm always talking to him by e-mail. It's the barley harvest I'm thinking of. I've got to help Burr with Grandma's barley."

Michael held out his arms to her. "Meredith, I can see this whole ordeal has taken its toll on you, and you aren't even telling us. That barley harvest isn't important anymore. Think about it. You've done all this for your grandmother. And now it's over."

"It isn't over. Burr—"

He interrupted her. "What you accomplished here this year was a . . . a fun experiment. But there is another gentleman who will own the land shortly. He's flying out the first of the week to inspect the place. If he chooses to harvest grain, then doing so should be his prerogative. If he decides to do something else"—and here he left a pregnant pause, as if he knew indeed what the man would and wouldn't do—"that should be his prerogative as well."

She tried to make them understand. "I know Grandma's gone. But after the work, finishing the harvest would mean so much to Burr."

Michael stood up. "The suitcases are still in the car. I'll take them up. We'll have the guest room, won't we? I know where it is."

Barbara pulled off three diamond rings and laid them on the counter beside the sink. She took their coffee mugs and began to rinse them beneath water running in the sink. She pulled a tea towel from the drawer, unfolded it, and began to line the cups upside-down.

Michael said, "There isn't any use keeping a hired hand around now that your grandmother is gone. We've discussed it in the car driving over. You know him well, don't you? If I write out a check this afternoon, will you hand it to him and tell him it's a bonus because he's done a lovely job? Find out if Fiona owed him anything that she didn't pay him last week. And you'll need to tell him it's time to go out for a different job. No use keeping someone around. You be the one to tell him, Meredith. We're letting him go."

The morning of Fiona's funeral was a morning Meredith's grandmother would have relished, with the ripening grain wavering to some plainsong melody in the fields, the colors brilliant and gold as summertime can be, the sort of day children loved. The great blue of the sky stretched cloudless from horizon to horizon, from the Wind Rivers west to the Absarokas northwest and across the land to the south and east that lay hilly and open as far as the eye could see. This distance formed a perfect circle of plains and buttes and mountains, all that was Wyoming and that Fiona had held dear, a solemn embrace.

It would be one of those days of summer when children could bake outside all afternoon without heeding the sun, giving breathless homage to the glittering warmth, to long unplanned hours, to all that would soon, when school started, be gone.

As Meredith drove with her parents in the black limousine to the funeral, she could close her eyes and tell by the fragrances what fields they were passing, for the road was perfumed all the way. They traversed miles of the sweet purple-blooming alfalfa, the green redolence of sugar beets, and the wild pitch of sagebrush. Oh, and the acres and acres of barley, the heady dust-nut fragrance, the crop that had been her grandmother's livelihood, that had made Fiona so hopeful and so proud.

Meredith clenched and unclenched her fist against the window glass, tears squeezing from beneath her lashes and tracking along her cheeks.

Michael saw his daughter crying. He cupped the back of her neck with one hand and jostled it. He said, as if he talked to a young girl instead of a woman, "Honey, we're proud of you. You did a great thing here. You made your grandmother's last few months very happy."

Meredith closed her fist, rested her nose against it, and couldn't answer him.

"There were times we didn't think you'd done the right thing. You've proven us wrong in this. There's no way any of us could have known that this would happen so fast."

She found her voice and answered at last. "Thanks, Dad. I'm glad you think I did the right thing."

"Your mother and I both think so, don't we, Barbara?"

"Yes, honey, we do."

The family limousine pulled up in front of the church. From all along Main Street, Meredith could see people coming, dressed in dark suits and black polyester dresses they must have kept in closets for years for some such occasion. Sam Grigg was just locking the door to his pub, his fiddle and bow tucked neatly under one arm. Someone had taped a "Closed for the Trichak funeral" sign at an odd angle on the barbershop door.

Taylor and Evangeline Kew made their way with laboring, sad steps toward the cemetery. Joe and Mavis Hester, who had come from the Sarvisberry Inn arm in arm, met Taylor at the little iron gate and shook his hand. Lorna Johnson arrived with a plate of M&M's cookies in one hand. Ralph and Mildred Carney propped the gate open with a heavy smooth rock that happened to be lying nearby. They stopped beside the engraved headstones of several friends before they made their way to the small, dignified group and the open, freshly dug grave.

It had been just like Fiona to specify that she wanted her service on a day they could gather out of doors. There had been strict written instructions left in favor of it. Sam Grigg walked to the head of the assembly and nervously adjusted the only tie he owned. He cradled his jaw against the chin rest of his fiddle and raised his bow. The simple penetrating tune sang out down Main Street and across the farm fields, a song no one but Sam knew the name to, the music as enchanting and as inherent to this place as the wind.

Meredith had never before come to the Melody Flats Cemetery. She'd passed by the rusty old fence on her way to other places along Main Street, but she'd never stopped to look in at the handful of graves or to think about them. Not until she stepped into the churchyard, with Michael and Barbara flanking her, did she see that Burr Colton had already come.

He stood with his back straight as an ax handle, his hands clasped together over the brim of his hat, his legs spread, his dog, Cy, content to loll at his feet. He'd borrowed a suit from somebody, a dark wool with trousers that hung an inch too short for his rangy legs. The collar of his borrowed shirt fit mercilessly around his neck. The jacket fit way too tight, too. The stretch across his shoulder blades made his back look broad as Wyoming. And when she saw the way he'd combed his hair wet, smoothed it down slick as a ball to get rid of all his curls, she felt a knot the size of a river boulder in her throat.

Meredith stopped where her parents stopped, where the family was expected to stand at graveside. He looked at her across the hole in the earth with a sorrow too deep for talk. He opened his big right fist and then he closed it again, dropped it clenched against the wool of his pants leg.

He turned away and focused straight ahead at the big rectangle dug in the black, warm soil, his jawbone set square and firm as a hoe handle. Burr stood with his knees locked and his eyes watering. She saw him take a swipe at his face as quickly as if he swatted away a fly, but he managed to use his jacket sleeve to spread wetness from the corners of his eyes all in the same motion. Beside them, Ralph Carney said to his wife, "I've seen pictures of this old churchyard when folks had to drive half a mile from Main Street to get here. Nothing used to be out here except for the old parsonage and the church and open fields."

How different this graveyard seemed from the expensive mausoleums Meredith had seen in California, with their trimmed hedges, manicured grass, and painted fences. Here, the sky seemed close and warm, and the sun gilded the long billowy grass that grew over the tombs. Russian thistles stubbornly flagged the headstones and the walks. The intrepid purple blooms and spiny leaves winnowed through every length of the rusted fence, the bristly seeds catching stockings and trousers and the pastor's billowing black robes.

"Been too long since I've visited here," Michael

said. "It's been twenty years or more since I've been here to see my dad's plot. It'll be nice to know she's beside my dad after all this time."

"This place could be pretty if they would keep it up better," Barbara whispered. "Someone needs to straighten up and mow. Maybe we ought to pay to bring in a gardener once a week."

"Wouldn't do any good in the winter. This place is armored in ice and snow."

"What do they do when they have to bury someone in winter?"

The minister of the Melody Flats Community Christian Church called for the pallbearers to step forward. Michael went, and Lester Irons and Taylor Kew. Burr followed Ralph Carney and Joe Hester. Cy trotted along, too. They mingled around the oak casket, not knowing who should start, until the pastor directed them and they lifted the casket where it should be set.

Across the way Lester Iron's grain crop matured in the sun, his newfangled $40,000 air-conditioned combine parked and ready alongside the fence. On the other side of the little square of fence, on the opposite side of the Kmart, the farm country stayed open and free. The cows were feeding in the distance, and there would always be plowing in the autumn and spring. The breeze would forever stir the many-colored fields and the sage and the grasses that ran on to meet the sky, in a place as alive and undeathlike as any Meredith had ever seen. She felt an odd burgeon-ing within her soul, an uncanny lifting, as if some-one had taken her hand at that very moment, as if someone she loved stood beside her and pointed out the landscape.

Almer Moley adjusted three index cards in his big fingers while Sam Grigg lowered his bow and the music sighed off into nothingness. Almer cleared his throat. Then he put his notes down to his side and didn't read them. "Fiona wrote out this whole thing about how she wanted her service to be," he said, his voice gravelly and faint with emotion. "She wrote in there that she wanted me to stand up here and say something, on account of me knowing her a good part of her life and being her friend."

As Almer spoke, Meredith raised her chin and kept a tiny smile on her face, proud and serious and sad. Cy had inched forward to be beside her, creeping on her belly with her nose and her eyes lowered the way she always crept when she knew she'd flat-out disobeyed a command.

The pastor quoted Scripture, and Almer kept talking. "There's plenty of stories I could tell about Fiona, I tell you that. And I wondered all night if that's why she'd wanted me to do this, because she'd decided I'd say something about her person that she thought folks ought to know.

"By the time the Lord took her, she was about as old as some of these first homesteaded farms out here, mostly as stubborn as the land, and I think as wise. Most of you know how much she loved this place, that she felt tied to it, and even when things would've come easier if she'd left and gone off with her son to California, she wouldn't go."

He stopped and studied all of them who stood

before her, as if he needed to make sure of something before he went on.

"Guess the best story I can tell you is that story of the little boy she took in once, a baby that was born right here in this parsonage, to a little girl in a family that's long since moved away. She'd driven up here to do some weeding and pull thistles out of Ray's grave. And that preacher, he ran right out of there and says, 'I've got a girl in the parsonage in need of some help right away.' So not only does Fiona Trichak leave this grave right here"—he pointed at Ray's headstone—"she went running inside and delivered a baby for that girl."

Around the burial sight, they looked among each other, heartened and pleased despite their sadness because they'd learned something new of her.

"That girl couldn't take the baby home. She'd come to the church to have it because she was afraid her father would kill it. You've got to understand how times were then. It was an awful drought and the Depression to boot, only the Depression wasn't felt so much here. Folks here already lived in a depression, trying to farm when the grain buyers wouldn't pay at the end of the year the same money that the farmers had put in, in the beginning. The last thing a wifeless fellow could do those days was lose his oldest girl, who'd been running his household, to nurturing an illegitimate baby. So Fiona kept the boy." Here, Almer glanced around and found Michael in the crowd. "She and Ray had always longed for Michael to have a brother. She and Pastor Charles Burleigh went inside this church late that night, before everybody'd gotten home from over at our place at the harvest dance, and christened that boy 'David Wilkins Trichak.' Wilkins, after his real mother."

Burr caught Meredith's eye. His grandfather. Missus Trichak had delivered a baby with his grandfather. Missus Trichak and Grandpa Charles had known each other, then, a long time ago. He said this boy's name to himself. David, the boy in the picture on the Christmas tree. David Wilkins Trichak. And something about that name, the rhythm of the words, stirred Burr's memory, only he didn't know why.

"That little boy died while he was still young. While everybody was working in the fields one day, he found a match on the ground and struck it, and the whole barley crop caught fire, and David got trapped. Fi left the combine standing in the fire, that thing she put so much hope in, and she went running through that burning grain, scorching her legs, trying to get to him. Michael tried to get to him, too, but it wasn't to be. That little fellow was gone out of their lives almost as fast as he'd come into it."

Everyone saw Barbara encircle the arm of her husband's suit coat, her fingers long, white, beautiful, with fingernails manicured vermilion. She arched her dark brows and glanced up at him, myriad questions in her eyes as they stood in the shameless blaze of the sun. He laid his hand over hers on his suit coat sleeve and rubbed his wife's bejeweled fingers.

"Fiona told me this story once, only once, and

then she never spoke of it again. That night, after she'd made all the arrangements for David's service and burial, there came a knock on the door and Kay Lee Wilkins stood there with her arms out, the young girl who'd given birth to that boy five years before, and she said, 'You were right when you said when somebody dies or is born, that always changes things. You were right when you said having a baby'd make me be the same person, but a different one, too. I was giving birth, and you talked to me about dancing and music, remember? How a dancer changes her steps as the music shifts.'

"Fiona hadn't wanted to see her that day. She wanted to close the door in Kay Lee Wilkins' face. But she kept staring at those empty arms held out. The girl said, 'Papa said I could have him, if you'd let me. Papa said I could carry him back and bury him on our place, where he'd be close. I got the forty dollars to pay the funeral home.' Fiona invited that girl in, and they both sat beside David and grieved for him together. And Kay Lee told about how one lady had stopped her in the street just that morning and had said, 'The Lord giveth and the Lord taketh away. That boy was a sin child, Kay Lee Wilkins. A sin child.'

"When Kay Lee Wilkins told that, Fiona paced around the house. Then she started gathering up pictures of David so Kay Lee could have them, those blurry black-and-whites they used to have back in the thirties. I remember she told me she had one of David riding in a wagon with Michael pulling. There was another of David setting up on that old tractor with Michael behind. She got together all of those pictures, frames and all, and put them in an old canvas bag for Kay Lee. She handed them over as if David's life had never happened to Fiona at all. 'Kay Lee, there's no such thing as a sin child. No matter how a child is conceived, by the time that baby comes into the world, there's not any sin left. God loves a child too much for that. Our David's in heaven now, pure and simple.' Then she said, 'You want David over there with you, you send your pa over here to help you carry him. I want to see your pa and look him in the eye after what he made you do.'

"The Wilkinses, they were about the poorest people in Melody Flats. To that time, they'd never bought an auto. They just kept up their old buckboard wagon and a team of bays, matched in color and in stride from when times had been better. And Old Man Wilkins drove Kay Lee back to Fiona's, and Fiona handed that boy over in that little pine box to Kay Lee. She said, 'I agree he ought to be buried at your place, Kay Lee. I raised him some, but you're his mama.'"

Here, out in the breezy field at the cemetery, the pastor rested his big Bible on his hipbone and jostled his sleeves so Almer would get the idea that he'd talked on long enough. Almer got that idea, but he kept going anyway. He had a bit more to say, to finish up.

"It was a way Fiona had, of always looking at people and knowing who they were and where they belonged even when other folks didn't know it. That's the best thing I can think of saying today, while we're telling her good-bye. This was her gift. She helped people get to be more of themselves, the good parts of themselves. And she never let her own wants get in the way of that. Never. Not in all the years I've known her."

The service over, Michael stooped beside his mother's grave, a boy again as he grieved, a boy despite the wrinkles at the edges of his eyes, his graying stubble beard that had grown out this week since he hadn't shaved. "I've never forgiven my mother for that," he said for everybody to hear. "I've never forgiven her for giving David away that day to be buried somewhere else. I was eleven years old, and she'd given away my only brother. I kept thinking, If I died, maybe she'd give me away, too. Maybe she'd let some other strange person come take me and bury me, too. Like she didn't want anybody to know we'd ever belonged."

"Oh, no." Almer strode to Meredith's father and clasped a gnarled hand over Michael's big shoulder, clasped it tight over the fancy tailored broadcloth of his friend's suit. "It was the only way she knew of helping Kay Lee grow up and her pa to start forgiving. Fiona Trichak loved that boy as much as if he'd been her own. She loved him as much as she loved you. And most of all, she loved the two of you together, what you could have become, running that farm."

"You never told me this story, Dad," Meredith said. "I asked you about David and you never said anything about having a brother. And neither did she."

"Used to sit with David on the front stoop of the porch at the house and show him how to whittle. Used to show him how to hold Grandpa Ray's old horn-handled knife so he wouldn't cut his fingers. We made whistles, funny-looking things. But boy, did they blow. All my buddies used to tease me because I wouldn't go fishing with them. I'd stay around the place and keep an eye on David while Mom was busy getting ready for harvest in the fields. Helped him carve his own initials into his own whistle. He carried it around for a good year, blowing it, proud as punch of the sound it made, and making me and Mom crazy. Aw, what the hell. It was a long time ago."

No one but Meredith saw Burr scrounge in his trousers pocket to find the whistle he was always carrying, the odd little hand-carved one his grandfather had left for him to find. He looked at the initials. D.W.T. David Wilkins Trichak.

And Burr remembered.

He remembered how he'd held this in his hand for good luck the night he'd first walked into the harvest dance. He remembered how he'd fallen and how he'd dropped this, how Missus Trichak had picked it up and examined it before she'd invited him to the house for a meal and a decent bed. He remembered and he realized the truth. Missus Trichak had known he had this whistle, this tie to Melody Flats and to her life, all along.

*This was her gift. She helped people get to be more of themselves, the good parts of themselves.*

*And she never let her own wants get in the way of that. Never.*

He lifted his eyes and found Meredith looking directly at him, her expression gone soft and grave. He tossed the whistle an inch or two into the air and caught it cleanly inside one fist. She came across the grass to him, stood in front of him with a trembling smile tilting her lips. He laid the whistle in her hand, watching it roll and take a perfect center in her palm. "You give this to your father, won't you, when things have gotten quieter? He's the one who helped David make it. He's the one who ought to have it back now. For a keepsake of his brother."

"But it's yours. Your grandfather gave it to you."

"You don't have to tell him where it came from, if you don't want. But I think he ought to have it." Then, "Checked the barley in the field this morning before I drove off. It's getting to milk stage. Another month and it'll be ready to come off."

"Maybe there's another kind of harvest than one that's in a field, Burr. Maybe we're in the middle of reaping something someone sowed before."

"All those things my grandfather said in the letter. Maybe he thought if I came here, I could bring a part of him, too. Or find the part of himself that he'd run from. It's odd, isn't it? She hired me because of him. I keep wondering, did she hire me because she wanted to grow a last barley crop? Or did she grow a last barley crop because she wanted to hire me?"

"Knowing her, I think it would be the second." Meredith surveyed the sky. "I wonder how well they knew each other. In the church building, she's always polished that plaque with his name on it. She polished every plaque, every picture, on Sundays. But I never watched her, never noticed if anything was different when she got to his."

"What would be different?"

"If she slowed down. If she looked at it longer than the others, if she acted as if she still missed him after all these years."

"I let her read a letter from him once, Meredith. I told her that he'd died and I let her read what he'd written. She could have said something to me then——"

"No. She would never have said anything. Not if they'd hidden it all their lives. Not if that was how they'd decided they wanted it to be."

Their eyes clashed together like heat lightning.

It was Burr who first said the words recklessly, giving voice to this prospect that stirred imagination, to the clues that gave it credence. "Wouldn't it be something. Wouldn't it be something if they'd loved each other. But no one ever knew."

Meredith ran her fingers over the wrought-iron fence that edged the cemetery. She felt as if she touched somewhere beyond the horizon, or beyond all direction, some place deep within the earth. "Where are you headed now that all this is over? Kansas? Texas?"

"No," he said. "Not going any place like that anymore." He raised his head and his eyes followed the countryside, the farms, the Wind Rivers and the Absarokas, the newborn, endless Wyoming sky. "I've thought I might go back to Belle Fourche. May be tough, facing everybody back there. But there's been wrongs that need to be set right. I'd like to go back and do some talking with my mother."

"I'll be going back to med school in weeks," Meredith said, her voice quiet and sure. "Until then, until school starts, what would you think if I went with you?"

# Epilogue

The rickety makeshift stage in Almer Moley's barn almost wasn't big enough to hold the musicians these days. Used to be, it was just music that spilled from the old stage. Now it seemed that it was always musicians spilling over as well.

Play they did, no matter how much trouble they had balancing on the platform. No one could convince a single one of them to give up the one night of the year they took the spotlight in Melody Flats. They played and the Fremont County folks paced heartily through jigs and square dances and "The Salty Dog Rag" exactly as they'd gone through them the past sixty years or so, twirling and stomping beneath the rafters, setting cobwebs to billowing in the eaves.

Sam Grigg had gotten new rosin for his bow. He'd given Taylor Kew two black eyes by leveling his elbow with his fiddle and flailing his bow back and forth, forgetting to watch if anyone else might be standing in the way. Joe Hester still picked the strings on his banjo so fast, you couldn't see his fingers, letting his notes mix proudly with the zingy strums of Taylor Kew's mandolin. Another fellow had joined them, the fellow who had purchased Fiona Trichak's old place. He blended in with the reedy cry of his harmonica, molding the songs with his lips and with his hands.

To the side of the rickety platform stood Burr Colton, fingering chords and picking at guitar strings like nobody's business, his hat pulled low over his eyes. For he was a landowner in Melody Flats, too, thanks to a small adjustment Fiona Trichak had made in her last will and testament one afternoon when she'd gone to town to run errands. Michael, her son, had realized a healthy profit from the sale of the house, the barn, and two fields, the twenty-acre parcel to the left of the road and the twenty-five-acre parcel to the right of the road. But the largest field of all, the acreage that contained the granary, Fiona had left to Burr. Folks had gossiped about it for months after she died. No one could figure why Fiona had done such an odd thing as that.

The musicians played and their feet and the dancers' feet tapped and skirts whirled in rhythm to the tunes, and the big deep strings of the guitar beat on, strummed on, like a person's heart. People danced back and forth in squares, away from each other, then close. Their feet tapped, four quick steps, heels beating sharp on the hard-wood floor with all the hay swept away, a chain-through with hands and swing. Folks went outside to take a breath or to smoke or to get a bottle of something to spike the Shiloh punch brought in by the church ladies.

A woman stopped in the doorway, watching them while they danced and played. She'd come in on a plane and had rented a car, hurrying on the mountain roads to get there in time for the music. She smelled like the out-of-doors, like California, reminiscent of sunshine and breeze and fresh-washed linen. Burr saw her, although the other musicians didn't. He stopped playing and propped his guitar against the corner, balanced it carefully between the edge of the stage and the barn wall. "Don't knock that over, fellows," he warned. "You go on playing without me."

"Oh, look there. She's arrived at last." Sam Grigg gestured with his head over the top of his fiddle bow. "There's Meredith Trichak. Come into town for a visit."

"Can't believe she's almost finished with her residency," Taylor Kew said. "When Fi died and Meredith left this place for California, we thought it'd take her forever to finish up."

Sam said, "Well, it didn't. All things come to an end after a while, like the seasons."

Joe Hester thumped Taylor Kew on the leg. "Keep playing, would you? They're all dancing and I'm losing the beat."

"Leave me be. It's always a big event when Meredith comes home." Taylor thumped Joe Hester on the back. "She's going to be our town doctor. So folks won't have to wait for Tuesdays to go to the clinic. Nicer you are to her now, the easier it'll be for you to get an appointment with her later. Doc Trichak. That's got a nice ring to it, now, doesn't it?"

Sam nodded his head over the fiddle again, as they watched Burr weave through the crowd. "Best not speak too soon, Taylor. Could end up being Doc Colton, too, couldn't it?"

Outside in the barnyard the seasons had begun to turn again, the nights gone crisper, the stars thick and unbearably close, as if they could be grabbed in a handful and held, shimmering. In Melody Flats the crops had all been harvested, sold away to seed companies or stored for the winter in silos. The ground smelled of heaviness and loam, dark with promise, almost ready for its autumn plowing. Dried leaves soughed across yards. And as things were put away for the winter, it wasn't with defeat but with ordered preparation, a carnival dismantling and preparing for its next opening all at the same time. Autumn, with its exquisite certitude that crops would soon be growing in the fields.

In the Moleys' old barn, Meredith saw Burr coming for her. He smiled, an open, gentle smile, the sort of smile that didn't hide anything, the sort that bespoke homecoming.

He adjusted the brim of his Stetson and beckoned to her. She began to beat her heels in rhythm against the old splintery floor. As the fiddle player changed to a different tune, she stepped into Burr Colton's arms and they began to dance.

# Don't Miss DINAH McCALL'S
## Stunning Debut

# DREAMCATCHER

Amanda Potter escapes her obsessive husband through the warm embrace of a dream that draws her through time. Detective Dupree knows his destiny is intertwined with Amanda's and must convince her that her dream lover is only a heartbeat away.

## And published under her own name,
## Sharon Sala...

**DEEP IN THE HEART** Stalked by a stranger, Samantha Carlyle returns to Texas—and her old friend John Thomas Knight—for safety. The tender lawman may be able to protect Sam's body, but his warm Southern ways put her heart at risk.

**LUCKY** Despite her vow never to be with a man like her gambling father, Lucky Houston is drawn to Nick Chenault, the owner of a Las Vegas club. Only by trusting Nick can Lucky put the past behind her and discover a love that can conquer the odds.

**DIAMOND** Legendary country singer Jesse Eagle knows it's love at first sight when he sees Diamond Houston singing in a two-bit roadhouse. He is willing to risk his career and his reputation to make Diamond his own.

*Harper Monogram*